"A girl comes into he[r] Susan Wingate's poi[nt] Moon Hungers...a he[artfelt] novel about overcon[ming] *Foreword Clarion Re*...

MW00960507

"...well worth reading. It shook me to my core, and while some readers will want to proceed with caution, I would strongly recommend this book to people in their late teens and upward." - Jo Niederhoff, *CityBookReview*

"From the ashes rises the phoenix...HOW THE DEER MOON HUNGERS is a powerful and memorable saga that is hard to put down and lingers in the mind long after the story is over." -Diane Donovan, *Senior Editor, Midwest Book Review*

"Vivid characters, a harrowing storyline and gratifying ending. What more could a reader want? Everything that can go wrong in Mac's life does—her parents divorce, her sister dies, and she's arrested for something she didn't do. She has to learn how to assimilate it, learn from it, and move forward. But that won't be easy." —Terry Persun, *Amazon Bestseller*

"Mac and Tessa are part of my life now." —Billie Hobbs, *Independent Editor*

"I found HOW THE DEER MOON HUNGERS amazing!" —Kathryn Lane, *Award-winning author of the Nikki Garcia Thriller Series*

"I was terrorized. Then, I cried." —Elizabeth Ajamie Boyer, *Author of Memories of War*

"a coming of age story that is both intriguing and captivating." —Donna Feyen, *More than a Review*

OTHER FICTION BY SUSAN WINGATE

Storm Season
The Lesser Witness
The Dementia Chronicles (memoir)
The Last Maharajan
The Deer Effect
Way of the Wild Wood
Troubled in Paradise
The Bobby's Diner Series
Sacrifice at Sea
Hotter than Helen
Bobby's Diner
Of the Law

For information contact:
Roberts Press http://robertspress.wordpress.com Book design
by Book Covers by Roberts Press Book cover by Warren
Design

Wingate, Susan HOW THE DEER MOON HUNGERS by
Susan Wingate 1. Coming of Age 2.Young Adult fiction-
fiction, 3. family drama-fiction, female protagonist. 4. Small
island town, 5. Pacific Northwest, 6. Sister Story, 7. Peer
pressure, 8. Marriage & divorce

ISBN: 9798629230182
First Edition: July 2020 10 9 8 7 6 5 4 3 2 1

HOW

THE

DEER

MOON

HUNGERS

You are not your own. —1 Corinthians 6: 19

HOW

THE

DEER

MOON

HUNGERS

SUSAN WINGATE

Roberts Press

for families whose lives have been ravaged by
drunk driving

A *SORT OF* PROLOGUE
Tessa

My new body bubbles like a fizzing soda pop as I sit atop the chopper's rotor—a ballerina on a jewelry box, an ice skater in full-tilt pivot. Dizzying. But the *thwak-thwak-thwak* of the rotor cuts the air, nothing like a jewelry box song.

I jump down, buzz straight through the glass-enclosed cockpit, sit atop the head of a young man administering pain medicine intravenously. I move over to sit on the woman's shoulder. She's trying to stop my bleeding, applying gauze packs, slapping up bags of blood to fill my leaking veins.

The pilot speaks in hushed tones, tells air traffic control he's ready for takeoff. When the chopper lifts off the ground, I slip through the bottom but zip back inside or outside at will, perching on either of the landing skids. A big red cross tells people this is an emergency vehicle, one used by the local hospital. The chopper is flying my body to Harbor View in Seattle where they will stop trying to keep me alive because . . . they can't. Only God can issue that order. And He's not. He's calling this daughter home. But not right this second.

The paramedics are keeping my heart pumping; but with a crushed neck, they're only performing their duties until a doctor can call time of death when we arrive, when they move me to the ground and roll me into the emergency room.

The woman acts in quick, sharp motions. She has a child around my age. She's transferring the experience as if I'm her own child. The young man has no children, just a dog named Boxer, a short-haired, fawn-colored pooch with soft eyes and a square face.

"Beth," he says. His words jar her. He sees she's about to unravel. "Beth! She's not going to make it. Pull it together."

"Shit, shit, shit," Beth whispers. Even under the rumbling engine from the helicopter blades as they cut the wind, as they bend slightly forward north over the water toward the mainland where they can officially call me *dead,* he hears her.

Beth pulls it together as Justin, her colleague, insists. She fiddles with the tubing, the one administering fluids to my body. The fluids pour freely out onto the gurney between my legs, my body incapable of functioning. My heart is beating from a persistent dose of epinephrine and an oxygen bag pushing air into my lungs—lungs that are filling with fluid. The monitor whistles. The two try another method. They switch places. The tight interior makes movement difficult, but they appear used to these actions—stiff and exact. Another bell goes off. Blood pressure plummets. Pulse speeds. A penlight flickers on. Justin's.

"Eyes glossy, unresponsive."

Another alarm sings. "No pulse," Justin adds.

"You take the chest. I'll bag and count."

"One . . . two . . . three . . . four . . . five . . . six . . . seven . . . eight . . . nine," the woman EMT counts.

"Bag . . . . . . one. Bag . . . . . . two."

"Repeat."

"Bag, one. Bag, two."

"Pulse!"

They stop.

Justin listens with a stethoscope. "Weak. Thready." The dinging of the blood pressure monitor continues. "Pressure's too low."

The pilot chimes in. "Descending."

I sense the shift the paramedics experience as they feel their stomachs lift from the straight drop of the chopper descending to the heliport sitting directly above the ER on the roof of the hospital.

The air whips at a slower pace now. The pilot has cut power to the rotor blades.

When the chopper bumps to a sitting position, he kills power to the engine.

A team of hospital staff wait with more equipment, more supplies, another bag on a wheeled pole. They rush the chopper when it lands. An ER doctor calls, "TOD!"—time of death—when they get my body inside to an emergency room.

ANOTHER *SORT OF* PROLOGUE
A Chorus in Effing-minor

MacKenzie

"Ohmygod!" Gemma's voice pulled me through a funnel into a pipe so narrow I couldn't breathe. I turned to run but my legs melted into the ground. I tried to crawl but the ground in front of me turned to quicksand and I began to sink. The muck slipping around my neck, to my lips, my nose, my eyes. I held my breath. But I forgot and opened my mouth to scream for help…

Something lifted me out of the muck, and I took a gulp of air.

"You're not here!" The Hulk beckoned. "You're in the safety zone."

He lifted me high over his shoulders, slinging me up where I clung to the log of his neck to stay put.

"Don't watch," he said.

But how could I not?

Then he pulled the man out by his collar in one motion, swift and violent, the man's legs swinging like ramen noodles hanging off chopsticks.

"Put me down!" he cried out once, his arms flailing.

But The Hulk refused to stop and instead popped the man in the face with one of his green mitt of fists and bloodied his nose—blood pouring out, his cheek bruising instantly, tears welling and sluicing out of his eyes.

I was losing my grip around The Hulk's neck from all his jerky movements, from him pounding the man into mincemeat. Through it all, the man was begging for forgiveness, for mercy, but The Hulk showed no mercy. Why would he? The man had just ruined everyone's lives.

The Hulk hit him a second time.

I yelled again for him to stop.

The man's baby blues spiraled around like pinballs banging inside his head and clanging out a clatter of *pings* and *boings* as they zinged back and forth inside his sockets. He groaned.

"Please. Please," I begged The Hulk. I was exhausted, my arms weak. I couldn't hang on much longer.

He must've noticed the desperation in my tone because he said, "Stop! Stop!" Then, "You're not here. You're not here. You're safe now. Your friends don't define you."

What? What are you saying?

Strange thoughts fluttered through my mind but, just then, he yanked me off his back and around to the ground—fast.

Suddenly, I was sitting on the side of the road. When more people showed up. People I didn't love. Tessa was lying flat on the ground. She had a bouquet of spring flowers clenched in her hands on top of her stomach. She saw me staring at her, lifted her head in my direction, and winked at me. Then, she laid her head down and started picking the petals off the flowers, saying, "He loves me not. He loves me not. He loves me not."

I giggled, covered my eyes with my hands and answered, "It's 'He loves me. He loves me not.'" But when I looked back to her, she was gone.

PART ONE
the beginning

"a flower knows, when its butterfly will return,
and if the moon walks out, the sky will
understand; but now it hurts, to watch you
leave so soon, when I don't know, if you will ever
come back." —Sanober Khan

1

The Day Before

I, one Miss MacKenzie Becca Fraser, was never
one for saying *fuck* much. But as with life, things
change.

The year before, Dad removed Tessa's training
wheels. The bike had grown up, was halfway between a
tricycle and a teenager's bike. Her eyes glowed when
the trainers came off. Her smile? Buoyant. My bike
was what Tessa called a *big girl bike*—a beach cruiser
in Tiffany box blue. Mine didn't have ribbons shooting
out of the handles. Can you imagine me going to school

with ribbons out of the handles? My peeps would never let me live it down.

The evening before what people called *the worst thing that's happened on the island since Becca Winthrop went and flopped over dead of heart failure at the liquor store*, we set off on a night ride—Tessa and me. We left Mom at home stirring up dust with her favorite electric broom. Tuesday was a lazy fall night, one with the sun and moon in competition for the evening sky; with the sun being selfish for time, trying to hang on to day even though it knew it should just stop shining, give up, and go away. We'd stuck playing cards in the spokes of our tires to add to clicking crickets, tree frogs chirping, a not-so-distant fox hacking out a cough to alert its scattered pack of food found—a doomed rabbit or kitty kibbles left out on someone's porch. Up the hill, deep in the woods, an owl's Psalm echoed back from its mate as if they were holding invisible hands across the horizon, not wanting to let go. Their song played while we rode.

We'd split the deck of cards, each one clipping twenty-six onto our tire spokes to deter animals from darting out into the lane ahead. Because that was all we needed—to crash into a raccoon crossing the street. Not much good for the coon either. But the road was deserted, and I kept Tessa in front, keeping my eye out for her.

Tessa rode her bike fast like she was angling to lasso the moon, which sat high at the end of the road over Old Man Johnson's cattle farm. The big, yellow ball lolled around atop a silhouette of gossamer evergreens framing a large swatch of grazing land.

Wind fluttered that silky sable ponytail of hers as we came off the downhill side of False Bay Drive where the road at the end of summer stripes a path of thirsty grass along the strait, where cows graze in a pasture trimmed by a stand of golden poplars, crooked and bending toward the north sky away from steady winds coming off the water. Most people think that on our island in the Pacific Northwest, we live in slickers and galoshes year-round. But that's the secret we have. Seattle gives our island a bad reputation, makes us soggy when we're not. We live in what meteorologists call a banana belt or a rain shadow, so our island lacks the lush, drippy rainforests often found in other parts of the Pacific Northwest.

Each downstroke of my pedals matched rhythm with the plastic ribbons whipping off Tessa's handlebars, whizzing like a thousand bees around her hands. When she skidded to a halt in front of me, I yanked left, my wheels slipping as I swerved to miss her, no doubt balding a spot on the tire's rubber.

"What's wrong with you?" I demanded, anger flashing hot in my cheeks and pooling into my chest.

Tessa didn't seem to hear me. She was gaping up at the sky with that moon gaping back at her.

"What?" I repeated, but this time we were both fixed on the dang moon.

"Do you see it, Mac? The deer?" Tess was in the habit of starting, finishing, and rereading Thurber's *The*

White Deer for, like, the millionth time—a read *way* above her grade. In fact, she often fell asleep with the stupid book open-faced on her chest. Then the next morning she'd stick a crow feather in the book to mark her place and set it on her nightstand, ready for her evening read.

"There's no deer in the moon, dork, but there might be a man if you look hard enough. You need to read *real* stuff. You're getting weird."

"See its horns?"

"Antlers." I told her. "A hungry moon like that likes to eat seven-year-olds for dinner."

"Nuh-uh," Tessa answered.

I rolled my bike backward, parallel to hers, close enough to sneak my hand around the back of her head and yank her ponytail.

"Don't," Tessa yelped.

I enjoyed hearing her whiny kid voice. Mom called it *plaintive*. But Mom liked to make things sound more sophisticated. Her beaten-up chest of drawers was a *chiffonier*. The mossy stone patio, a *pergola*. Mom wanted more out of life, and I suspected she harbored a few regrets. "Our island didn't hold a candle to New York City," she'd complained one night. "Not even to Seattle. At least Seattle has an international flair," she'd said.

Mom could have been a model if she'd pursued it, but she'd fallen in love, had kids. The what-happened-to-my-life syndrome seemed to have snagged her in a net she couldn't get out of. She often talked about things she would do after Tess and I were out of school, when the house and her life were her own again. A longing filling her words, just enough for me to sense an underpinning of resentment. Her gaze would shift to the window, outside, away and away, but not for long; and she would chuckle. Then, she'd sit upright and say, "Oh, we wish on stars and mushroom caps for moon dust and fairies." I don't know where she got that phrase, but Mom always trotted it out when she got wistful. Maybe it came from Gramma Kiki. Who knows? It really doesn't matter, but the oddity of a phrase like that will stick with you.

And although our island boasted an international school—Spring Street School—our town was mostly country, with nothing international about it. We didn't even have a stoplight. Just stop signs and, of late, one abused turnabout.

When I glanced sideways at Tessa, she was straddling her bike as she stared up at the moon. I noted a certain otherness in her expression, as if we weren't alone, as if the ghost of that deer she'd spotted in the moon had plopped onto her shoulders and was weighing her down. Her eyes seemed dark with worry and as deep as a pair of bottomless wells, shimmering with unshed tears. I think about that worry sometimes. It haunts me still.

"Come on," I said. "We'd better get home. Mom's already in a snit."

"I wonder what the deer eats, Mac. Do you think it's hungry?"

"One thing it doesn't eat, Tess, is cheese!" I said, laughing, but Tessa didn't get it. She didn't know then, or ever, about the man in the moon or about the cheese the moon was *allegedly* made of.

I used to like the word *allegedly*. I'd learned it as a vocabulary word at the start of my junior year, and I got it right on a pop quiz in homeroom spelling. The teacher even had me write my sentence on the board: *Gemma allegedly hid the pencil from me, but there was no evidence to prove that for sure.* The sentences I would write with this word now could not be more different: I was *allegedly* taking care of Tessa when we went to the park the day after looking at the deer moon. And I was *allegedly* not watching when the car hit her.

Allegedly became an important word for me after Tessa died. It's weird to recall how much I liked the word in my junior year but hated it afterward when I heard the cop use it.

"*Allegedly*," he'd said, "the younger one was in the older sister's care." And then, as though no one understood, "The older one was *supposed* to be watching the younger one." He said *one* as if we were buttons on a conveyor belt at some stupid button factory. The jerk.

After Tess died, I started counting the days of the moon as it sketched out a path in the sky from crescent to half to gibbous to crescent again. I called it moon spying, and every month when the moon was ripe, I used to rush outside to search that big ol' cheese wheel. Maybe I'd spy Tessa riding on the back of the deer ghost, but mostly I just hoped she might see me searching the moon for a glimpse of her.

2

About Gemma

My affection for Gemma was nothing but
intellectual. Certainly, not sexual. I want to reiterate
that.

Gemma Painter burst onto the island scene when I
was about ten. I remember the day clearly. Mom had
given birth to Tessa the year before. The island was in a
state of what I like to think of as a *kerfuffle*. Quite a bit
of turmoil. Dad was drinking more back then, so it was
natural when Gemma and I became friends, two birds
of similar nests, with her parents known for kicking
back a few. I remember that day like looking at my
palm. Knew every line, every pause, every word she
said.

We walked together between classes. She showed
up after spring break which, back then, held a net of

hope for the end of the year, the rumbling under a blanket of warm crystal days. It had rained earlier that morning, but by the time we walked out of our classroom, the sun had bullied the clouds out of the sky.

Small talk:

"Have any brothers or sisters?"

"Nah," she said, then added, "you?"

"My mom just had my sister."

"Whoa!" Gemma said about Tessa's age difference. "An error in judgment? Or did the condom break?"

The comment startled me. Felt raw and bold but funny and secret all at the same time. We'd just met, for crying out loud, and there she was laying it out just like that—unfiltered.

Gemma was my age, a month older, but years my senior in maturity. Right away, I liked her. If for no other reason than her startling wit and apparent inability to buffer, pause, or rethink. To be safe. To lie. To fib even. If only a little.

Maybe it was just with me. Maybe it was just back then. Maybe I mistook her inability to hold back what she felt, to speak her mind, the opposite of fibbing. She spoke the way older kids spoke, not kids our age. Like her parents might be the sort of people who didn't allow baby talk at the dinner table.

"God no," I imagined them saying, "we want *our* child to understand *words*. Not 'goo-goo, gah-gah.'"

In our first seconds getting to know one another, the thought of someone speaking baby talk to Gemma was simply ludicrous, like tits on a basketball. Didn't fit.

Gemma was the round peg. Baby talk? The square hole. Although, she wasn't bold like that around adults.

I'd met no one like her. She intrigued me. By the end of our walk between classes, an urge had already washed over me. Like . . . I needed her. Does that make sense? Like I needed to fill my brain with all things Gemma, all things she knew about which, at that time, were all things I didn't know about. Like condoms.

Stupidly, I asked, "What's a condom?"

"You're such a child."

A child. A dagger straight to my heart. But it didn't stop there. She followed the strike with a punch. "Sorry," she said, "I don't associate with *babies*."

My heart ground to a stop. My breathing picked up as I tried to urge my heart to keep on beating. "I am *not* a baby." And, if you've ever had to say something like that, you know upon saying it that you sound more like a baby than not.

"You're child*ish*," she explained. "My IQ is 161." She stopped walking. I stopped. Her eyes inspected me as though I were alien, checking me out up and down. Then she said, "Your IQ . . . *maybe* 145. If you're lucky." She turned and walked forward.

"What's IQ?" I yelled, running up behind her to catch her.

She blew out an audible breath. And, in her most instructive tone, she said, "Intelligence quotient." By then, she refused to look at me. Acting as though I were a pariah. Not worthy of being near her.

But I needed her. Right? I mean, she couldn't dare jilt me, not so soon after meeting me, after I'd fallen for her. A bond with her grew, one I had with no one else our age.

Mrs. Lackey had put us together. A foregone conclusion, kismet it seemed with hindsight. I had been studying an assigned chapter in biology. Mrs. Lackey instructed fifth grade science classes. She was also the wife of one of the better-known real estate agents. Anyway, she'd stuck Gemma at my table. "Get to know one another," she'd said, her red lipstick covering mouth split into syrup. "She's new," she added.

Like, duh. Like I didn't know since there are like three people who live on our small island planet. Right? I mean, everyone knows everyone here. Anyway, I took Mrs. Lackey's suggestion and my new responsibility seriously and started chatting up Gemma. Getting to know her. After class, and breathless from the run and anticipation about the lie I was going to tell, I said, "Mine's 157." I chose a random number, ending in a zero or five just seemed like an obvious lie. Which worked. Because she stopped, moved in close, squinted deep into my eyes. She said, "Liar."

"Nuh-uh." That made her roll her eyes. "I heard my mom and dad talking about it. One of my teachers told them at a parent-teacher meeting." (Here I made my voice deeper like the teacher talking) 'Your MacKenzie here is *veeery* bright.' (Back to my normal voice.) *Smart,* she said." But Gemma wasn't buying any of it, until I said, *Different, talented.*

Stopped her in her tracks.

"Are you sure?" she asked.

Muscle memory took over from some previous lie when I didn't want to get caught. My head bobbed little tiny bobs. My eyes widened. "No lie," I added.

She paused, rolled her eyes, then continued to walk. "Maybe," she said.

"Where do you live?" I asked, trying to change the subject. But she knew. I could hear it in her voice.

"Argyle Street."

"Cool."

"By the Jehovah's Witness freak show."

I saw her face turn to mine in my peripheral vision. When I looked at her, her eyes were prying as if to say, "You're not one of *them*, are you?"

I pointed to my chest like, "Me?" And shook my head no.

"Which side?" I asked. Of the street, I meant.

"Kitty-corner, across from their . . ." She cocked an eyebrow, then said, "church."

I giggled. She had an illicit smoothness that made me drunk. Made me laugh.

"Sometimes we go to the Presbyterian Church. Where do you go?"

Big mistake.

"Church? Ohmygod. No pun intended. We don't *go* to church. Church is for weak-minded sheep. For people who need to be led to the slaughter. The easily influenced. We believe, if you must know, in science, in truths proven. Not some unverifiable hocus-pocus that makes people kowtow to a *higher* power. Ohmygod. There's no such thing."

Mom didn't allow Tessa and I to talk bad about other people. She'd say, "You never know what is going on in someone else's life. Try to be nice, *always*. Even when people aren't nice to you." Mom's *peace be with you and also with you* talk. A nearly daily occurrence.

No wonder Dad left. Mom would say things like, "Now, go out and be kind, exchange good for good, respect everyone, give no evil." Yada yada. I couldn't blame Mom, given her upbringing, but she wasn't exactly making an example for us either, not taking us to church regularly. Or at all some months. So, live by your words, Ma, is how I interpreted her. Like, always do the right thing. Unless, of course, it doesn't fit into your schedule du jour.

Mom would send me and Tessa off, each with ten dollars for *tithing*, it's called, giving to the church. After a while, we got wiser—a religious concept and all, one might argue. And, instead of giving the whole twenty dollars, we would only give one of our ten-dollar bills to the church, and we'd spend the other. Some of it, anyway. After buying candy at The Little Store, we'd each split the change and pocket the rest of the money. Being the older sister, I needed more so I kept more. Tessa stowed hers in a fat, green and blue Seattle Seahawks piggy bank. I kept mine in a Doc Maarten shoebox in the corner of my closet under a soccer ball.

Back to Gemma, though. I was losing her after telling her about church, so I tried to recover by saying, "We go for the money."

Obviously, this confused her because she stopped again. "What? The money?"

"Mom gives us money to give to the church. We give half and keep the rest." This I said in a whisper, close to her face, close to her eyes. Close to my *lying* eyes.

Her jaw dropped. A hand rose to her lips. The ensuing laugh wasn't a giggle, a chuckle, or a chortle. None of that. No. Instead, she barked. Like a dog. Well, almost. It was one large bark of a laugh. Big and hilarious.

My face hurt from my lips being so wide, laughing with her. "You tell anyone, and I'll tell people you're an atheist. People around here don't like atheists much." I showed her I could be cunning too. That I knew the word *atheist*. Learned it at church where there's nary an atheist a-pew.

I was ripe for Gemma, who was all about no-holds-barred living for the moment and challenging the status quo. If she had rules, you wouldn't know it. Maybe her singular rule was the sign she hung on her bedroom door: NO BULLSHIT HERE. But her rules were always in flux, ever-changing, always on the fly, whichever way the ball bounced.

Gemma freed me. Her adaptive, defiant nature gave me wings. Butterfly wings. Being near her broke me free from a smothering cocoon of motherly love. Of

having to take care of a little sister, of the anguish of
Dad leaving and Mom crying at random. Near Gemma,
I tumbled effortlessly, willingly, alighting on sweet
flower petals known as *Gemma*. Her pollen made me
dizzy. I was living a double life. One with Gemma, then
one back home with family.

Please. And don't get me wrong. Like I said before,
these new feelings weren't sexual. It's not like I wanted
to sleep with her or anything. I mean, I like boys. I
might better describe the sensation with Gemma as
liberty. My chains loosed around Gemma. My mind
became *inquisitive*, ever searching, wondering, thrilled
about learning. Hungry. No, *starving*. Yes. That's how I
should describe what was going on in my mind. I
starved for knowledge around her. We seemed to starve
together, wanted to devour the universe—one Gemma
had split the veil of. A universe sheltered from me. An
abstract of question-and-answer. Digging until you hit
pay dirt. Every amazing thing kept under wraps.

Until now.

3

About Bill Pauling

Each time the door to The Legion's Bar opened,
horizontal smoke ribbons filled the darkness like a sex
of rhythm pulsing from a local band, The Henry James
Band. On stage stood the lead singer, a mellow-voiced
tenor named Tom Henry, known around town as the
island computer techy dude. He also frequented the
only ashram on the rock. Picture this: a guitar on dry
grass next to his crossed legs, maybe brushing against
his loose-fitting, ivory cotton pants while sitting on a
boulder meditating. But under the smoky lighting, he
looked like a rock star, jamming away on his acoustical
guitar, bumping his lips softly against the mic. An
allure about him, women watching, men watching their
women watching him, anesthetized by the music and
magic of the band.

No wonder people gathered at places like this—
grainy speakeasies where laws weakened and,
occasionally, fights broke out. Where women left their
men. Where men got caught violating the laws of
monogamy behind a bramble tangled in the wire railing
on the downside of the deck out back. Where a murmur
of rumors scrawled across stall doors by bathroom
visitors—an etching of town lore.

Most likely, none of that was happening tonight.
Not with Undersheriff Zac chatting up the bartender,
asserting his authority, fully uniformed, flak-jacket fat,
gun holstered. Apparently, he decided to question
people leaving who might be stumbling out drunk to
drive in a blitz of stupidity, or perhaps he was searching
for underaged customers on the premises. One could
only wonder.

My sight eventually adjusted where I could make
out people moving around—dancing, standing, heading
up to the bar. Where I could see club chairs, stools, a
couch with a woman with beer in hand, balanced and
slumped on the arm of the sofa, leaning into a
conversation with two men and another woman who
filled up the seat.

It took longer for our noses to adjust, to get used to
the assault of sour cigarettes so we could lower our
hands from over our mouths. Gemma gave me a look
like *Good God* and stuck out her tongue like she could
puke. That's when I pointed. Gemma followed the
direction of my finger.

We spotted all four of them slouched in a bust-high line like statues. The top of the bar severed them at the torso, each with an arm set upon the bar, a wet highball cupped by an alabaster carving of a hand in a museum of beer, whiskey, and drunks. Finally, one of them turned to speak, the movement bringing them to life.

It was Mr. Painter, Gemma's dad, who spoke. The other three laughed—Mrs. Painter, Mom, and Dad. It was then Bill Pauling strode in and sat down next to Mr. Painter. At that moment, I realized how much younger our parents were than Pauling. He wobbled, glowed, happy with the alcohol he'd already consumed—perhaps on his way for one more stiff one—and scooted up to our parents, sliding one leg over a stool beside Mr. Painter. Nearly fell off, but with the help of the bar and Mr. Painter, he didn't land on the floor.

Undersheriff Zac glanced over, a departure in his talk with the bartender. He lowered his head like something one of my teachers would do to a rowdy student. Pauling waved, his hands explaining the misstep. *I'm good. I'm good*, my lipreading skills told me he was saying to Zac. Then, the old dude slapped one hand down, attempting to laugh it off. The bartender moved away from Zac, pulled the lever of a draft down, filled another mug with beer, and slid it with a fresh napkin to Mr. Pauling who, sipping greedily at first, settled back, and then suckled the mug every so often.

Mom had told me to stay at the Painters that night. Tessa, age two by then, got a babysitter, a neighbor girl—one of three kids—whose own mother, Shona, also had a toddler in diapers. She told Mom that Tessa was welcome anytime, that she was company for her toddler and that she didn't mind the extra *little one* around the house. Shona's husband worked four days in Seattle during the week at Microsoft. Shona was often alone, so the added little body helped distract her thoughts, she'd said. I think Mom envied her money, her independence during the week, staying at home and doing whatever she wanted, albeit with a small clutch of children at her feet. Mom sometimes jokingly called her Madonna. Not the *Vogue* singing Madonna, either. The one living in the *Louvre*.

We weren't permitted to step *one foot* inside the bar at The Legion. So, instead, we called into the room using our polished whisper-yell. It's an attention-getting tool students often use in study hall or when a teacher leaves a room. Gemma whisper-yelled first from outside the front door, a spring-hinged monstrosity which closed at a snail's pace against my back. The heavy metal door pressed me closer to Gemma's back, with me resting against her.

"Mom!" Gemma and I called out in unison, after not hearing our awesome whisper-yell, once our bravery kicked in.

Mrs. Painter's eyes shot up. So did my mom's. Gemma's mom sort of rolled her head away, bent toward Gemma's dad, touched his arm like a dog begging for food, and whispered into his ear. There was a familiar parental talent being exposed. Because, at the same time, Mrs. Painter and Mom both lifted one finger each in a wait-a-sec-motion to us, leaving us frozen— half in, half out of the door, bent at the hips, waiting.

First, Mr. Painter tried to stifle a very audible *shit*. Failing, of course. On purpose? One can only speculate. Gemma and I knew them pretty well, being their children and all, as children know their parents—their facial expressions, their body language, the sudden lethargy having to explain one more thing or drive their children one more place or having to give one more dollar.

But we also knew they hated interruptions when they went out together, hated the interruption when each set of parents visited the others' homes, hated us interlopers when they met for drinks. Like drinking was a sacred ritual only allowed to a higher few, and when I say higher, I mean *higher*. Tonight was no different, and when he said *shit*, that wasn't different either.

Mr. Painter, with all the muster and lethargy required by parents, swiveled from the counter and crossed to the door. "What?" He couldn't have hated seeing us more. After asking the question posed, which was a more rhetorical statement if anything else, he waved us back out of the door toward the void of nighttime behind us while simultaneously saying, "Out."

He joined us on the concrete ramp that led to a sidewalk flanking the road.

Gemma started, "We wanted to know if we could go see *Hunger Games*. Jennifer Lawrence is like, awesome. Please."

"You're supposed to be doing homework."

"We're done. Finito! Can we, Dad?" Gemma was putting on her sweetest *please, please, please* face for him. For *us*. Her hands clasped prayerfully, making tiny bounces as she begged.

"Go," he said, "Shit. I don't care."

Gemma clapped her hands madly. "Thanks, Daddy," she said. Then pushed out one of her hands, open-palmed, for cash. "Mac needs money too," she said. Sweet smiles all around from Gemma.

"You girls," he said. Turned, disappeared inside. We waited a minute . . . maybe two. And blessed be all the saints and angels, when he reemerged, he bestowed a twenty for me (I assumed from my parents) and a twenty for Gemma.

"Thank you," I said to Mr. Painter. But mid-sentence, the door pressed wide behind him and out walked Mr. Pauling. He grappled for the metal railing running down a hip-high block wall to keep people from falling off the ramp. It reminded me of those guard rails found on steep mountain roads. He nearly body-checked me when he fell toward the railing.

"S'cuse me, girls!" he said and burped without even saying *s'cuse me* again. The lean of the ramp sped up his footing, but it slowed when the ground leveled out. A trail of yeasty breath followed him.

Gemma said, "G'night, Mr. Pauling!" Then, under her breath, she said, "Ya old drunk."

"Hey," her dad scolded. "None of it. Or you can kiss off the movie."

"Sorry!" Curtsying, Gemma put on her appropriate *I'm-so-sorry* face, grabbed me by the arm, spun me to the street, and skipped us down the ramp. When we got up next to Mr. Pauling, she said, "Bye, Mr. Pauling!" Looked back at her dad and lifted her hands in appeal. "Come on, Mac!" Then, she dashed off in front of me, making me run to catch up. And we both blew down First Street, angled across Spring Street where we raced to the doors of the theater.

For a while now, since they'd moved to the island, the Painters had hung out with Pauling at The Legion. That's where Mom and Dad had met him.

The Painters, each recalling how they had first met Mr. Pauling, took turns telling it like roles in a stage play. Each recited the tale, vying for time in the limelight, both wanting to tell it from their perspective, respectively one-upping the other's embellishing facial tics, altering their voices, their movements methodical, John Wayne-ish.

First, Mr. Painter would speak. "He was the first person," then Mrs. Painter adding, "other than Monica, our real estate agent," then together, "who we met on the island." And Mrs. Painter, including Mr. Pauling in their storytelling would say, "Right, Mr. Pauling?" Who nodded off sleepily due to a number of beers we'd watched him consume at the kitchen table.

So, it seemed the Painters held some loyal affection for him. I guess they sort of felt protective of Mr. Pauling—a protective loyalty. Is that a thing? A thing so infused in the skin of their story no one would recognize as false. Not right away . . . or ever. Not only with the Painters but also the entire island carried this bond of loyalty for Pauling. A loyalty saturated from years of hearing stories about him—his historic valor in Vietnam, war medals, a missing wife, childless, and alone—that none of Mr. Pauling's *episodes* (we call them episodes out of respect) were ever fully his fault. He had become a loveable, old, drunken war hero that everyone knew and revered.

"He was a Vietnam vet, for God's sake," Mr. Painter had said after Pauling had endured a row with the round-about tree by the marina. He'd turned too soon and slammed his car into the trunk. "He earned his drunk," Mr. Painter added.

After all this time knowing Mr. Pauling and how the community accepts him, maybe I'm supposed to figure out that loveable old drunks need protecting.

But protecting from what? From people? The police? Other cars?

Or . . . from themselves?

4

At Home, Before the Bike Ride

Tessa ran down the hall past my bedroom door. She was crying again. With the back of one hand wiping her nose, she blubbered almost indecipherably, "I'm not yours!" all the way down the hall.

Dad once said, after a few lovely minutes of respite from crying and yelling, "In about ten seconds, the crying will begin." Sure enough, each time something didn't go Tessa's way, she broke out into tears. Not immediately though. More like a floodgate opening slowly as each eye filled to overflowing with tears, silent crying at first, then sucking back, Tessa's precursor to a big wail, then crying. Like her physical sadness had to catch up to her emotions.

Dad didn't even have to speak. *See?* was written all over his face.

I was taking account of my previous solace, longing for the disruption to go away, internally remarking on my surroundings, pausing before having to check on Tessa. I focused on the five and a half mason jars that sat on my dresser, each filled with varying colors of beach rocks, *all* of them heart shaped. It's amazing how many heart-shaped rocks you can find on any given day, weather permitting, as Mom says. The beach rock collection started because of Gramma Kiki. She got me hooked because of her ginormous collection. She dedicated one entire china cabinet to beach rocks alone.

By the time Tessa's sniffling began, notes of toasted grilled cheese and butter still hung thick in the air from supper. I liked mine with pickles fried in between. Mom liked tomatoes in hers, and Tessa's was without any adornment. *Cheese, please. Only cheese. White bread, toasted.*

And, the way she ate? Good gravy. Envision a starving raccoon. Like the food would crawl off the plate and get away from her if she didn't wolf it down superfast.

Once, after watching her decimate a hamburger, I told her she looked like a little pig. Mom said, "You ate like that too."

Tessa howled. I made a face at her then glowered at Mom. Happy times.

But then Mom said to Tessa, "You're gonna choke if you aren't careful." Something she'd said to me often enough. Mom was already done with her food and clearing her plate when she said, "Hurry up." Which meant *go to your rooms*. Mom wanted to clean up and have *us out of the way*.

I had been lying on the bed finishing a homework assignment, a proof in Calculus, when I saw the landline's red button light up on the cradle and the digital display reading: LINE IN USE. After no more than thirty seconds, Tessa raced by my door crying.

I rolled away from my work onto my side. Mom was on the phone, but I called out to her anyway, "Why's Tessa crying?"

I heard Mom say, "Hold on." Then, to me, "What, Mac?"

"She's crying. What happened now?"

We didn't often hear Mom say the F-word, but she let it rip then. "Ben, I gotta go," she said. It was Dad. She was speaking with my dad and hadn't told me. I screamed, "Wait!" and leaped out of bed.

"Hold on. Mac wants to talk to you." She covered the mouthpiece and said, "Make it quick. You need to finish your homework." Her face burned red. Her eyes wild. She sometimes got like that when it came to Dad, so I didn't think anything unusual. I snatched the phone from her.

"Dad! When are you coming over?"

We'd stopped saying, "When are you coming home?" By now, after so many months, we'd deduced that Dad was never coming home.

Mom chimed in real quiet but enough for me to hear, "He's, um, *busy*."

I took it to mean, as Mom's demeanor intended, that Dad had someone there with him . . . a woman. She had armored up and was now donning her *fight tone*.

"Can we talk tomorrow?" I was giving him the benefit of the doubt. We agreed to reschedule a chat for tomorrow evening after he got home from work, after he showered and ate, when he was relaxed. But our tomorrow talk? Never happened, not the way we'd planned it anyway.

After hanging up, I said, "Why's Tess crying?" Still pressing Mom about our previous talking point.

Mom didn't seem to know but appeared rattled far more than her usual angry, unsettled state after talking with Dad. "How would *I* know?" she said. "Why's she *ever* crying?"

The apathy dripping out of her pores, of leftover poison from talking with Dad, floored me. It was one thing that she used on me, although hurtful. Quite another she used on Dad. Dad was old enough to handle himself, capable of either fighting or relinquishing a fight. But when she chose cool detachment about my little sister, I wasn't about to let her off the hook.

"Wow," I said, "nice." I matched her vitriol with equal sarcasm. "She's just a baby."

Her slender shoulders slumped, and with them, her eyes sunk with shame. Her shirt, stained from splattering butter from tonight's dinner, was twisted, and she tugged it straight. She kicked off her shoes, revealing chipped toenail polish from paint she'd applied weeks ago. To describe her, I'd use the word *haggard*. She'd lost weight since the separation. Her collarbone almost protruding under the sting from the overhead kitchen light. She took in a deep breath, grappled back to her chair, and let her head drop backward before she lowered it into her hands as she placed her elbows on the table.

"When?" Her voice was drawn, irritable.

"Just a second ago. She ran down the hall and into her room crying." My tone was defensive and accusatory. "You were on the phone. She came from the kitchen." It was hard being the only adult in the house.

Her eyes hardened back to a deep shade of jade, the blood retreating from the whites as her gaze ticked back and forth, pinpointing the exact moment just seconds ago.

"What did you do to her?"

She placed a hand over her mouth, the action pulling on her cheeks, making her eyes warp and elongate.

"Mac," she said, "will you please deal with it?" She paused, then explained, "The call with your dad and all. I'm done in."

The separation had gnawed away at Mom's usual cool. Her put-together, stoic, ready-for-the-day demeanor was crumbling. It was like she was eternally PMSing. Since he'd left and, I figure, started dating, Mom couldn't seem to drag a brush through her hair, couldn't hang up her forever-crumpled shirts and pants, couldn't stop being angry all the time. She was relying on me more and more, something I thought was cool at first but now it was grinding me to ash. Dragging the life right out of me. Tessa, too, who had to help me with whatever Mom was asking at the moment. "Clean the bathroom, load the dishwasher, dust the furniture, and make sure you get under the table, anywhere dust can collect! Water the dog and cat, clean the cat box, sweep in the areas of the front and back doors so you girls don't drag dirt in on your shoes! And, by the way, why is it you can't ever seem to wipe your feet? Why is it so difficult to wipe off your shoes?"

The pressure from their separation had built up in us, too, to holy-freaking, hot teapot levels.

So when Mom asked me to deal with this *thing*, this whatever the heck was chewing on Tessa, I responded with the same sarcasm she'd been teaching me to use for years, and said, "Of course, Mom. I'm only trying to finish my AP Calc homework, so that I can ace the mid-term, so that I can get into college. No big. Don't worry about me. I'll deal with *your* youngest daughter. *Again.* Since you can't seem to deal with *anything* anymore!" And I bolted out of the kitchen.

She was so lame. She'd turned into this pathetic excuse of a woman. And if I was disgusted by it, why shouldn't Dad be too? Why *wouldn't* he want the freak out of here?

Tessa was lying on her stomach crying, the pillow consuming her tears, muffling any sounds. Sobbing still choking her, seeming to accumulate within the hunch of her back. Each time I thought she'd stopped crying, another wave of weeping welled up after following an ebbing of silence between her sobs.

This wasn't her normal baby act. Something bad had happened, had affected her deeply. As I pondered what might've happened, she turned, wiped her wet lips, and yelled at me through a warble of tears.

"Did you know!?" Spittle dripped from her mouth. "Know what?"

But she didn't answer. Her face crumpled, and she went back to crying and pillow-planted her face.

"Tess," I said, my voice hushed, "I don't know what happened." Which seemed to make her more upset. I needed to finish my homework. "Oh man, Tessa. If you don't tell me what happened, how can I help you?" I'd used similar psychology on her before. This time it wasn't working. "Look," I went on, "if you want to talk about it after you're done crying, come into my room. But I'm getting a little overbaked dealing with everyone's issues. I have to pass this class or I won't get to college a year early. Okay?"

Of course, my explanation for not sitting with her while she cried only made her cry more . . . *and* harder.

"Okay," I pushed off her bed. "Look, I'll be in my room. Mi casa es su casa. Later, widdly-kiddly."

I thought the endearment might help. but it didn't seem to matter; and when I laid my palm on her bony little back, she recoiled under my hand. I figured I'd learn when I'd learn in due time, after her tears ran dry. After the baby act. What I didn't figure on was *what* I would learn. Nor did I figure on how the why's about what had upset Tessa would carve a rift between our family as distant as the moon. Because, how would anyone guess what Tessa had heard? But what's sadder is that she had to find out at her age.

5

At Home, After the Bike Ride

"Did I know what?" I said, revisiting her question to me.

Tessa's face wedged between the door and jamb. The door hid her frail limbs like a bookmark hidden between pages of a novel. She crossed her big brown eyes, scrunched her nose, and puckered her lips. I made the same face. She slid into the room, skipped to the bed, and flopped onto the mattress, landing halfway on sheets of homework.

"Hey. Watch it, bonehead," I said.

She rolled back, allowing me to gather the sheets of paper from under her and fold them into my textbook. She pursed her lips like she was keeping a big secret.

"Okay. Don't talk." I flopped my legs off the bed, walked out of the room to the bathroom, and cranked on the spigot. I heard as she scurried out to follow. Right away, she was leaning against the door watching silently, so I gave her my goofiest goof-sneer. I was watching her watching me through the mirror goof-sneering back. My hair sprayed out in all directions from the clip that held it. A tough homework session, for sure. I desperately needed a shower to drag my hair into submission. The color didn't even appear super blonde any longer, changing with every season, going from towhead to mousy. I knew by the time I reached my twenties my hair would be closer to Tessa's hair color . . . and Mom's.

I pushed a wild strand behind my ear, pulled out my toothbrush, and loaded it with green and white striped toothpaste. Tessa, the little monkey she was, copied. She pulled out hers and held it up for me to load. She hooked one foot around a small plastic step stool Mom had provided her to reach the sinks and slid it next to me.

"You can't use the other sink, twerp?"

She smiled. I stuck the brush into my mouth and goof-sneered as I brushed. Again, with Tessa copying me.

"Do you love me, Mac?" Tessa asked. Her words wrapped around her toothbrush, her gums foaming with paste.

"What a stupid question," I said through my own slosh of toothpaste. I wasn't sure, but I thought I'd picked up a gnat or two in my teeth on our bike ride earlier. Gross.

Anyhow, it was my responsibility these days to get Tessa ready for bed, so I started her bath. Mom had delegated the job because she liked to clean the kitchen before heading off to bed.

Tessa splashed in a whorl of streaky froth, opal bubbles hanging heavy off the curve of each bubble, stalactite opals dripping. A war of scents filled our small quarters, making me imagine we were inside a candy store. Hints of coconut, banana, peach, and bubblegum, and the faintest note of Junior Mints, Dots, and Tootsie Roll. Each burgeoning aroma from her several bottles of *Minnie Mouse* bubble bath collection. She loved using *all* bottles at once. Never just one. No, Tessa dripped a soup can of each into her steamy bath. With her skin shining, slippery like a tiny dolphin breaking the surface at Marineland, and with her slicked-back hair, she still appeared like a baby mermaid. Her baby cheeks still visible at seven, as though still round from milk feedings.

"How'd you get so cute?"

Her voice sage-like, she said, "My pants."

I nearly choked. "*Genes*, not pants."

She giggled and rolled her eyes, "Jeans ARE pants, silly." She was screaming over the sound of water gurgling from the faucet into the tub.

"Different kind of genes. Spelled different," I explained. I was sitting on the toilet next to the bathtub. I'd detached a scrubby netted sponge we hung off the

tile wall from its suction cup. Dipping it into the water,
I scrubbed Tessa's back with soft, circular strokes.
Mom always commented about how small she was
when she washed her—back before Dad left—her back
undeveloped and uniform without any girly shape yet.
Again, I said, "How'd you get so cute, turd?"

"Jeans," she giggled, then splashed me.

"You did *not*! I'm going to freaking kill you."

I pushed on her head like I was going to dunk her.
She screamed and wriggled, the worm. With me acting
all scary and mean. Growling like a rabid dog. "I'm
gonna getchoo, getchoo, getchoo." My voice
demonesque. My hands gnarled as a monster's. My face
frozen into a zombie mask. She screamed again. I
growled, "Mwahahahaaaaaa!"

But Mom came in and spoiled our fun. "I need the
bathroom. Can you hurry it up?"

Tessa and I were still laughing when Mom ruined
playtime.

"Killjoy!" Tessa called out, still giggling.

"Yes. Well. You're not the first to say that."

I rolled my eyes so only Tessa could see.
Obviously, Mom's comment alluded to something Dad
had said sometime in the past. Who knows when? If
ever? Mom was good at self-pity these days. And just
like that, our fun ended. The mood? Broken. A glass
shattering on concrete. Our time together ruined.

"Come on, Tess," I said. "Let's finish and dry you
off."

Those eyes of hers connected with mine in a silent conversation of disappointment. She flashed a glance to Mom, tipped her head. Then Tessa opened the drain and stood. As I wiped her down, I was checking out Mom, too, her face inches from the mirror, her fingers dragging swollen bags under her eyes, making them into melted candle wax.

I lifted Tessa and set her onto a bath towel and wrapped another towel around her scrawny body. "Hold on to it," I said, then got another towel for her hair. The towel wrapped around her head, making her a tiny version of an Egyptian princess. I picked her up and was carrying her out the door so Mom could be alone when Mom asked, "What happened?" I presumed her meaning why Tessa had been crying earlier.

"Don't know," I said.

"Well, figure it out," Mom demanded. "I can't have this hanging over my head."

I wanted so badly to say so many things: *Then you ask her! She's your daughter, not mine! What's hanging over your head?!*

Instead, I zipped it. Kept it all to myself. A daughter knows when to speak and when to hold her tongue. Especially with Mom's irritation crawling on top of her skin.

6

The Day of, Earlier That Morning

"Make her do her homework or something. I don't want her tagging along. Me and Gemma have plans," I said.

But Mom was in no mood to barter. The floors need vacuuming. The furniture, dusting. The kitchen smelled of bleach water and toast from breakfast. Small puddles of water shone on the blue counter tile under the occasional sunbreak. Pieces of browned bread scattered the breakfast table. The coffee maker urn steamed, emitting a nose of charred coffee from four hours sitting on a searing burner after Mom first woke up. That was five o'clock. She hadn't slept well since immediately before Dad left seven months ago. Well, seven months, six days, and thirty-four hours ago. To be precise.

Lately, Mom hated anything to do with housework, got really cranky cleaning of late too. Always wanted us *out of the way—outside or riding bikes at the high school.* I knew I wasn't going to win an argument right now, but I was still going to give it my best.

"MacKenzie Becca Fraser, I am in no mood to discuss this with you."

Told you. Not after using all three of my names. In that tone. Stopping action. Refusing to make eye contact. I'd lost the battle before it had started.

"Why can't you lock her in her bedroom if she bugs you so much?" Then I added, "She bugs me, too, you know." A special whiny tang laced with each word.

"Now," Mom said. She had put down a proverbial foot.

I didn't want Tessa with me today. Gemma and I had *big-girl* plans which certainly didn't include a little sister tagalong bugging us all day long. I whipped away from Mom, leaving her with whatever imaginary fungi she was bent on defoliating.

"Don't get testy with me, young lady!" she called after me. But I was already slamming my door. A great start to a crappy day—babysitting Tessa. And even with my door closed, she didn't stop. "The least you can do is wipe down the table!"

No. Thank. You. Mom.

It wasn't a big table. She could get it clean in no time flat. Buck up, Mom.

"Tess!" I called. "Come on. I'm gonna be late 'cause of you. Hurry up!"

"Quit yelling," Mom said. Her voiced pitched. Angry. Loud.

OMG. My eyes burned a hole through my wall at her, at Tessa too. They were royally jamming up today's plans.

7

Five Days Before
Mackenzie

"It's big girl stuff. You're not old enough."

"Am too!" Tessa scrambled back into her bedroom and slammed the door. She yelled, "I hate you, MacKenzie Becca Fraser. I hate you!"

"You shouldn't tell her she's only a little girl," Mom said.

"I didn't."

"She made the inference. She's advanced for her age. All that reading."

"You used to tell me the same thing before Tess showed up. Why is it okay for you to say but not for me?"

"I did not."

"I was nine by then. It's sort of crystal clear. You did," I repeated, paused, and breathed. "By the way, why the long gap in between?"

"What are you talking about now?"

"Between me and Tess."

Mom stuttered. "It's none of your business." She refused to answer. She glanced back at me when we both heard Tessa sobbing again from within the sad confines of her room.

"Big baby," I mumbled.

Mom's face expressed everything I needed to know. Told me I had to go make up with my sister. The same thing I'd been doing for the past seven years of my life. I couldn't wait to get to college. Like a balm, the thought soothed my angst, swept me forward twenty-one months— packed, waving teary goodbyes, kissing Tessa on the forehead, hugging Mom and Dad (they'd decided to get back together in my fantasy), on a long bus ride south out of Washington through Oregon and into California, landing me on the hallowed steps of Stanford University.

Mom's voice broke the illusion.

"Fine!"

Of course, her bedroom door was unlocked. Inside, I found her in the favored pitiful position, face pillow-smashed, sucking in big air balloons of sorrow. She locked the door when she read, a big *Do Not Disturb* signal to all of us. But when she was sad, in need of condolence, she left her door unlocked. Tessa enjoyed make-up sessions, all the explaining and groveling, all her forgiving. To be honest, I guess I enjoyed them too. Each time the gap of our years tightened. We became closer with each life lesson taught, me wiping the tears from her blotched, chubby cheeks. Never missing a tickle session sending howls and giggles through the house, our music of reconciliation.

"Gemma and I like boys, and we talk about things seven-year-old girls shouldn't hear."

"Like sex?"

"Tess! I'll tell Mom."

"Sex is gross."

"Yeah, well, maybe. I wouldn't know."

She smiled at my confession. "You haven't yet?"

"OMG. None of your freaking biz, creepazoid." Her eyes fixed on my face, trying to glean the answer. "No, not yet. But, again, none of your business."

She flipped onto her back and shuffled her butt against the pillow into a sitting position.

"What then?" she asked.

"What do we talk about?"

She nodded, like it was a big secret about to unfold.

"Well, stuff like if so-and-so likes Gemma and if another so-and-so likes *me*. That sort of thing. And college. Gemma wants to go somewhere near New York City."

"You're not going that far, are you, Mac?"

"I don't know. Maybe."

Tears threatened the brims of her eyes.

"Not too far, though. My dream college is Stanford. They have an awesome math program. Maybe closer if I can't get in. Maybe UDub. But sometimes you have no choice."

"Whattidya mean?"

"Well, you have to apply to colleges, and not all the close ones might take me. I may get into say . . . MIT in Massachusetts, or Princeton in New Jersey. You know? They're both great colleges for math."

"I think I'll die if you leave, Mac."

"You have a few more years of school here and a few more years until you're old enough to move out on your own. You have your whole kid life ahead of you. Stop thinking about older girl things, Tess, and just try to be a kid. If there's one thing I know, I wish I had spent more time being a kid." I let the wisdom of my age seep in.

Finally, she said. "I'll try. But I love you, Mac. I want to be with you all the time!" Her smile was goofy. Why was this the first time I really noticed she was missing a front tooth. I knew the tooth fairy had come, remembered Mom talking about it, had seen her smile, tooth missing and all, but it was only then it hit me as something precious and unforgettable.

"You could fit a straw through that hole."

"Stop it!" She blushed and covered her mouth.

I laughed. "Yeah, well, creep. I love you too." I pulled open the drawer in her nightstand, grabbed her SpongeBob brush, motioned her to come closer. She scooted into position next to my right leg, her back to me. I dragged the brush low at first on her natty curls.

But the wisdom hadn't ended. "Growing up is tough business, especially at the age of seven. You don't know Gramma Ellie, but she used to say, 'Keep the past in your heart, today close around you, and tomorrow behind you.'" Dad's mom, Gramma Ellie, had told me that a few years before she died. Tessa was still in diapers.

"The past . . . where?" Tessa tried.

I tapped my sternum. "In your heart," I said it slow with her saying the words right along with me, "today close around you, and tomorrow behind you." Then I said, "You don't know Gramma Ellie because you were still Diaper Diane.

"What's it mean?"

"Gramma's saying?"

She nodded.

"It means always try to forget the past and not dwell on the future, keep it out of sight, behind you. She used to also say something about past, present, and future. That they call it *present* because it's a gift."

Tessa thought long about that one. I finally combed out the rat's nest on top of her head. A slow smile coursed into place and anchored there.

"You need to brush your teeth and do your homework. Can we agree that after I come home, I'll tell you all the juicy details about me and Gemma's talk, okay?"

She grabbed me around the neck and said, "I love you, Mac. But I'm not staying home with . . . . . . *her*."

"Crap. Okay. Whatever, you little turd."

She laughed and jumped off the bed.

"Love you back," I said. And as we walked into the hall, I followed up with, "Turd."

8

The First Call
Uma

MacKenzie's words distorted to the point Uma Fraser had to tell her daughter to quit screaming, settle down and start over, for crying out loud. She was pretty sure; however, that Mac had inserted Tessa's name somewhere. Something happened, something about Tessa. But with Mac's mouth plastered against the cell phone receiver, Uma heard only a garbled mush of words.

"Good Lord, Mac, settle down, stop screaming. I can't understand a word you're saying. Now, please. Calm down and start over."

However, when Mac stopped screaming, she started crying. No frantic words forming, just sobbing. Uma could do nothing but listen, console her, wait for a breath.

"Honey, come on. What happened?"

A whiff of wind wafted through the line. The day was breezy and gray. Uma could tell Mac had pulled the phone away and was wiping her nose, heard the sniffling. She turned her attention to a bucket of lavender water where she'd plunged the ropy end of her *Tornado* mop. As she waited, she lifted the mop up and down by the shaft, dunking, redunking a few times, hoping to dislodge all the grit hiding within the long strands of blue and white yarn. The mophead needed replacing soon. The blue and white had gone grimy, morphed into shades of gray. Uma calculated the cost of several other things that needed replacing, other things she needed to buy. She mentally calculated the cost of things she needed to the balance in her checking account. Her heart fell as she weighed the cost of food, a mortgage payment, the electricity bill, gas for the car, all her bills to a measly paycheck from working a mashup of several jobs. And . . . she worried.

But when Mac didn't stop crying, Uma's attention returned to her daughter.

"Honey," she said, her voice louder than normal because it seemed that maybe Mac had lowered the phone from her ear. "Honey!" she repeated louder.

Mac's voice sounded morose, bunched in with phlegm and choking on tears.

"Mom," she wept into the phone, "Tessa," she got out. "They flew her to the hospital."

Uma stopped breathing. Had her heart stopped? It seemed her heart was no longer beating, but when she checked, it was not only beating but galloping, threatening to split her chest open. Hair on the nape of her neck prickled. Her stomach clenched. A flash of cold sweat beaded along her brow, her upper lip, and the skin on her arms. She couldn't speak.

"Mom?" Mac said. Her voice quailed.

The words coming from Uma sounded gravelly, "What happened?"

"Mr. Pauling." Mac began to cry again.

"Oh Lord."

The mop handle loosened from Uma's grip, but she held on. She needed something to steady her. Needed something to control.

"Where are you?" Uma asked.

"Roy's."

"I'll be right there." And she hung up.

There are things we remember when tragedy strikes, and things we don't. We remember strange details that seem senseless at first, but then end up becoming important when we look back. Uma was thinking about each second after Mac's call, remembering how she leaned on the mop handle against the sink because she didn't want to fall. She recalled finding her keys, which were never on the table, but that day by some miracle they were. She remembered the click and bleep from the key fob as it unlocked the driver side door, and another bleep when all doors unlocked. She remembered seeing Tessa's pink sock lying on the passenger side seat precisely in the spot Uma left it after struggling it off her fat toes when she'd bent around between both front seats to pull the sock from her foot. Tessa was sitting in her big-girl bumper seat, in the very spot where she was parked now. Uma hadn't bought larger socks because funds were low.

Things she forgot were the engine turning over, backing out of the driveway, making her way to town— to Roy's—spilling from her car, racing to Mac, shaking her by the shoulders, thinking *shaken baby syndrome* and stopping the attack.

She let slide to the interior of her mind, the deputy guiding her to a picnic table and lowering her into a chair, how he separated Uma from Mac until they were united again in the backseat of the police vehicle, when they were clutched together, their hands in a death grip, squeezed together so tight that they felt like one.

9

Uma's Call to Ben
Ben

Ben Fraser got the call at 1:13 p.m. on Saturday.
His estranged wife kept her tone terse, calm—calmer
than what he might've imagined—given her news. She
relayed that Pauling hit their youngest daughter. With
that beast of a car, she added. Of course, he was
inebriated, she'd said. At the scene, Tessa's situation
was dire, critical condition; they had flown her to the
trauma center at Harbor View in Seattle before she
could get there, she said. Then came the long-awaited
typical Uma dig, the one she let fly every call. "If you
wanted to know, that is."

What a thing to say, let alone think. He adored that little girl. Of course, he wanted to know. She was the baby, Mac's sister.

He ditched work. No excuse tendered. Not like him to walk off the job, but words weren't coming without cost, the ache in his gut like he swallowed concrete for lunch. No way words would be forthcoming, not without losing control. Better book than blow. What would the guys think? You don't show weakness while breaking rock at the quarry. Tears were not an option. Even the slightest show of fragility, the guys would eat him alive.

Ben hesitated inside his truck. All his thoughts banged against each other, making a pinball machine of his brain. He must compose himself. Must drive the speed limit. Watch for other kids playing on the road, like Tessa, on their bikes . . . lest, they, too, became decoys, mere targets for anyone driving carelessly.

How many times had he glanced at his cell when the thing blipped? Or unwrapped a hamburger coming off the gas stations from The Little Store onto Spring? Heat rose in his face. How many times had he also jumped into a vehicle after drinking a couple glasses of Zin at a restaurant? His head light, swimmy, certainly not incapacitated but not sober either.

He pulled from the quarry's parking lot onto Rogers Road with intention, stopping at Roche Harbor Road, checking both directions, ready to give it gas, to turn right, but his foot wouldn't move off the brake pedal. From this commanding position in charge of a 7,000-

pound four-by-four, a deep rumbling mounted. He
thought initially the rumbling grew from somewhere
under the truck's hood, somewhere within its engine,
but then his foot slipped off the brake pedal and the
truck nudged out onto Roche Harbor.

He grappled at the steering wheel, threw the gear
shift into PARK, making the truck lurch to a halt. The
rumbling was everywhere now. In the engine, inside the
cab, outside, lying on his skin, in his veins. His eyes
burned, his mouth plated open, and the rumbling
became a wailing, like a banshee keening out the death
of a family member. The moans poured from his soul,
moans nothing could stop. Swallowing air he tried to
stop. His face was wet with tears as he drummed up the
scene Uma had described. She'd gotten there after
they'd moved Tessa, and yet his mind filled in details.
Pauling's car was a boat. A deadly boat.

He didn't know the last time he'd cried. His father's
funeral? Yes. A long while ago. That was different. A
child's death is a black and hollow mark. A blip. An
error. Children are deemed to outlive their parents, not
the other way around. But his mind was racing, getting
ahead of facts. Uma said Tessa was alive, didn't she?
Now, he wasn't sure. The car was a tank. How might
such a small child live under an attack with such size,
such weight? No. He knew he had to stop. Think *alive*.
Keep thinking *alive* then she'll be alive. She'll stay
alive.

Something down a ways off the road moved. A lone
deer, a buck with a three-point set of felted antlers, the

felt always drumming up images of wetland cattails. It
ducked from under a hedge of blackberry, headed
perpendicular to the road, ready to cross. The length of
the hedge trimmed a sharp angle at the corner where
he'd thrown his truck into idle. The buck paused before
setting its forehooves into the ditch, then skipped up
onto the roadside. At the same time, from around the
blind corner, another vehicle sped a few hundred paces
south of his truck. Ben wiped his nose with the back of
his wrist and laid on his horn. The deer's legs skidded
out from under its body in four directions, splaying. But
it quickly rebounded, found its feet and galloped
crossed its path safely to the other side where it
vanished into a tall spray of evergreen, oak, alder, and
willow, all the makings of the island's woods. A
moment of victory swelled. He'd hunted blacktail like
that one but wasn't about to witness one plastered on
the grill of a car in front of him. Didn't want to witness
the dismemberment a car could exact on a living thing.

He wiped a hand over his hair. The oncoming car
set its blinker to turn left and slowed in front of Ben. It
was Dave, the island's master stone mason. He was
rolling down his window to say something when Ben
gunned the gas and turned onto Roche. Ben wasn't in
the mood to explain anything to anyone. Certainly, not
the boss. He didn't care if he might be fired. A
ridiculous thought, of course. He wouldn't. Dave would
understand. Anyone would. And, if he didn't, well . . .
screw him. All he wanted was to see Tessa. He had to
see her before . . . before *what*?

Keeping his hands steady on the steering wheel, he refused to think she might die. Their baby girl was not going to die. Not if he had any say in the matter. But, of course, he didn't.

10

About My Mom

My third year alive, I became aware of the strain within our home. One of my very first memories looks something like this: Mom is rocking me on a knobby rocker that I swear could hold four people, but this time it's just me and her. She's not breast-feeding me but holding a bottle of chocolate milk over my face—the plastic nipple gripped tight between my wet lips while I suckled. The aroma of Jergens lotion and sugary milk rise from the hand she's using to hold the bottle. Her hand so close to my face, I feel the tiny hairs on her knuckles. The nutty chocolate sends me into ecstasy and makes me giggle. Mom coos. The moment, sweet and serene, explodes into crumbs when the door slams, someone putting an exclamation point on a final word.

Mom jumps. My tiny form jumps.

The bottle wrenches from my lips.

Dad is yelling.

"Ditch," he said. But something was wrong with the word.

"Shh. You'll make her cry." Mom's face went moony. Worried, she checks me.

Her body tenses, her eyes scared.

I cry.

"Is it true?" he asks.

"Not now," Mom says.

"When? Why? We could afford another one."

"Right," she says and laughs but not because of humor, because of sarcasm, disbelief, wanting to sliver open one of his veins to reduce him to rubble.

We can barely afford chocolate milk. She holds up my bottle, the one I'm screaming for. I want more milk. Now, I'm wailing.

"Not even a conversation? You just make the decision? It's over? And, poof! Done?"

"It's my body." She pauses here. "Not yours."

I am not letting up. Sucking pockets of air, I go silent. I can't cry. I can't breathe.

"Now, look what you've done." She glowers at him.

"Your body?" he says. "What about what was inside? That was mine too! You had no right. Not without talking."

I'm turning blue. Mom lifts me into a sitting position. My breathless crying opens into a whale song loud and feral . . . finally, air, air, blessed air.

Anyway, I don't exactly remember things smoothing out, but they must have. Until I was seven. When Dad brought up the *termination* again. About terminating *it*. He'd said *it* like *it* was some unidentifiable creature crushed under a flyswatter. Something long dead. Or just killed.

Swack! What the hell was it? Like that.

Mom, "Not now."

Dad, "Yes. Now. Is it true?"

Mom, "I'm not talking about it."

She tipped her head, her eyes traveling to me. Crayons on the floor—sky blue, emerald green, strawberry red, sun yellow, paper white, grape, indigo. All flung willy-nilly around a book filled with sketches of kittens, frogs, butterflies, puppies, elephants, hippos, flowers. Tall, spiky grass fronds, loopy petals, miniature trees, fat suns rising behind trees with rays shooting out seven broad strokes and a big egg yolk center. Grasshoppers hopped, ants labored, worms inched. There were bees with honey jars, beetles with polka dots, snails sliming trails behind them. My coloring book with its powder gray pages felt warm under my fingertips, under my wrist where I lay my arm. I crouched over the book on my knees, drawing outside and inside the lines, whatever happened to happen. At seven, I didn't much care.

"I don't give a flying fu—."

Ben.

She stopped him from saying something.

My head turned. Mommy was upset again. Daddy was mad. He almost used a bad word.

"We'll talk later."

"You bet your easy ass we will."

She blushed.

The door slammed. The truck grumbled to life, an earthquake of sounds but longer, unmoving from the driveway, revving, revving the engine. Then, kablooey! A shockwave. The shrill squeal of tires, the smell of rubber drifting through our open windows, the chassis creaking as each tire bounced over the curb, another squeal, and gravel spraying behind the truck. Finally, the tires taking hold and the zooming throttle speeding out of the neighborhood, away from our house until the din goes deaf, becomes a ghost.

Mom cried. Not like someone had died but with worry like she'd broken someone's expensive bottle of perfume. And something had broken back then. With me crying over my coloring book, still trying to choose a stick to use, the fresh one or a pointy one, round and used or clean and new. And the searing screech of tires circled back ever near.

He burst through the front door. His face tomatoey. He raced at her. Her chair sat between the counter and table facing me on the floor. He leaped across my book, smashing my sun yellow crayon in the process, and pushed Mom hard by the shoulders, her back slamming into the counter. The sound she made reminded me of a lamb bleating.

She grabbed his forearms to stop whatever was coming next: a beating, a slap, letting her fall, but that would be impossible. Maybe then slamming her head against the counter.

Would he do that? Would he kill Mom?

I dropped my crayons, scrambled over the floor under the table, ducking there for cover.

The end of the world is nigh! Men on street corners dressed like Jesus, chanting, wearing dingy robes, holding signs. *Do You Know Jesus?* and *The End of the World is Nigh!*

"Ben!" Her voice warbled with fear . . . or maybe rage.

"Answer me! Is it true?"

Mom didn't speak. She was crying again.

From where I hid, I could only make out from Mom's torso down. Her neck and head above the plane of the table. The chair leaned at an angle, balancing her frame, precariously askance. Her feet hovered over the kitchen floor. Her tennies bent from the flex of her toes inside. So, were her eyes closed or open when he cuffed her, when his right palm stung her on the cheek? *Crack.* Two shallow breaths escaped her mouth then a whimper. He struck her again. *For good measure!* Gramma Kiki would say. But most often, Gramma Kiki was referring to a second dollop of whipped cream over a bowl of cherries.

The feet of her chair landed in place. Mom's legs tight against the seat of her chair pulled under like a scared dog's tail, her feet shook as they connected with the floor.

Dad's legs now stumbling as he backed away. He turned and his steps lit up, guilty. He grappled with the kitchen door handle. The door opened. There, I could see him fully. He glanced down where I hid. His face was morose, lined, tight, tormented, a mix of fury and sorrow. He wiped his nose. Stepped past the threshold and vanished.

He didn't return for weeks. They exchanged calls, although Mom often refused to answer his. Other times, she ran to reach the phone. Mom often repeated a script she'd memorized with calls she made to Dad, a script of commands while waiting for him to pick up.

Come on, Ben. Answer. Come on. Please. Answer.

These calls were often coupled with crying. Hers and mine. I didn't know why I was crying, maybe simply because she was. Maybe simply because I missed my dad. But I remember us crying often back then.

It's funny what we remember. Why we remember. Usually triggered by some phrase, a song, a lawnmower kicking up cut grass, a full moon, puddles of rainwater on the street, seeing flats of cherries at a roadside vendor.

Then, you're sixteen. Say, you're in jail. A chair gets knocked out from under someone. It teeters just before crashing to the ground and . . . *voila*! A scene, from when you were seven, unfolds like the ragged pages of a tattered coloring book. A glimmer fleeting like the ribbons on Tessa's bike, the memory flutters to the front of your consciousness but fizzles out seconds before you remember why you're seeing the scene. Before understanding its import.

A thing that sticks with me like moss sticks to a rock is a thing about Mom and all the choices that day. Like, which crayon to use, which color—blue or orange. Mom's denial or telling the truth. Dad's attack or refusal to attack. But mostly, I remember wondering how things got so scary. And then how the scary stuff sort of drifted out of sight. For a while, anyway.

11

About My Dad

"I'm a regular Joe," Dad often said about himself.
Mom used to smile when he said it, but later it was like
she didn't hear him, or she'd ignored the statements
altogether. You could never tell with Mom.

"She's more a society bee," Dad would say. Then,
"She's too good for me."

After a while, I guess Mom started believing what
he was telling other people about her.

Anyway, the laundry list that makes up my dad is
like this:

Born on the island from a long-time family but not
what they called an *old* family. Far different from a
longtime family, and farther flung from a new family,

transplanted from Renton nearly fifty years ago. Longtime families had staying power seventy years plus. Lots of them were born on the island. But even seventy years is still a long time, not old. Better to be born on the island during, say, prehistoric times to get an *old family* ranking. Longtime families garnered respect, owned plenty of property—undeveloped and otherwise. In town and out, in the country, on the water's edge. Old-time families, like Mr. Johnson, had ranches and grazing land, hundreds of acres or prime real estate.

Dad met Mom at a stone mill in Renton. Dad had worked in hard materials, as they called it, for a few years by then. He was an apprentice at that time working with granite, semiprecious stone, quartz, beautiful stuff, but river rock, too, when my parents started dating. He laid and carved stone for floors, walls, showers, fireplaces—you name it. You wanted something built from stone, Dad was one of the guys who would come out and chip the stone right there on-site.

What he couldn't do or didn't seem to have the aptitude or maybe a desire to do, was run a stone business.

Mom showed up at the mill to pick out material for a woman who liked her *eye*, Mom would explain later to people who asked how they met. Mom's *eye* caused her clients to assume they might not have the taste or talent. People would ask Mom what she thought about this or that color, this or that fabric, this or that type of carpet, wood, or because of Dad's influence, stone.

They always wanted her expert opinion. One woman who hired Mom on an hourly-fee basis plus an increase of fifteen percent above the cost she could get, needed expertise for a particularly difficult and angular bathroom. "She doesn't have the time," Mom would say, "and I need the money." Mom was always drumming up business on the side. Mornings, she was a part-time bank teller and, in the evenings and weekends, she worked on her interior design business.

It's funny how time and circumstance intervened. That particular day she saw Dad, walked over to help him. He smiled *that smile he has* and chatted her up. Mom felt *all a-dither*. This is where the story gets gross. Her body reacted to him and *why not, God?*

But really, I get it. Dad's rugged looking. He's strong, tallish, not too tall. He has the sweetest smile, a gentle smile.

However, if provoked, he's fiery. I've only seen him get physical that one time with Mom when I was a kid. Although, he'd gone on about his college days. I'd also heard some island stories about Dad and his buddies. He must've been a handful when he was a teenager.

So, the deal is, Mom got all hot for Dad. *Ew.* One thing led to another. She moved to the island. Thought it would be idyllic, and it is, but it's also remote. Many folks, after buying their over-priced homes, realize they miss the convenience of the mainland, a city with all the amenities—sliding grocery store doors, stop lights, a Costco and Home Depot. So, they tear out, take a loss

on their investment without pause because they got bit
with island fever. Some people, not everyone. Others
love the reclusive setting, like me. You can't be a
society bee with only three flowers in the garden.
Society bees require English gardens thick and dripping
in an array of wildflowers, periwinkle to saffron.
Society on the island offers two shades of blue. You're
either with the in-group or you're not.

Honestly, though, people who can't handle it slough
off the island like dead skin off locusts and leave our
place shinier when they go.

After they married, Mom's old urges began to
surge. She wanted her career back. Wanted to fly down
to Seattle, dine at The Dahlia Lounge—one of her old
haunts. Wanted dinners out most nights, but on Dad's
income and with a child in tow, funds weren't exactly
pouring in.

She wanted a new purse for every season of every
year. New shoes for the purses. What she got? Me and
stone dust off Dad's clothes.

Cornered doesn't come close to how Mom reacted,
even with the man she presumably loved. Dad tried
romance, brought her flowers. *Nice, but no cigar,
mister.* Candy? *I'll get fat. Take them to work or in the
trash they'll go.*

"What about a baby?"

Mom stuttered. Paused. Was that a smile Dad saw
cross her lips? Sure was.

He'd been talking to the guys at the bar. They
suggested the idea, the baby idea. "She's unsatisfied

because all women want a baby," they'd said. "It's their nature."

Dad, "She was so pissed off. Didn't want anyone to know she wasn't happy."

Oh please. When will you two ever quit telling this horror story?

Mom, "He told me *after* I got pregnant that he was telling all his guy friends how unhappy I was."

At this point in the story, I typically get nauseated and have to excuse myself.

Dad, "Mac gets embarrassed when we talk about how she was conceived."

Dad! I'd scream on my way out of the dining room, out of the kitchen, back inside from a barbecue with neighbors to cover my ears in the confines of my bedroom.

They'd all laugh, Mom and Dad lost in their own story and whoever else, uncomfortable by the intimacy as it might be for others. The conversation turns to something more appropriate—high school football Purple and Gold, or the latest fight at Herb's. That Mark-n-Pak wasn't Mark-n-Pak any longer since it moved to the better location but how old-timers who knew better didn't use the reestablished name.

What's weird was that Dad never seemed to notice people squirm. Even at Mom's urging to change the conversation. Never evaluated people for anything but face value. What they said, they meant. He didn't notice sideways glances, the slight shake of their heads, shuffling off to get another beer, excusing themselves.

He took people at their word. Like when Mom agreed to have a baby. He believed that she wanted a child. The one that turned out to be me. He believed her.

I did too. Until she got pregnant again. Unexpectedly. The big blowup. After that, I wasn't so sure she was happy with me. She wanted something no one could place a finger on. Was it another child, though?

Dad, "What about some college classes?"

Mom: "At that piddly college?"

Dad, "What about these online ones? I hear they have online classes."

All bad ideas. She wanted something that not even she could put a finger on. So, why not have another baby? A ridiculous suggestion. Still, within months, Tessa was on the way. And there was nothing Dad could do about it.

12

What the Woman Saw

"The worst thing," she said, "was that I couldn't react." The woman looked like a tourist. Locals can spot tourists a mile away. Their clothing looks straight out of a department store, creases slightly visible from a quick ironing. No one ironed here. No one who had a life, that is. Tourists of a certain demeanor, a trancelike state walk in their ultra-white shoes through town. We can spot them anywhere. Tourists feeling swept away on a riptide of our town's *quaintness,* You have no idea how many times each summer we hear this phrase. Tourists awestruck by the island's beauty. The walking undead with their cash fluttering out of their wallets, willing participants in spurring on our GIP—gross island product. Making summers boom enough to sustain most businesses throughout the thinner days of winter. She wore a Huskies cap with straight, cropped hair meticulously tucked behind each ear.

The woman started swaying back and forth like a mother holding a child, but instead of a child, her arms were filled with a white terrier, a Westie. The dog began to wriggle, fighting to be put down; and with the woman losing the fight, she placed him next to her shoes and coiled the dog's red leash around her left fist. The dog launched forward, yanking the woman's arm out straight.

Workers inside Roy's Coffee kiosk nearly mashed their faces against each of two windows to see what was going on. One girl working held a hand over her mouth. Two Hispanic guys had ventured out near one white dude by the side door, his broom propped up in one hand. People began to mill in from around the corner. Townies and tourists alike piled in on top of one another to see what happened, most shaking their heads, hands raised to their mouths. Some spoke things like, "Ohmygod, ohmygod." Some whispered, "Tessa Fraser." The name floating on steam from the cappuccino machine above Roy's, above the woman, above the dog. Tessa's name bubbled in gauzy clouds above their heads and over the crime scene in a united thrumming of horror.

Were juncos chittering? Crows on the wing?

An abrupt bulb flashed, snapping an indelible image in onlookers' memories. Shifting the term *quaint* to *dreadful.* In the bat of a hummingbird's wings, the mesmeric atmosphere stripped clean, baring whitewashed molding to wood. Kelp sloshed its death scent from the bay and mixed with greasy hamburgers grilling. Gulls wailed in rhythm with the clank of masts from sailboats bobbing in slips of the marina. Burnt coffee molding on the tongues of people staring at the nightmare unfolding on one corner of town. Rorschach blotch on the ground where Tessa's blood flowed.

Mr. Pauling, the driver, now slumped on a metal woven chair under an umbrella at a table near the road in front of Roy's, not too near the woman where a deputy spoke with her. The red and white umbrella frisked against a brisk wind, the scalloped edges of the canvas goosing up the runner hub, a fleeting glance of the umbrella rib assembly like a square dancer's skirt twirling and revealing a bony set of legs.

"Ma'am," the deputy said, "if you can try to remember some details." The tip of a number two pencil ready, touching the sheet of note paper in his hand, a small memo pad encased in leather.

"That poor little girl," she said.

The deputy shifted his weight into a more even stance.

"You know they weren't paying attention," she said. Then, "Looked like drugs."

"Pardon, ma'am?"

The woman squinted and wiped moisture from under her eyes with her one free hand. "I can't remember anything; just all of a sudden that man there ran her down." Then she asked, "Dear God. How old was she?"

"*Is* she," he corrected, and said, "Seven, ma'am." The deputy continued questioning the woman, asking, "Did the vehicle slow down?"

"What? Um, no. Maybe. I'm not sure. Not that I could see." She let the leash uncoil. The dog stretched its tether to the max, the woman's arm stretched and bounced languidly as the dog swept the area, its snout down, running this way then trying to get to the bloody stain. "Bentley, stop," she commanded, but the dog's curiosity won out. "I have to get him out of here," the woman told the deputy. "Honestly. I didn't see much. All I know is they were doing something not right. You know what I mean? It all happened so fast." She was pulling the dog off, trying to get away from the scene. "Look, if you need me to answer more questions, you have my number. Right? Can we do this later? My dog and all."

"You'll need to fill out a formal witness statement. Come to the station tomorrow first thing."

"Thanks. I'm sorry. It's just—" she was about to say, but instead the deputy interjected, "It's your dog. Yes ma'am. Thank you."

13

Four Days Before

Dad had worked for three years on refurbishing an old abandoned hotel at the third turn of False Bay. Some people had pulled a winning Powerball ticket one year before the job started, bought the hotel, and started a major remodeling campaign. Residents along False Bay Drive complained daily because of construction traffic and trucks speeding along a twenty-five-MPH stretch of road. One old woman had clocked one of their trucks doing fifty she'd said. She'd stopped several workers, asking them to slow down. Stood arms wide in the road stopping vehicles. A real looney tune, but that's what you get living in this place. A real mix from upper crust to crusty bottom.

When I heard about the woman, I cringed, hoping the speeding truck wasn't driven by Dad but sort of knew it was. He enjoyed racing up and down I-5. Anyway, construction had siphoned off a large population of construction workers—stone masons like Dad, carpenters, cement guys, electricians, plumbers, glaziers—a fact that pissed off a population of locals who were having trouble finding help for smaller projects. So goes our island life.

Anyway, because of these people's hotel remodel, Dad had missed a few of his *custodial* visits during the few months since the separation. Once, he totally forgot, didn't even call until the following morning. His memory miraculously returned in the shower getting ready for work. I was pissed, but Mom was livid. She'd made plans. Wanted to go to a movie with a *friend* she'd said. Suggested Dad's bout of forgetfulness might be directly correlated with her plans. They had fought about something a couple days before. But you get so sick of hearing the same fight over and over that you block out their words each time they have the fight again. I was so sick of hearing them fight. So, I bottled up inside my room, slammed the bedroom door, shoved in my earbuds, and blasted the John Legend *Jesus Christ Superstar* soundtrack. You can only block out so much, even when you know Jesus is on your side.

The island wire was that Dad was already seeing someone so soon after their separation. Not seriously, but when word finally knocked on our door, Mom snapped, became unhinged. I heard the conversation ramp up.

She began calling him names: son-of-a-bitch, effing bastard, piece of dog crap (but she didn't say crap), sleaze. I snuck outside the kitchen, back to the wall, and listened. Tessa stuck her head out the door, but I waved her back inside her room.

He must've been trying to defend himself. "I have every right!" she said, her voice junkyard dog.

She clicked off the phone and slammed it onto the kitchen table. "That bastard," she hissed and began to cry. My stomach knotted. I hated hearing her cry.

Her head was in her hands, her fingers pressed into the skin of her forehead as though she were trying to keep her brains from spilling out. When she realized I was standing in the doorway, she said, "This is none of your business." And tossed a finger toward the door to get me out of the kitchen.

"Fine," I said, "you guys make me sick."

"Well, that's just a real shame, isn't it? You have it so bad."

But I'd walked off before she'd finished. Walked *out*. It took all of two seconds to spin the combination lock for my bike. I let the links fall near the front wheel like a dead snake, walked off, leaving the chain on the cement driveway. After jumping onto the bike seat, I took off. Headed to Gemma's.

It was midday. A Saturday. I knew her dad was probably mowing or hedging or pruning—his weekend chores fully underway. Imagined the smell of grilling meat, maybe hamburgers, a salad bowl on the counter, a chopping board wet with traces of vegetables. A beer in the cupholder of Mr. Painter's riding mower. Gemma on the front porch dorking around on her iPad or reading another novel, *Catcher in the Rye*, one Mrs. Danchin assigned in English for a book report we were supposed to write. I read Salinger's coming-of-age tale two years before but reread it for our class. This was Gemma's first go at the story.

"I want to marry Holden Caulfield," she'd said after only the first two chapters.

"He's fictional. You want to marry someone fictional?" I said.

"Anyone else better here on this piece of shit island?"

"Hey, Gems. Language," her dad said.

"Sorry, Daddy." She winked back to me.

Weather had begun to change, but we were catching the last few rays of warm sun before autumn set in. Mrs. Danchin got to assignments fast, talking about Salinger and his propensity to womanize. With a start like that? English class started sounding better and better.

When I bumped up onto their driveway, Gemma's dad was keying off the mower and taking a long healthy swig of beer. Grass clippings speckled the white socks pulled up to his knees. He sat on the mower as though it were his throne. Gasoline fumes permeated in heavy humidity. Where grass clippings had spewed from his mower lay long curving mounds that formed a labyrinth—a mouse-high hedge through the yard where he'd mowed. He slipped off a pair of red plastic ear mufflers and left them hanging around his neck. His Seahawk's T-shirt touted the number twelve for the twelfth man fans of the team. When he lifted his hands behind his head to rest, the armpits of the T-shirt glistened dark like two wet badges of honor.

"Hey, Mac!" he yelled.

Gemma looked up. "Mac!"

I dropped my bike where I'd rolled to a stop at the back bumper of Mr. Painter's car.

"Hey, Gem," I said.

"Want some water?" Mr. Painter asked.

"That would be awesome, sir."

The seat creaked when he twisted off the mower. He stretched into a straighter stance and limped up the stairs and into the house.

"Your face is all blotchy," Gemma said.

"I'm so mad."

When Gemma swiveled her legs off the swinging bench, I slumped my butt down next to her, close to the arm rail. "My house is totally effing effed up."

Mr. Painter came out with a bottle of water and handed it to me. He directed his question to Gem, "Mom wants to know if Mac can stay for dinner."

"Can you?" Gemma said.

I lifted my shoulders, but then nodded. It wasn't the first or the last time they had asked me in their roundabout way.

"I'd love to," I said. "Mom's manic."

"Sorry, kiddo," Mr. Painter said. "Well, you two want to partake in some girl talk, I'm sure, so I'll be heading inside."

"Thanks for the water, Mr. Painter."

"Sure thing, kiddo." He winked, spun off the porch, and headed into the house.

"Your parents are so cool," I said.

"They're nerds, Mac. Big-ass wonky nerds."

I laughed. Gemma had a way to make me forget my troubles.

"They're nice."

"Nerds in love. Mom was a book nerd and Dad a nature nerd. Now, they're pot nerds. Thrilled it's legal. But, here's the dealio. They will always be together because who else could stand either one of them." Gemma set her iPad on her thighs. "What happened?"

"They're fighting," I said, pausing, "again."

"You ready to try yet?"

I didn't respond right away. Instead, I considered the look in Gemma's eyes—a toss-up of mischief and sorrow for me.

"Getting there," I said.

She puffed out her disgust with me and said, "Chicken."

"I'm on the soccer team!"

"It's not like it will paralyze you. You won't go blind either. Despite *Reefer Madness* lore. God. They were so stupid back then. The 70s was like inventing the wheel for science."

"Tell me again."

"How many times will this make?" But she complied. "Okay, you feel happy and lazy. Relaxed."

"Will I choke?"

"I don't know. Maybe." She read my face and said, "Yes. Probably. But usually only the first time. Then you stop. You get used to it real fast."

Her mom broke our secret when she was standing at the screen door. "You girls want French fries or mashed potatoes?"

We both startled and answered her at the exact same split second. Gemma responded with mashed potatoes and I asked for fries. She laughed at us.

"Don't act like I didn't hear you. I did, you know. If you, Miss Mac, don't get permission from your mom, then Gemma won't be allowed to let you try any of hers. You're not eighteen. We don't let Gemma do it outside this house, you hear, and if I call your mom and she doesn't give the okay, no go. Understand?"

I nodded. I was still so weirded out and uncomfortable talking about pot in front of an adult. Even Gemma's parents who were way cool about pot *and* sex. They'd even started Gemma on birth control so if she ever ended up having sex, she wouldn't get *knocked up* as they put it.

"Oh, Mother dearest. Eavesdropping? Isn't that a sin or something? Now, please. May we have some privacy?"

"Not until you're eighteen. Then it's up in the air. But I mean it, Gemsy. Mac's mom has to say it's okay. French fries for our guest."

"Fine, Mother!" She paused, then said, "Come on. Will you please go?"

"*Gemsy*. I love it." I whispered and chuckled under my breath. "When did *Gemsy* happen?"

"Shut. It. Now." she said. Then, Gemma apologized for her mom's intrusion. But I guess because it was out, and Mrs. Painter was aware that I was considering smoking pot, I caved and told Gemma I'd do it, *in five days*. She clapped like a giddy dork, then we went inside and ate, and I ended up sleeping over.

14

What the People at Roy's Saw

The chopper lifted. Its rotor blade slapping a beat, then dissolving in the distance. "No, that's not what happened," the young man said in response to something his workmate had said. He wore a small silver ring pierced through his upper lip.

"Yes, sir. I saw it!" she said. His workmate was a young woman with strawberry freckles. "You weren't even at the window, Lex. How would you know?" She was shaking her head and squinting at him.

"I saw, Shelby. I was standing right here." Lex pointed the broom handle toward a side door which was open. "I saw," he said. Then, in his own defense, no longer directing his comments to the woman but to one of two male deputies standing at the curb directly in front of Roy's, he said, "I *did* see."

Paramedics and EMTs had come and gone when a large truck clattered to a stop in front of Roy's, grabbing the attention of the three talking. The vehicle's blue hull advertising *Island Towing* across the side shimmied into idle. The engine wheezed while it waited for the go-ahead to tow off Bill Pauling's car.

After the brief distraction, Shelby went on. People nearby held hands over their eyes, watching the chopper saw across the distant sky on its path south to Harbor View's trauma center in Seattle.

Locals from nearby businesses were now dispersing, still murmuring their shock. Their words like cremains in the ash heap of other island stories.

"He did *not* try to veer. He didn't do *anything*," the girl said.

Lex responded, "His car swerved." His tone was apologetic.

"Because it bounced to the right when he hit the little girl!" she exclaimed. The young woman appeared shaken by the event and was ready to cry.

"What's your name, miss?" the deputy asked.

"Shelby. Shelby Lowell."

"And you, young man, Lex, right? What's your last name?"

"Swaisey."

The deputy wrote their names on the pad. Again, he turned his attention to the girl.

"So, Shelby, tell me exactly what you saw." He paused and addressed Lex, "You next. Please let her tell me what she saw. If you could give us a minute?"

Lex stepped away, pulled out a pack of Marlboro cigarettes, tamped one out of the pack, snapped a blue flame out of a butane lighter, and lit his smoke. He slumped closer to the intersection and stood near where the woman had been standing with the dog.

"Okay, Miss Lowell."

"Shelby," she said.

"Okay, Shelby. Please tell me what happened."

But then her face contorted, and she screamed, seemingly out of nowhere, "Ohmygod! She's dead, isn't she?"

"Miss, please. We don't know that. Please calm down and focus. I need to know what you saw."

Shelby's hands shook when she tried to tuck a wild strand of long brown bangs into a fold of hair. The other hand hovered above her mouth—her eyes wild.

"Miss," the deputy urged.

"I've never seen a person die."

Tears welled in her eyes. She turned her head, pulled a rag from a pocket in her uniform, one used to wipe down counters, and wiped her nose.

"I'm sorry," she said, and tried to contain her emotions. "I've never . . . okay, um." Pausing, she continued to wipe her face. "The car bumped off the curb." She pointed to the exact spot. "Then took a hard pull to the right . . . there." Pointing again to where the big Chevy sat lurched on top of a wrecked fence at an angle as if it'd lost a wheel, but all the wheels were intact. "When he crashed," she said, "the car stalled, and the horn went off for, like, well, forever."

"So, who helped him off the horn?"

"Mac."

"The sister?"

"Yes. She's, well, sort of a friend."

"Sort of?"

"I know her. You know, from around."

"Okay," he said, "what did she do?"

Shelby's eyes danced, tried to land on anything but the deputy's eyes. She shifted from one foot to the other. "Look, I can't remember everything, okay? I mean…," she said letting her words fade.

"I know this is difficult."

"You didn't see Tessa get mowed down! So, no," she yelled, "you don't know how difficult this is for me. They are, were. Shit . . . *are* my friends. Is she dead? I mean, God. I've known Mac since grade school. She was four years behind me."

"Miss, please."

Shelby took a moment to collect herself.

"Okay, again, Miss. How did Mr. Pauling end up outside of the car?"

She turned, dropped her arms. Her mood changed and she shut down, went from sad to angry. "I can't remember. Look, are we done here? I still have to work. I could get fired. I have stuff to put away. I'm still on duty. Are we done?" Her hands locked around her waist. Her fingertips brightened under the strain.

"I'm sure management will understand, miss."

"Quit calling me miss." Again, she covered her mouth. "This is unbelievable."

Two more deputies showed up. Three sheriff's vehicles lined the ferry lane parking lot. Each car's emergency lights kept swinging in a lazy display, alternating between red and white. One of the deputies was hanging yellow crime scene tape to cordon off A Street at Nichols. Another deputy was hanging tape from Nichols along A to block Ferry Lot B and then between the pet store and the lot. From a bird's-eye view, the taped off area created one big obtuse triangle.

The owner of the pet store, Annie, and her assistant, Elaine, backed off so they were standing a few feet behind where the tape had been hung. Neither woman spoke to the other. Their faces took on a pallor of people who had seen the un*see*able.

"Shelby, can you please tell me how Mr. Pauling ended up on the ground?" the officer asked once more.

"I guess he fell out."

"I thought you said Mac helped him out."

"I could be wrong. Look, I told you I don't remember everything. And I'm not answering any more questions. I can't remember, okay? So, can I please go?"

"One more thing," the deputy said, and paused.

"What?"

"Where was the other girl?"

"Other girl?"

"Mac's friend," he said.

"Gem?"

He checked his notepad, "Gemma Painter, yes."

"She and Mac were by the pole, over there." She pointed to a short stretch along A Street where cars line up in the ferry holding lane, Lot B.

"And she did what?"

Shelby wiped her nose again. "Who? Gem?"

He checked his notepad. "Gemma Painter. That's right."

"Gemma stayed back. It was like, uh, she froze."

"So, just MacKenzie came up?"

"She didn't just come up, she tore up. Ran. Balls out." Then she added, "There was nothing she could've done. Tess was down by the time she reached the car." After saying, *down*, beads of moisture trickled onto her bottom rim of lashes, turning them a ruddy tone, darker than her strawberry eyebrows.

"I know this is hard, but is that when Mr. Pauling got out of his car?"

Shelby straightened her back and once again pulled at the errant strand of her hair. "Yes. It is hard," she said and looked over a shoulder to Roy's. "Look, like I said before, it's all fuzzy. I don't know. Now, I'm sorry. But, please. I have to get back to work." She turned from the deputy and walked to Roy's, checking once over a shoulder before ducking inside. She then slipped into view at one of the interior windows facing the ferry lanes.

15

Three Days Before

Mom sped around the house in a flurry. She came and went twice, once to the beauty salon and once to the clothing store. I couldn't leave because I had to watch Tessa . . . again, for the *bazillionth* time. Tessa was thrilled we were home alone, but I needed to do some homework and all Tessa wanted was to play. I mean, come on, I'm too old to play dolls or make mud pies. I'll never understand why Mom and Dad decided to have another kid so many years after me.

After coming home from the stylist, Mom dropped her purse and keys onto the table and booked it to her bedroom where she slapped a stripe of glossy goo on her lips, slathered her lashes with a dusky shade of mascara, then dashed out again to grab a new outfit. Honestly, how many times had she said we didn't have money for this and that? So, it sort of shocked me when I read the credit card receipt saying she'd spent ninety-eight dollars at Local, her favorite hair salon. And although her new do looked awesome, how was it she was able to find the bucks in our meager bank account to spend another how many dollars on the new clothing? I was just happy I got my allowance for chores. My nest egg had become quite a nice little wad of dough, a wad I intended to spend on clothing, shoes, and books for school. I even had extra to buy some items for Tessa too, who didn't drag down the money I got for allowance because, well, Tessa was pretty much as useless as *nipples on a doorknob* on chores—a Mom-saying after a glass of wine.

But I have to reiterate, when Mom returned from her stint at Local, she looked gorgeous. Radiant, even. And happy. I hadn't seen her so happy, so elated in months. Like the senior class had voted her queen of the prom or something. She was acting all giddy and goofy, running to the closet, then into the bathroom, futzing over this purse or that one. And shoes! Ohmygod. What shoes should she wear?

So, when I saw the money she'd expended, well, I couldn't really get upset. Plus, it wasn't like *I* was bringing home a paycheck every other week to support the three of us. And I'd heard all about how much money it took to support us—the food, the electricity, the water bill, the mortgage, school supplies, gas for the car, insurance payments, property taxes, income taxes. The list grew each time she spoke about our bills. "Dad was pitching in only enough for your and Tessa's food," she'd said, "because there's no custodial settlement making him pay more." She awfulized *he's stringing me along* and *it's probably a devious plan.* Because, as she'd pondered, he'd most likely have to pay three times as much after a divorce. Plus, Mom didn't really want him gone. She hadn't wanted the separation. It was he who left us. She didn't want a divorce. She'd only let her opinion about his measly offering slip once. Well, once before. Until the next day when she went from thrilled about life to flat, freaking furious.

16

After Dinner at Gemma's

Gemma was handing me a bottle of water after I
texted Mom explaining how I intended to stay
overnight, and that Mrs. Painter had already fed me.

I was cracking open my bottle when the phone rang.
It was *her*.

"What?" I said with more attitude than was
necessary.

"Make sure you help them clean up from any mess
you make."

"God, Mom."

"I mean it, Mac. Don't leave any messes like you do
here."

"Are you done?"

"What about homework?"

"Covered."

"Be home before I leave for work. You need to make sure Tessa gets to school on time."

"Fine." I didn't bother with a goodbye. After which, she sent *XOXO* with stupid heart bubbles blossoming up into my screen.

"So lame," I said. After which, I pocketed my phone and took a mouthful out of my water bottle.

"What's up?" Gemma asked. "Did demons return unto Mary?"

I nearly spit. We sat in the gloom of Gemma's bedroom. It never failed to amaze me how dark she liked it, her windows drawn with blackout curtains. Gemma's bed was big. Bigger than mine. A queen mattress. I still had a twin. It was embarrassing when she came to my house.

Gemma's bed had this thick, sloping wood headboard with a matching footboard. The setup made the bed look like a boat, which by the way she'd draped a dream tent over since I'd last visited, a tent that *turns your bed into a magical dream world*! And inside? A resplendent display of stars, moons, planets, and comets, giving the effect of sleeping under the night sky. Since fifth grade, when I first stayed at Gemma's overnight, she had always placed some kind of cover over her bed. So, just since last time she must've traded in the pup tent for the dream tent.

Since puberty, which Gemma refers to as *the pubes*, she's kept a smallish green chalkboard with a warning posted on her door. During her period, she keeps it on the outside. During such grisly times, she like to write things such as KEEP OUT OR DIE, and often, MONSTER VISITING, DARE TO ENTER! Things like that. Once she'd even written: BEEEE-ATCH INSIDE! Today the chalkboard was inside. Today, she'd written BOO! With a little stickman ghost with its hands in the air and long, oval eyes, and a scary hole for the mouth. I had to snicker since in just a month we'd be heading into Halloween season. Other days of the month, she'd write short philosophical-leaning phrases like *When in doubt, believe*. Gemma was my funny friend. Almost always, she could make me laugh.

"I wish I lived here," I said.

"No, you don't. My parents are always locked in their room, *napping*. In other words, banging it out. It's gross and embarrassing."

"Gah, Gem. Why'd you tell me?"

She giggled and pulled out one of our assignments for first hour in AP class—a 600 level class, 629, in precalc. We were covering advanced study of polynomial functions, finite sequences, exponential functions, trigonometry, conic sections, data analysis, vectors, limits, probability, and statistics.

"Look at this," she said, reading from the book. "In mathematics, a polynomial is an expression consisting of variables (also called indeterminates) and coefficients, which involves only the operations of addition, subtraction, multiplication, and nonnegative integer exponents of variables. An example of a

polynomial of a single indeterminate x is $x^2 - 4x + 7$."
She held an LED mini flashlight over the book. "The
product can change as x changes," she said.

"Or as the multiplier changes," I said.

"Exactly. This crap is easy."

"Do you have another iPad? While escaping hell, I
forgot my stuff."

"Oooey," Gemma popped up, put a hand on her hip,
and mimicked my mom. "You'll be in so much trouble
if you don't get your homework in on time, young
lady!"

"An iPad, lame-o," I said, to which Gemma opened
the top drawer of her dresser and pulled out a Pro
version.

"It's small," she said, and held it to her chest.
Gemma's parents had upgraded her to the 12.5-inch
2017 version.

"It's great. Mine's the same."

"You poor mistreated darling. How do you survive
the abuse?"

I reached out my hand, "Give it, weirdo."

"Wanna play D&D after?"

"Sure." I paused while I powered on the iPad. "Did
you talk to Jacob about me?"

"I was wondering when you were going to ask.
And, yes. Yes, I did."

Gemma was playing cat and mouse, killing me in
the process.

"Okay! So, spill?"

"He wants to sit with you for lunch tomorrow."

"Oh crap."

"Oh crap. Oh crap," she mimicked.

"What should I do?"

"Umm. Sit with him at lunch sounds like a possibility, ditz."

"What should I wear?"

"Now, see. I also know you don't have anything *at all* to wear for situations like these. You know, kiss-me-now clothes . . ."

"Stop it. Oh, wait. What *am* I going to do?"

Gemma pushed off the floor and sauntered to her closet, swaying her butt with exaggeration the entire way. When she got there, she slid the doors hard and fast, making them slam open. She then proceeded with an over-the-top model gesture, you know, the whole arms up and down, displaying the overfilled contents inside. "This is where magic starts and ends."

She slid several hangers back and forth on the clothes rack. Dresses, shirts, slacks, their silky weight undulating under her force until, "Ah! This. You're going to have to find some decent shoes. Your feet are smaller than mine."

"Oh, hell no." Not about the shoes but about the outfit Gemma had chosen.

"What? Too . . . me?" Gemma giggled.

"Mom'll *kill* me," I said.

"Come home with me after second period break and change here." Gemma winked the wink that always persuaded me to do something I shouldn't. Then she said, "Ol' Uma'll never know." She was the Cheshire cat hanging from a branch. "Come back here after school and change back into those raggedy-ass denims. Yer mom'll be clueless."

17

What Lex Swaisey Saw

By the end of Shelby's interview, Lex had finished his cigarette. As the deputy approached, he pinched off the cinder near the middle of the stick, flicked the nib onto the pavement of an empty parking spot off the side of Friday Harbor Pet Supply. Still hot, the ember curled up until he crushed it into nothingness with the toe of his work boot.

"Lex Swaisey, right?" the officer confirmed.

Lex nodded and crossed his arms over his chest, his posture held in a question mark, his brown eyes streaked with red. A scruffy, mottled beard leading from a set of shaggy sideburns stippled around his upper lip, under his chin, down his neck, and under his

shirt like he'd run head-long into a storm of facial hair.
He wore a once white apron over a red and green plaid
flannel shirt. The apron tied off above his belt—green
canvas strap looped within the waistline of his baggy
jeans.

The deputy showed him his notepad, pointing to a
spot on the paper. "Got the spelling right?"

"That's *Patrick's* spelling. Our name is spelled S-w-
a-i-s-e-y. With an S."

He scratched out the name Swayze and rewrote
Lex's name correctly. "Got it." While writing, he said,
"You said you saw something different?"

"Well, yeah. But like Shel said, I was inside."

"You think he tried to avoid the girl?"

"Like I said, I was inside. But his car took a hard
right. To me, I mean, if you asked me, he tried to miss
her."

"Where were you standing?"

"Sort of outside the door, over here."

"Sort of?"

"No. On the side of the building. More outside than
inside, I think."

The deputy's pants swished when he walked. A
radio sat strapped on his left shoulder and whispered,
clicking on and off into a coiled wire leading up the
nape of his neck where it wrapped around his ear and
ended with an earpiece inserted into his ear canal. A
bright, six-pointed badge rested high on his chest with
the insignia of the San Juan County Sheriff's Office.
The badge displayed a number, indicating his level of

service and the authority granted to him by taking his oath. The charcoal gray uniform bulked out around and under his arms and above his belt, creating hard lines from the standard-issue flak jacket he wore under his shirt.

Lex and the deputy shuffled out of earshot past the tape on the ground, past Pauling's empty car, past Gene sitting behind the steering wheel of his big, blue tow truck, waiting for the okay to clear the scene and move Pauling's vehicle from in front of Roy's. Bill Pauling had already been taken to the station at the courthouse for booking.

"I was here, like Shel said, at the door. Sort of just inside. I was sweeping," Lex explained when they reached the spot.

"Tell me exactly what you saw," the deputy said.

"The accident or before?"

"The accident, then before."

"I heard first."

"Whattidya hear?"

"Someone yelled, screamed, 'Oh my god!' and I looked up. I think it was the lady with the dog. You know, who screamed. But really, you're always kinda watching things in town. Something's always going on, ya know?"

"Yes, I do," the deputy commented. He eyed Lex fast, then lowered his gaze. "What happened next?"

"The car kind of, you know, jumped." Swaisey's arms lifted. "Then it . . ."

"It?"

"The car. It turned to the right." His arms followed the car's path. "Ending there."

The deputy prompted him, "Like he was trying to avoid the girl?"

"That's what *I* thought. Yeah. I mean, Mr. Pauling's, like, the nicest old dude. You know? He wouldn't hurt a fly."

"You know Bill Pauling?"

Lex nodded, then said, "You know, from around. He's a church person. Goes to the one on the corner."

"The Presbyterian Church?"

"Yeah. Is it? Sure. I guess."

"What else can you tell me about Mr. Pauling?"

Lex paused, then said, "I dunno." He shifted his weight and looked south, away from the accident. "It's kinda mean."

"What's kinda mean, Lex?" the deputy said, cuing him to continue.

"I guess he's, well, some people call him . . . you know, like, he's sort of the town joke. Used to be an old saying, 'keep the kids in after dinner 'cause Pauling's out driving.' But I never saw that. He's always real nice to me, sir. Always ordering a latte with a humongous glob of whipping cream and chocolate syrup. A cheese Danish. He loved those." He caught himself. "I mean loves them."

"What about the girl? Did you know her too?"

"I know her sister, Mac. Sometimes she hangs around, but I didn't really *know* know her. Never talked to her. 'Cept 'Hey, kid,' sometimes. She was sorta quiet. You know, to herself."

"So, he tried to avoid hitting her?" The deputy said, returning to the original question.

Lex squinted. "That's what it looked like to me."

"So, before?"

"Yeah. Man, I hope it's not true."

"What's that?"

"Man, there's enough of this shit, sorry, stuff on the island. Even got caught up a little myself." He rubbed the ring through his lip. "I'd hate to think Mac was doing this crap."

"What crap?"

"You know, the drug thing."

"She was doing drugs?"

"Shit, man. I think so."

"You think Shelby saw?" The deputy was writing again.

He shrugged. "You'd have to ask her. But I saw 'em smoking. And I know for a fact she's not eighteen. I thought about asking her out but then found out she was underage and bagged the idea. But she like freaked. I mean pot doesn't make you crazy like that. Coke mixed with pot will. Like PCP, almost."

"Are you high right now, Lex?"

"Pot's legal."

The deputy wrote something on the notepad. Still focusing on the pad, he said, "What else did you see?"

"Maybe they passed something between them. I think? Shit, man. This freaking bites."

"Yes. It does bite." The deputy wrote a little more before stating, "Okay. I think we have enough. What's your number in case I need to call you with further questions?"

After Lex Swaisey gave the deputy his cell phone, he walked back inside Roy's where a slurry of nuthatches fevered at particles on the ground near the side door but flitted off when Lex approached. The birds flew to the bent wooden fence downed by Pauling's car and branches in a throng of wispy poplars that hung in an alley between the backs of buildings facing Nichols and Web Street. Lex began to sweep crumbs and dirt out the door and onto the pavement of Roy's drive-thru once more.

18

Two Days Before

The day Mom spent all that money on herself,
acting like she was the princess at the ball, she came
home like an ugly stepsister. Tessa and I recoiled when
the door slammed. Tessa had gotten her bath. We were
lying in her bed, me at the top and Tess at the foot, in
opposite directions so her feet were against my hips and
mine were near her shoulders, close enough I could
poke my toes in her face and make her giggle and
squirm. And, yes, she was reading *The White Deer*,
chattering about the weird little monarch, Clode, and
his sons—Thag, Gallow, and Jorn— and, of course, a
princess.

When Mom slammed the front door, it was with such force that Tessa's doorknob rattled. We both jumped. I looked at Tessa, then her pink alarm clock. It hadn't been all that long since she left, maybe an hour, if that.

Something or *someone* had provoked her ire. The phone rang. Mom picked it up. She yelled so loud that her voice distorted. And from her one-sided conversation, I knew she was screaming at Dad. Again.

"Don't listen," I said. My voice conspiratorial, whispering.

Mom stomped through the house past Tessa's door to the master bedroom, all the while laying into Dad. She went a short way down the hallway grumbling and sounded a guttural, "Son of a bitch!"

At first, I thought she stubbed her toe, but the grumbling and foul words persisted.

Tessa said, "Uh-oh."

"Shh. Don't say anything."

I snuck to the bedroom door and tried as hard as I could to become invisible, standing there against the wall. Tessa usually kept her door cracked open unless she was upset, then she kept it closed, slamming it for added effect. It was funny how much Tessa was like Mom.

"Your effing (but Mom didn't say effing) girlfriend?"

Then, "How humiliating! In front of the *entire* town!"

Her words became shaky.

"Oh my God. I'm the laughing stock!" Then silence surrounded by a lullaby of tears.

She gasped when the landline rang. I nearly broke my foot scrambling over to see who was calling. It was Dad.

"You son of a bitch! You asked your girlfriend too?"

I can only imagine Dad's response, which couldn't have been very long because Mom laid into him.

"Why did you even ask me to dinner?" Then, "I thought you wanted to talk about *us*? About *reconciling*. As if there's any chance of that now. Well, asshole, you're off the hook! Don't ever call again. If you want to talk with your daughter, (and I thought, *daughters*, Mom, *daughters*), you can call her cell phone. Hear me? Do. Not. *Ever*. Call. Me. Again!"

She slammed the receiver with such force she could've cracked the plastic when it landed on the cradle.

I dimmed Tessa's light and scrambled into bed with her.

"Pretend you're asleep," I said to Tessa.

Mom came barreling back down the hallway toward the kitchen. A cupboard opened. Glass clanked onto the countertop. Tears. Sniffling. A cupboard door slammed. Another opened, the lower cabinet. Grumbling a lonely argument. A heavier sound clanked against the countertop. A bottle. Wine. The pop and squeak of the cork. The *clup, clup, clup* and squeaking of the cork being pushed back inside the neck of the bottle.

Another cabinet door slammed. Silence. A deep breath from Mom. Stomping on the tile floor of the kitchen, a chair skidded away from the table. Mom sat. Breathing in, Mom drank more. The lullaby turning into a choir of tears.

I put my finger to my lips to make sure Tessa remained quiet and whispered, "Don't move."

She shook her head violently like all of this was scaring her, but said, "I need to pee."

I rolled my eyes. "Really? Gah. Okay. Come on."

We snuck out of Tessa's and slipped across the hall into the bathroom we always used. And we almost made it. With my hand steady on the knob, I made sure the door made zero noise opening and closing, but when Tessa finished her business, and because I forgot to tell her, she flushed the toilet. *Faloosh*.

Mom heard. Of course.

"Is that you, Mac?"

I mouthed to Tessa, "Way to go."

I popped my head out of the door, "Yeah. I had to pee."

"Tessa with you?"

"Sound asleep," I said. My eyes flashed open. I mouthed, "*Go, go!*" Making a hand slice across my neck, indicating to Tess not to make a sound, gesturing for her to get back to her room. Putting both hands together and placing them on the side of my head in a pretend-you're-sleeping gesture.

"Did I wake you?" Mom said. She was still in the kitchen but standing from the sound of the chair sliding across the floor. Her steps crossed the floor, nearing the entryway just before the hall.

"Move, move, move." Mouth-syncing the words again, pushing Tessa into the hall, back inside her room. I flipped off the light, and whispered, "Pretend you're sleeping."

I had gotten good at lying when trying not to upset Mom. "No. I just woke up," I lied. "I'm going back to sleep."

"Oh," she said. Her steps stopped at the edge of the kitchen. "Okay. Goodnight," she said. She retreated back into the kitchen and stopped at the counter, refilled her glass of wine.

19

A Text from Gemma

By the time Mom shuffled into the kitchen that morning, my Cheerios had coalesced into an ooze of milky oats with a few Os still holding their shape. The message had me so stunned. I almost didn't notice her. Before she could see Gem's message, I clicked off my cell.

"That Gemma?"

I slopped a spoonful of mushy cereal into my mouth. "Mm-hmm."

Mom's eyes were glassy and swollen. She dropped her gaze, reconnected with me, opened her mouth to speak, but didn't.

"She okay?"

"Gem?" I said.

She poured day-old coffee into a mug and nuked it. The humming microwave became our morning music. While her coffee heated, Mom bent over the sink, opened up the cold water, placed a hand under the faucet, and drank straight out of her palm. It reminded me of an old Western movie where a dying man crawls on hand and knee across the desert hardpan to an oasis where he drinks, and drinks, and drinks.

Mom stopped drinking when the microwave dinged. She maneuvered so that her head would not move without her shoulders moving with it. She had what I'd heard called *the spins*. Once the mug was up to her lips, she blew and sipped, blew and sipped. Every so often she would groan.

Then, Tessa walked in all glowing and cheery and behind her, April and Walt, our cat and dog. The faminals, as Tessa liked to call them, a truncated version of *our family of animals*.

"Morning," she chimed.

"Not today," Mom said.

Tessa had been all *bright, alert, and responsive*, to use a term our vet once said about one of the cats we had to put down. After Mom's comment, Tessa's glow dimmed.

Mom's response confused Tessa for a second, then her face seemed to flash back to the night before when I made her pretend to be asleep.

"Tess, come here. I'll fix you a bowl of cereal," I offered.

Mom groaned.

"Excuse me," I said. Mom shuffled closer to the middle of the sink out of the way so I could snag a bowl from the cupboard.

As I shook out some Cheerios, Mom groaned again. She set her mug down and hightailed it into mine and Tessa's bathroom, not bothering to close the door. Another groan and Mom yarked into the toilet.

"Gross," Tessa said. Not bothering to quiet her voice.

I placed a finger to my lips.

Whispering, I said, "Mom's sick. Eat your cereal."

A small mound of Cheerios crumbled when I began to add milk.

Tessa said *when* for me to stop pouring.

While putting the milk back into the refrigerator, Mom nudged the door closed.

My cell phone buzzed with a text message from Gemma. I thought I'd choke on my Cheerios when I read what she had to tell me.

Gem: Yer M&D in a big scene at Vinny's last night

Me: Shit. What'd U hear?

Gem: Dad's girly showd up. Totally curving your mom. Julie had to quiet Uma down. Tight mad.

Me: Shit. Who? What she look like? You know her?

Gem: My dad says cute. Blonde. Young. R/E Agent. Not sure on name. Dad didn't say.

Me: F.U.C.K. Man. Ok. Tx.

Gem: ROFLMAO

Me: Not me. 🙁

That day, I learned the word *pariah* and what it means to be a one—one of The Lame—the dregs in school. I'd suffer the looks and whispers from different clicks—popular girls, loadies, Bible thumpers, and every different ethnic group *including* their varying subcultures.

You walk down the hallway, and it's like the Red Sea parting. Waves of girls and boys all silent as you pass by, all expecting—no, not expecting—*hoping* you melt down under the weight of their silent stares, or worse, their snickering.

And why? Because my lame-ass mother and father can't seem to hold it together for more than a few lousy minutes at a time. Certainly, not when they meet face-to-face. Not anymore.

I had to reread Gemma's messages several times. It wasn't that I didn't understand. I mean, I heard Mom erupt into the house the night before. I understood her message, but I needed time to wrap my head around yet another upheaval. Dad's leaving was good for a year. Now this. And was another shoe about to drop?

Embarrassment is a funny thing. It makes you drum up scenarios that probably will never come to fruition.

Believe me. I know. Since Gemma's text message, I had been drumming up thoughts that some young blonde woman, whom I'd never met before, was going to be my stepmom.

20

What Gemma Saw

Gemma's hand shook as she rubbed a small vial of lavender oil onto her wrists, then jabbed a peppermint candy into her mouth. Glassy eyes set off her hazel irises, making them seem almost teal. A steady breeze rustled her strawberry blonde curls, stringing her hair across her brows. Her hand continued to shake as she moved a strand of hair off her forehead. She kept the other hand wrapped tight around her torso covered by a cable knit sweater the color of a clear morning sky. Olive khaki cargo pants and a pair of sequined Skechers finished her look.

"She's like my sister too," Gemma said. Her eyes switched between the deputy and Roy's.

"Are you okay?" the deputy asked.

Gemma turned away. She was still crying and shook her head *no*. But she was also stoned.

"Are you high?"

"No!" she exclaimed. "I'm only sixteen."

The deputy squinted at her and wrote something in his notes.

"Can you tell me what happened?"

"Mr. Pauling's car came careening around Nichols and crashed into the fence after piling over Tess. How could he not *see* her? She was riding her bike. How can you not see a *little girl on a bike*?"

"She didn't see his car?"

Gemma became upset again but got out, "She was watching us." Her words crumbled into sobs.

"Watching you?"

Gemma nodded, keeping her eyes diverted. She placed a thumbnail between her teeth. She shoved the other hand deep into her pants pocket.

"Watching you *what*?"

"Nothing. I mean. We were just hanging out. You know, talking. She was always tagging along. Mrs. Fraser made Mac bring her to town sometimes. Like today."

"On bikes?" The deputy's voice had a twinge of disapproval.

"I know, right?"

"Is that Mac's bike there?" He indicated to a powdery blue bike on its side, the single one of two bikes at the scene not lying deformed and mangled, a backpack slung off the front like an extra rider on the handlebars.

Gemma's eyes shot to the road where they had been standing when Tessa was hit. And after shoving both hands into her armpits, she said, "Yeah. Don't worry. I'll get her bike home for her." Gemma half-pivoted then refocused on two other deputies who were talking to Mac. Gemma removed one of her hands and started to chew on her thumbnail.

"We'll handle it," the deputy said. "Are you nervous about something?"

"You mean other than Tess being crushed by a car?! No, why?"

"Like I said, we'll take care of the bike." He paused, then asked, "Did the car slow down?"

She returned her gaze to Roy's where another deputy was speaking to some woman who looked like a tourist with a dog. Both women, Gemma and the tourist, at the same time spotted each other. But the woman with the dog pulled her eyes away as soon as their eyes connected.

"I'm not in trouble, am I?"

The deputy stopped taking notes and lowered his notepad. "Why would you be in trouble?"

Gemma shrugged. "Not sure. Just asking."

She pivoted again, noticing nothing in particular, The Studio Fitness Center, cars down A Street toward the ferry, up Nichols as it led away to Mosquito Fleet Mercantile.

"You seem nervous. Am I making you nervous?" the deputy asked.

"No. Jeez," she said. She blew out a puff of air.

The deputy lifted the pad once again. "One last question," he asked, "did the car try to slow down?"

Gemma faced the deputy but focused on his notepad, not his face. She answered, "No. It didn't. Now, can I go home? My mom doesn't even know. She needs to know. Mac and I are besties. I *have* to go."

"Sure," the deputy responded, "but stay on the island. Don't leave. I may need to get more information from you."

Gemma nodded then jogged off toward Argyle.

21

Questioning Bill Pauling

"Sir, I need to ask you a few questions."

Bill Pauling's eyes drifted right then left. He lost his balance and stumbled.

"Whoa!" the deputy said. "Let's sit you down." The deputy led Pauling to an umbrella-covered picnic table outside Roy's and helped him into one of the metal chairs. He grunted as he lowered his body. Pauling's stomach hung like a three-gallon water balloon over his belt. His broad chest floated inside a blue denim shirt with Dickie's, the manufacturer's logo, stitched into the left breast pocket. He wore his shirt tucked in, the belt pulled past a comfortable point enough to wrinkle the shirt and pants where the strap was cinched around a pair of denims a shade of brown as close to baby poop as any designer would dare.

Burnt sugar and roasted coffee effused from Roy's. Beads of sweat speckled Pauling's forehead. His pink skin puffed around his eyes and lips. Capillaries blistered the skin of his nostrils, webbing out over his cheeks then sinking deep into his loose jowls.

"Wha— happen?" Pauling slurred his words, which were made more indecipherable by the wet mucosa of his lips. A slurry of blood trickled into his right eye, staining the white sclera with red, overflowing, and finally streaming from his cheekbone. His left cheek had a fresh bruise puffing up in a warped and irregular shape. But none of Pauling's injuries were life-threatening.

"You were in an accident, sir. Got a nasty bruise and a cut," the deputy said. "Can you tell me what happened?" the deputy asked.

"I don't know," he fumbled with his face, with the bruise, then the gash. He inspected his bloody fingers and with bemusement said, "All a sudden my car stopped. Jerked me hard."

"How'd you get that bruise, sir?"

Mr. Pauling simply shrugged. "I had an accident. *You* said." His words sounded childlike, as though he'd messed his diapers instead of mowed down a human child.

"You weren't wearing your seatbelt?"

"Was too!" he objected.

"Have you been drinking, sir?"

"Wha—?" Pauling sat forward, "No. Uh, no. 'Course not." He shook his head once, making the gesture more a violent tic than a refusal.

"So, you won't object to a breath test?" the deputy stated.

Pauling wiped a hand across his face.

The deputy gestured to a female deputy. The female deputy neared and at the same time, she unclipped a black hand-held breathalyzer from her belt. The male deputy continued to ask questions. The female unwrapped a protective plastic from a new mouth tube. She knelt in front of Pauling to explain what was about to happen.

"Sir, I am going to administer a breath test. If you refuse, I will be forced to take you into custody. At that point, you will be placed in a jail cell. You have the right to speak with an attorney. If you agree to this breath test and you are legally impaired, you will be charged with driving under the influence, but unfortunately, we will have to hold you for hitting the little girl. At which point, you will be arraigned in the morning. After that, assuming you can post bail, you can call someone to pick you up and take you home. It's much better if you comply with our breath test, sir. But it's probably best if you spend tonight with us, assuming your test comes back positive. Either way, noncompliance gets you an automatic stay in jail. Understand, sir?" she asked.

Pauling's head bobbed and drifted.

"Do you understand what we're telling you, sir?" The female deputy repeated.

His eyes lingered on his car and Tessa's mangled bike.

"I was in . . . an acciden—" he didn't pronounce the last letter.

"Yes, sir. You were," she confirmed. "Can I administer a breath test, sir?"

Pauling leaned forward and puckered his mouth.

"Give me a sec, sir."

Bill Pauling didn't stir from the pose. He waited for the female deputy to proceed. She inserted the mouthpiece, pressed a button, and said, "Okay. Ready?"

Pauling nodded once, his eyes swimming.

"Take in a normal breath, sir, then blow out."

Within seconds the breathalyzer registered Pauling's intoxication level, an alcohol-to-blood ratio.

She glanced up at the male deputy, holding the breathalyzer up so he could see. She stood and said to Pauling, "Sir, the machine reads zero point one nine. Do you know what that means?"

"Nope." He sounded amused. His eyes fluttered. He slumped, allowing his back to settle into the chair.

"On a scale, zero point one nine means you're legally intoxicated, sir."

The male deputy said, "Sloppy drunk, actually. Look, sir, we need to get you up and into our vehicle."

"Okeydoke," Pauling responded. As he rose, one hand slipped off the arm of the chair and he fell back onto the seat. It began to topple, but the deputies caught the chair before allowing Pauling to fall. He chuckled.

"S'close one!" Pauling said.

With both deputies assisting, on the count of three they lifted him under his arms. As they guided him toward their vehicle, the female deputy said, "Away we go."

"Away we go," Pauling said.

22

The Sheriff's Office the Day After

I stared at the floor. Between the squares of each tile, a gritty checkerboard pattern fossilized within the seams from dirt collected over decades of traffic through the lobby. The tiles themselves were clean but mottled in a fake-stone design of pebbles appearing like gray jelly beans.

Mom and I sat on two of five putty-colored chairs lining the wall kitty-corner to the dispatcher's station and running alongside a set of meeting rooms behind us. Another meeting room directly across from where we sat displayed several interior picture windows with horizontal mini blinds hanging halfway down. The walls were painted eggshell white over block construction.

Through the window, I watched as the lower half of the deputies' bodies breathed, bellies expanding and contracting as they moved. Both men wore black uniforms, thick black leather belts that holstered a can of mace, a baton, and a gun. One man was overweight. The other, a little less. Apparently, fitness was not a stringent requirement for deputy positions in the San Juan County Sheriff's Office.

Occasionally, Mom's hand would move off her lap to her face, where she would wipe the corners of her eyes with a soggy wad of tissue. On and off, she placed her hands over her face, completely hiding it. Her chin would dimple, the palms of her hands wet with tears when she brought them down to wipe on her skirt.

It was around this time that Mom stopped hugging me. Actually, it was minutes before, when she arrived at the scene. She held me at a distance, her hands gripped both my shoulders, her eyes frantic, searching. For what? I'm not sure. Fear, maybe? Guilt? Certainly, for me to explain. But then suddenly, she changed her mind. She didn't care what I knew or what I had to say and released me to stand near the spot where Tessa had been struck down.

By that time, thank God, the deputies had placed absorbent sheets over the blood spill. The sheets reminded me of extra-large blue puppy pads you get at pet supply stores. Their bright plastic lining contrasted against the charcoal pavement. And all I wanted was for

Mom to hold me, to tell me everything was going to be all right. I wanted to feel her heart against my cheek. My baby sister had been crushed under one of Mr. Pauling's tires, and it was my fault. I wanted her to tell me it wasn't my fault. That it was a freak accident. That it was fate. That you can't avoid fate.

But she didn't.

She walked over to *the spot* to look at an imaginary holograph of her baby daughter lying on the ground.

Truthfully, it wasn't like Mom could hurry and have another baby sister. It's not like buying a replacement cord for a laptop. I mean, I wish it was, but wishes are feathers in the wind; wishes aren't meant to last.

Mom pulled her skirt longer, tighter around her legs and tucked the hem under. For what? I don't know. So the hem of her skirt wouldn't accidently drift over into my space, accidentally come in contact with me. She'd stopped answering my questions, acted like she didn't hear me.

Across the hall, the deputies tried to keep their voices low. Still, their words seeped through the glass with a strange reverberating quality, in a bizarre buzz of feedback. Maybe Mom was trying to hear, too, and that's why she wasn't speaking to me.

Their voices pitched higher, then lower, droned, and subsided. Their inflections, their anger crawling through. My breath caught when I thought I heard something—*negligence* and *homicide*? But then they quieted down again, and I couldn't make out with certainty through the glass if one of the deputies was correcting the words. My ears began to acclimate to the weird resonance. No, he was not saying homicide. It was *manslaughter*. Also, *possible reckless endangerment, disregard, elicit substance, a minor in possession*. Words all strung together, one-two-three, like years in a sentencing hearing.

Suddenly, a familiar voice drew our attention to the security room. We saw through a glass door panel two uniformed deputies assisting Mr. Pauling. They stopped in the security room between the outside world and where we sat in the confines of the sheriff's office. In a louder than normal tone, Mr. Pauling stated his defense, slurring how he didn't see her—which I took to mean Tessa—until it was too late.

Mom's breathing became raspy. Her knee began to bounce a double-time rhythm.

The female deputy held her face low to the dispatcher's window, spoke to a dispatcher. Pauling staggered up next to her, bumping her sideways. The male deputy straightened Mr. Pauling, pulling him closer and away from the female deputy. The door clicked and swung open. Rachel Boykin, the female deputy, leaned against the door, holding it open while the male deputy, known around town as Deputy Dave, led Mr. Pauling in. But it was like they all slammed into an invisible wall when they stopped short.

"Dave. Now!" Boykin said. I also know she said *shit* under her breath. Her eyes jumped between us and Deputy Dave. To Dave, her eyes flashed anger. Back to us, they spilled over with pity.

I know pity. I've seen it. The island grapevine snaps like a bullwhip. Teachers at school. Hell, the freaking custodians heard about Dad leaving Mom. I'd walk the halls and the sweeping halted. In the playground, landscapers stopped using their blowers. Like, *ohmygod, how will she ever exist without a father*? Well, you know what? We do just fine, thank you very much. All except here, with these deputies.

Mom began to moan. See a sister getting flown off to a trauma center is a whole different sort of pity. This sort of pity makes the stomach jump. To read the face of the ER doc walking toward the three of us, his head hanging in a way that told us the forthcoming news was bad. Not wanting to make eye contact because he'd just pronounced your sister dead. That's another sort of pity.

The gal, Rachel, raced from behind the dispatcher's station when she saw the perpetrator near our family. With burly arms flexing against a set of sleeve tats, she hustled us out of there and into Interview Room B behind us. She flipped on the lights, gestured for us to sit down at an oval table with a set of six wood chairs surrounding it. She helped Mom into one of the chairs. By the way, these chairs were *far* less comfortable than the ones in the main area.

"Ma'am, would you like some coffee?" Rachel Boykin asked. Her voice was breathy as she glanced to me, asking, "Pop?"

I nodded. "Coke, please." Mom didn't say anything. It was as though some invisible man had his hand across her lips. Rachel's focus flitted between me and

Mom, then she decided to give up, to leave without forcing the issue about the coffee. And it was strange that after all that, she didn't close the door when she left. So, when Deputy Dave walked Pauling down the hall to where I presumed they would place him in Interview Room A, Mom stiffened. You couldn't miss the yeasty booze slither off him and into our room when he passed our door.

Then, the telltale *click* of the latch when the door closed from inside, their mumbling still leaking through the wall. To me, it brought up memories of watching *A Charlie Brown Christmas*, his mother scolding Charlie Brown in a series of *waa, waa, waas*. Deputy Dave kept his tone steady, but in the steadiness was a stern tone you couldn't miss, even through a wall.

Then, everything got busier.

Assistant Prosecuting Attorney Jenny Bartlett walked into the room across the hall where the other two detectives were continuing to discuss the crime scene, possible charges, evidence regarding Mr. Pauling. Certainly, they intended to charge him for running down my sister.

In the mix of *waa, waa, waas* coming from the deputy with Pauling and from across the hall with the two detectives and now the PA, the world seemed to shift.

No. Not shift. Everything rocked.

I heard someone mention my name. Mom did too. With her hands clutching her knees, she pressed her chin up, and sat forward. And as if Mom's body owned magical power over them, their words drifted in clearly to our room.

Charge the sister as an adult and possible negligent endangerment, then, *definitely for the controlled substance of an opiate.*

Opiate? What the eff?

Mom's head jerked in my direction. Her eyes fumed.

Blood rushed from my scalp. My skin went clammy. A million pins prickled every follicle. Every hair spiked. My heart sprinted.

Every cell in my body screamed, *Run! Run! Run!*

But where? I rose to my feet. Mom motioned me down. My hands perspired. No matter how many times I wiped my hands on my pants, they wouldn't remain dry.

One of the deputies exited the room across the hall and came into ours with APA Bartlett.

Bartlett didn't waste time. "Mrs. Fraser," she said, "the PA's Office is set to go on several charges. Two for Pauling—first degree manslaughter and driving a car while under the influence." Then the deputy laid the big, old, stinking egg. "Another charge for negligence against your daughter, MacKenzie. As well as trying to sell a controlled substance."

"Pot's legal!" I cried out. "I wasn't selling . . ."

But Mom cut me off by lifting one hand. Then she rose and stood face-to-face with Jenny Bartlett. There was this long awkward pause, long enough to think she was done talking until her face went red and she clenched her fists. I swear, I thought she was going to clock the woman.

But, barely making a sound, she said, "We want a lawyer." And, with merely the weight of a leaf pressing her, she leaned in and said, "Now."

The APA and deputy left. Mom didn't sit back down. Instead, she walked in front of me and, with her hands behind her back, she grappled for my hands and shifted me into place behind her, hiding me from whatever was about to happen next.

23

The Left Behinds

Certain things triggered fantasy. Like, Mom had kept every detail in Tessa's room the same as the day she died. Suddenly, I'd find myself floating. Then, boom! I ricocheted lengthways under the ceiling, my hands and feet—hell, my whole body—no larger than the size of a dragonfly. But there were no double wings creating motion. I didn't need wings with sheer will instigating each movement. If I summoned my body to the left, to the left I flew.

Like I said, everything in the room had gone untouched. Her bed in a crumple of sheets and pillows. *The White Deer* on the floor where it'd fallen after she got up that morning. The nightstand drawer gaping halfway out, revealing her pink diary. Its brass lock gleaming but the book staying mostly hidden.

April in a neat coil on Tessa's favorite pillow cover, a cover pocked and gray from years of sleep. April's odd marks blending into the cover, from the black spot between her eyes to the copper, white, brown, and cream blotches of her diminutive body. Tiger, a ratty old green and black stuffed turtle, lay in the middle of Tessa's bed with its head cocked to one side and a gash along the seam on its neck.

Next to the pink iPad on her white Bombay dresser, deer and unicorns leaped and bounded across a metal lunchbox. The quote, "Deer are simply unicorns in the making!"

A book with her spelling homework sat beside the lunchbox, a pop quiz she'd used as a bookmark in *I am Amelia Earhart*, a picture book assigned her class for reading, an assignment she'd complained to Mom about because she had been reading well past picture books since the age of five.

Dad had started her on crossword puzzles, easy ones, of course, but still. It was the same age he started us both on word puzzles.

On the other end of the dresser sat a SpongeBob brush with a month of Tessa's hair twined between each inch-long bristle. Her toothbrush matched the hairbrush and stood upright in a translucent plastic tumbler Mom had moved from the bathroom.

I zipped lower to glance at Tessa's treasures on her bookshelf—books like *Bambi, The Banyan Deer, Deer*

Dancer—some erect, some askew, but all in order by author. Several crossword puzzle books lying flat acted as bookends for other books.

Zipping still lower, sets of small shoes lined the closet floor, from Skechers to Nina Riccis for dressy days. Tessa's shirts and pants folded and stuffed into cardboard boxes that acted as extra shelving. Only three dresses hung, one black with a lace collar, one red Christmas dress, and a floral print on a creamy background, each nearly brand new because she hated dresses. She got that from me, both of us happiest in jeans, sweatshirts, and tennies. Also, on the floor of the closet she kept a kiddie makeup kit, a chess set, and three fuchsia golf balls in a net bag next to a kid-size golf club—a six iron. On each one of Tessa's left-behinds, I would alight a few seconds at a time, long enough to draw in the essence of her—her energy, her smell, her quality.

I swirled and swirled, my wingless form knocking against the ceiling until exhaustion set in and I landed right of the bed next to her favorite book. I muscled a big blue ink pen out of the nightstand drawer from next to the diary and touched it to the pink leather before scribbling some sentiments onto the book cover.

24

About Tessa

If animal spirits are a thing, Tessa's animal spirit was the deer, but only as a runner-up to the unicorn. She cried like the baby she was when she learned unicorns didn't exist. Of course, maybe where she went—that place on the other side of our comprehension—unicorns do exist there. And if they do, I bet she's riding one now or feeding it sugar cubes. But she's hanging out with unicorns for sure. Deer too. She'd never abandon one for the other. Tessa was nothing if not equitable. A true fair square.

Tessa devoured anything deer. Deer eyes hypnotized her. Their grace, their being in a spot one moment and the next? Into the woods. I once read a

poem to Tessa where the author described deer as LSD
deer with hallucinogenic disappearing acts. Blink and
poof! They're gone. LSD. Tessa didn't understand LSD
but agreed with the poem's concept.

Four years ago, we nearly lost Tessa. She was three.

We were all at Jakle's Lagoon. She was doing her
thing, taking in the beauty along the wooded path,
checking out salal and blackberry bramble, bending to
touch checkered lily, lagging a step or two behind me
and Mom and Dad. I was fascinated with how the
treetops tightened if you stared straight up at them.
How they appeared to be trying to catch the sky, the
gathering uppermost feathery branches distorting the
view. Sunlight danced within the fissures made when
gentle breezes pushed through the treetops, allowing
shimmering rays between branches, leaves and pine
needles. As many feet as years, one hundred feet above
us, tree trunks all forming a tent over our heads, a tent
that moved along with us as we walked.

The three of us dominoed into each other when Dad
came to a stop.

"Shh," he said, pressing his hand behind his back to
stop us. "A deer."

It nibbled on ivy clinging to the trunk of an old
growth hemlock. His head shot up when Tessa gasped,
lifting a rack of antlers. "He had to be four years old,"
Dad said later that evening. The deer bounded off for
safer cover deep into the woods,

Once lagoon-side, we fell into step again. After picking up from where we left off, our family unit felt out of kilter. Mom noticed first, then Dad, then me.

Tessa was gone.

"Tessa," Mom called out. Her tone bordering on frantic.

"There she is!" I spotted her bowling down a subtle slope chasing after the buck, her long hair flailing behind her after each uneven footfall, bounding over downed logs and mossy rocks. She'd fallen back and ducked into the woods after seeing the deer.

It was seconds until Mom noticed the odd quiet, as she'd retell the story. Tessa always hummed or chittered about something—the nettle, a pile of dog poop, bees. But her chatter had stopped. Once we learned she was no longer behind us—Mom would say—we went into panic mode.

That's when Mom darted into the woods. A few seconds later, Dad took off. I tailed after everyone. We busted through a thicket of salal on the path and scrambled down the uneven landscape after Tessa, who was still after the deer.

Dad and I found Mom and Tessa in a chest-crunching hug, with the deer a few feet away nibbling on a patch of browse leaves of sea breeze greenery. Mom's face was wet. Tessa kept saying, "Deer, Mommy, deer." In her tiny Minnie Mouse voice.

If not the woods, we'd lose Tessa in the grocery store or when she took off on her trike and rode all the way, a good mile, to the bay. Once, she turned down

Old Man Johnson's private road and pedaled all the way down to the beachfront trimming his ranchland. To this day, I can't imagine what people thought upon seeing a toddler riding her tricycle down a county road all alone. Mom nearly busted an aorta about that one.

But that was Tessa. We were always losing her. So, now that she's gone, well, it seems like one of those times when she just decided to pick up and take off. But this time, she left us forever.

25

Two Days Later
Gramma Kiki

Gramma Kiki came to stay with us for *a spell*, to
help with funeral arrangements, also to help *get you
through this* she said. As though we might just as
simply step into a portal that would zip us into a space-
time continuum where our memories get wiped clean—
a place where we'd forget about what had happened to
Tessa or forget about Tessa completely.

It took two days for Gramma Kiki to arrive. She
needed to make her own arrangements. Had a cat, a
bird, and a dog all living with her in Tacoma at a senior
retirement complex that didn't allow people under the
age of fifty-five to stay longer than a week at a time. A

couple of her girlfriends, Laurie and Jan, agreed to alternate days tending to her animals until she returned.

Gramma Kiki was nearing ninety years old. Mom had five older siblings, all tall boys. Mom was, in stature and gender, the *odd girl out*. She'd said so on more than one occasion. The brothers all stood six feet and taller, same as Gramma Kiki, same as Popeye, but he'd long been out of the picture since his death eight years ago from a full-on myocardial infarction. Doctors said *widow maker*, all droopy-lipped and consoling eyes. A widow maker it was. Precisely what happened. But Gramma Kiki rebounded and seemed to be over Popeye's death. At least, that's how things appeared. She spent years grieving his loss. Then . . . snap. She was fine. Compared to the loss around our house feeling as fresh as a slap across the cheek, the cheek still bruised and swollen.

"Jan's taking cat box duty. She doesn't mind cats, but Laurie's allergic," Gramma Kiki said.

She released Mom's frail form, gripping her shoulders, speaking directly to her as though trying to locate some hidden treasure.

At this point, she hadn't yet looked at me, which was highly unusual. I always felt like I was her favorite. And the slight felt intentional, her eyes avoiding me, landing anywhere near me and uncomfortably fixated on Mom. I mean, it was like she knew I was standing right there but couldn't be bothered.

"Oh, that's good," Mom said—about Gramma Kiki's pets.

The words came out as inaudible as a whisper. It was Mom who wriggled free from Gramma. She stepped back from the door, guiding Gramma Kiki in, with Mom whirling inward, a samba, the lead and follow.

"Mac, hug your grandmother."

Finally, contact. A one-armed pull and release. Outside, the afternoon held a tang of Hawthorne berries in the mist. The weather as cold as Gramma's hug.

"The marine layer slowed down the ferry," Gramma Kiki said.

The explanation: the damn weather delaying arrival.

The sky, a perfect ashtray smudge, replicated the mood inside the house. Outside, everything was the same. No mourner traversed the streets beating their chest. Each cookie-cutter house was built on a cookie-cutter street in our cookie-cutter town. A bell tolled a somber note near the marina. Before I closed the door, I snatched Gramma Kiki's overnight carry-on. By then, I had metamorphosed into the family bellhop. And, by the way, what the hell had she packed? Gold doubloons? The thing weighed a ton. Gramma called back without turning, saying she'd packed all her pills and was sorry about the weight. Question: how many freaking pills keeping one person alive weighed that much? I grabbed the bag's leather strap, tugged it near the kitchen entryway, and left it mashed up against the wall.

Mom and Gramma walked off, heading for the living room. It was strange, Mom had this habit of

placing one hand against the small of Gramma Kiki's
back because, well, I don't know why. To protect her
old bones from a fall if she toppled? But now, Mom
plodded ahead of her. Guess today she wasn't much
concerned about Gramma taking a spill.

They veered left into the living room, Mom's body
a crumpled question mark. Her navy blue sweats hung
loose off hips accentuating her puny form. An old rag
of a T-shirt, one of Dad's leftovers, added to the effect.
Her size and poise contrasted with Gramma Kiki's erect
posture, her gliding gait.

Gramma commiserated, repeating phrases like,
"There, there," and "I know, honey," and "Shh, shh,"
and "It's going to be okay." Funereal tones.

Sidling close against the wall, my stocking feet
pattering, I slid down to the floor where I listened, fully
expecting Mom to out me, to blame me for the accident.

"We need to get food in you," Gramma Kiki said.

Mom objected. Couldn't stomach food.

The mere suggestion gushed saliva into my mouth. I
hadn't eaten all day and it was closing in on dinnertime.
I don't remember trekking back to the kitchen, but
somehow, I was standing at the cupboard pulling out
three cans of soup. Life took on a choppy weirdness
because, flash! Next, there I was at a drawer, can
opener in hand. Flash again. At the microwave.
Buzzing nuclear heat through the broth. Flash, pulling
down bowls, setting in spoons. Breaths carried me in
stops and starts, never walking to these spots, instead

carried along not by my own will but by sheer breath impulse, swapping places, unattached to the ground.

Flash. Fanning out soda crackers onto plates.

Flash. I jerked and thudded back to Earth when I heard his voice, dropped the spoon into the bowl, splashing soup onto the cutting board, one I'd gotten out as a tray for Mom.

"Kiki's here?" he said. Dad was leaning against the refrigerator. "Sorry," he said, about the mess. Then, again, "Kiki's here?"

"Just," I said. "What are *you* doing here?"

"I came to," he waved his arms around as if swatting at flies, "you know, help, I suppose. I don't know."

"Well, *Dad*," I put a *buttload* of emphasis on the word *Dad*, "we don't *need* your help." I grabbed Mom's cutting board, pushed past him, bumping his left elbow, and left him in the kitchen by himself.

26

Three Days After
Paper Wings

The flashes, the strange transporting, continued with more fervor.

I had snagged a box of tissues and snuck off into Tessa's room to lie on her bed, breaking Mom's rule to not go into her room. It started this way: I began journaling. Trying to find the perfect words to express my everchanging mental state. I was sad. I was angry. I was laughing, then felt guilty about laughing. My emotions were running rampant, so I thought I should chart the changes. At first, I scribbled on the cover of Tessa's book. The first word reed thin, meaningless. Not descriptive enough to express the loss. Words came out rough. I needed the perfect phrase to immortalize something that was slowly turning into a lost memory.

Scratching out that word, I wrote another, then another. Finally, I landed on one that described my madness, one that expressed the flashes true to their nature, their true obsessiveness. I opted for *delirium*. Delirium encapsulated the fervor my moods had taken on during these flash points. Like wormholes slipping through antimatter of our home. Mom's mood seemed to ignite my delirium. I could see in her face she felt the delirium, too, like an augur drilling bone-deep, gnawing into marrow, boring into our souls.

The day after . . . you know . . . after Tessa died. During dizzying bouts of disbelief, of horror and sadness, came the numbness. The mind finds ways to cauterize the tsunami of emotions quite on its own. Without permission. The mind's way of blocking further onslaught of sadness and sense of hopelessness.

And yet, for now, I floated in some weird wormhole stratosphere within our home, trying to find sanity in a place that had lost all meaning. How can you find meaning when you're living in a looping rewind, seeing the same scene over and over of . . . you know . . .

I prayed and prayed. To wake up. To go back. To become Superman. To spin the planet in the opposite direction, to alter time, the past, if only by the beat of a hummingbird's wing. Not enough to change anything else, just enough that Tessa wouldn't have died.

My motto: Don't cry. You don't cry about something when you caused that thing to happen, when it's your fault. You bite your cheek until it bleeds. You feel you're going to cry? Shut up and lay into your cheek.

"Are you *daydreaming*?" Mom said. Accusation filling each word, almost as though she could see a thought bubble above my head; yet when I looked at her, her eyes never connected with mine. If they had, maybe she would see my pain, wouldn't hate me anymore. I remember thinking how happy it made me that she had said anything to me at all.

The silent treatment was the norm. She'd gone deaf and mute. With me, anyway. A venomous tone with Dad when they spoke.

"If you care at all," she'd said into her cell. She was sitting in her bedroom across the hall from mine. I could hear her through my door. She went silent for a moment, then said, "I'm sorry. That wasn't fair." She had called him about Tessa's service. About him helping with the cost. About decisions to bury or cremate. Deciding cremation. Less expensive and better for the earth, but I knew the expense outweighed any environmental consideration. Anyone listening on could've figured that out.

Mom's first call to Dad, the day of . . . you know . . . ended abruptly after Mom told him they'd flown Tessa to the hospital and that she was on life support. Adding, they were hoping for a new set of lungs, a good liver, and a heart—the lifesaving fresh organ trio. Then, thank God her head hadn't been crushed. The phrase had caught in her throat. Like, if the brain had been crushed, well, there'd be absolutely no chance in freaking hell that she survived but, oh, three out of four isn't so bad. What the—?

But the ER doc had given us a thimbleful of hope, told us the paramedics report stated Tessa's eyes were fluttering before they moved her from the scene. At first. But after? All bets were off.

After getting priority status for the ferry, the ride across the sound, plus the ensuing drive to Seattle had been brutal. The roomy interior of Dad's truck still felt like we were crammed to the brim with twenty-six-foot-tall clowns complete with softball-sized red rubber noses, oversized plastic shoes, and enormous bouquets of balloons. Yet, just the three of us were inside. And the balloons, shoes, and rubber noses? Nowhere to be found.

Tension can be a prickly thing. The reality? We were back to where we were before Tessa was born. Just the three of us. They had been happy days once.

Now, cruising along in the double-cab purgatory, every molecule of antimatter was drenched in palpable misery.

That was two days ago. After banning me to my room—where my sentence was listening through the walls to hours of Mom crying, talking to herself, wailing into her pillow, and walking the halls—the flash points took on form.

And so it went.

First, Mom was in the bathroom. The crane of the faucet as it opened, water splashing onto porcelain.

Then she walked down the hall, her feet padding on the carpet past my door and toward the kitchen. The metal leg of a chair scraping the floor. Then nothing for ten minutes until the moaning started fresh with mournful anguish, followed by the choking from lack of air, and bursting forth into the howling—a blind dog lost in the desert soon to die of thirst. Next, her socked feet padding the other way in front of my bedroom. Tessa's door opening. And Mom whimpering her name, saying, "No, no, no." Sputtering in BB gun repetition. Mom crumpling to the floor.

And me? Days—I suffered flash points. Nights— numbed into bouts of troubled slumber.

I believe the brain takes a vacation during trouble.

Next, I'd get a stiff case of drowsiness. Couldn't keep my eyes open. However, when I could manage to wrench myself awake, what came slamming forefront was Tessa. First, on her bike. Next, on the ground. Then how the fabric of our lives got snagged into death's ever-churning meat grinder, turning us into pulp, and spitting us out like ground meat onto the dirt.

Later, I'd hear Mom thumping within Tessa's mausoleum, the place we once knew as home.

It was somewhere in these forty-eight hours after *you know* when life transformed, when dreams crystallized, that I found myself on the rooftop with duct-taped canvas wrapped around a set of stiff wire hangers, the canvas spanning the area between the wire, creating two opposing and giant wings.

There I stood, the contraption strapped to my arms, around my waist, secured under my armpits by way of old leather belts—belts Dad decided to leave behind after leaving *us* behind. The wings connected low against my spine which allowed a certain flex to open and close when I flapped. In theory, anyway.

Staring from two floors below me, Walt, Mom's dog, barked. And barked. So much it surprised me that Mom didn't come out to check on him. But she didn't.

My toes threaded the edge of the roof, dangling precariously over the gutter as it creaked under my weight. When one of the gutters slumped, water sloshed out onto Walt's head. He shook and shimmied all the way to the tip of his tail. After, he stared up again, keeping his eyes pinned on me and, yes, still barking. Mom never showed. Even through all of Walt's racket.

My flight plan: I'd need to clear the cobblestones of our walkway. Need to avoid the terracotta angel and cat statuary, both staring blankly to the front yard, just sitting there perched on one of three stone plank steps. 'Course, I'd need to miss Walt. I didn't want to kill him if I crashed. April, my calico kitty, was inside, so I didn't have to worry about her. Still, I didn't want to be responsible for Walt's death too. Give Mom more ammo to hate me.

I figured if I *did* plummet onto the stone cobbles, the terracotta angel, cat statuary, or stone steps, maybe I'd die too. If I *did*, I wouldn't have to endure life without Tessa or life with a mother who wished I'd died instead of Tessa. Both options worked. If the wings worked, well then, I'd get a little more time on this big, round ball of clay. And, if the *other*, maybe I'd get to see my little sister again zipping around her deer moon. After all, if I took a header then no more sorrow, no more pain. Win-win.

Unexpectedly, a gust kicked up. The current used an invisible pair of hands and shoved me squarely between my shoulder blades.

Honestly? I didn't want to know what was going to happen next and closed my eyes.

For a second, Mom's face flashed behind my eyelids. A vision of her finding her eldest child in a broken crumple, shattered on the cobbles, Walt crazy yapping as she rushed to me.

Her face made me pause. Second thoughts invaded. My heart jump-started into gear, beating rapid-fire, playing bongos. A queasy sense of vertigo washed over me, and I tried to catch my balance. But, with that dagnabbit wind nudging me, there was no hesitating.

Of course, I lost my balance.

And tripped.

Tumbled forward.

And then . . .

. . . the most amazing thing happened . . .

The wings held. The duct-taped canvas proved up to the task. I arched my back, angling the wings higher. I tipped my chin up to avoid head-on impact, avoiding a Humpty Dumpty. With all the muscle power I could muster, I yanked both arms down in one big flap. My body shifted upward. I flapped again, pumping harder this time, wrenching me higher away from Earth with each pull of the wings. My legs strained, toes pointed behind flattened into a prone position, sending me sailing in a direction across our front yard toward a tightly-packed bank of trees trimming the circular drive. If the cobblestone could crush my head, the trees could tear off my wings, sending me smashing to the ground.

Again, I wrenched, my head craning to the right and a near miss seconds before my tryst with the trees. With my head to the right, I was flying in a circle but not simply flying, I was soaring just not far off the ground. Walt was going apeshit-mad chasing me, trying to snatch a toe through my socks. I flapped my arms twice and climbed higher. Repeating, I rose into the ether, floating high above Walt.

"Ha! You little shit," I said, "you can't catch me now!"

Higher still, my body soared, getting farther from the cobbles, scaling the trees, and far, far away from home.

PART TWO
the middle

"You aren't falling apart. You're well beyond that. You're just rattling along now. Elven dolls doing what little you can to gather the pieces as they fall away." —Darrell Drake, *where Madness Roosts*

27
Drawing the Short Straw

Gemma's parents wouldn't allow her to testify. Their lawyer advised against allowing the cops or prosecutors to speak to Gemma. And since we were both minors, her parents could refuse. That's what my lawyer told us. It blew me away.

She'd cut me loose. Left me hanging. Left me holding *her* bag.

Great friend, Gemma. You're a real peach.

After the sentencing, everything moved relatively quickly. The PA was going balls-out on Pauling for driving under the influence and going after me for possession of drugs overall, specifically for an MIP—minor in possession—but mostly for the controlled substance of an opiate. State laws stated that for an MIP with more than one point five ounces of pot, especially opium-laced pot, prosecutors could warrant a felony charge and a max sentence up to five years, not to mention a hefty fine of up to ten thousand dollars. Mom and Dad both flinched at that. No worries about me being sent away for five years . . . good riddance to you, young lady.

But the lawyer, Mark Markel, Esquire, explained that an MIP marijuana felony charge was unlikely to be prosecuted since the marijuana statutes had slipped down to *who gives a shit* levels and equal to an MIP alcohol possession. An MIP alcohol charge brought a tap on the nose, a small monetary fine, and zero jail time.

Markel further explained that because there were witnesses willing to testify in court about me selling pot to Gemma ,and not the other way around, I might be charged and sent to juvenile detention. Here's why. Because the sale of drugs by an MIP was a more serious offense for two reasons. First, I was a minor. Second, I wasn't a licensed seller of pot. A seller could very well get five years and a monetary fine from a sale to a minor.

Now, triple the effect the freaking pot had been soaked in an opiate solution. A glaring explanation of the woozy sensation after only a tiny hit. How many details had I blinked out after seeing Tessa run down?

"I doubt they will pursue it, however," Markel told us.

"That's good," Dad chimed in.

"I didn't sell Gemma anything," I told them all.

Mom ignored me and asked Markel, "So, what happens next?"

"They will arraign her, and she will offer a plea." He pointed the next question to me. "What will you plea?"

"You mean, guilty or not guilty?" I questioned.

The lawyer nodded at me. His eyes uninterested and condemning. "Yes."

"I'm not guilty. I told you, I didn't sell Gemma that pot." A telltale tingle burned behind my eye sockets. I wrestled back a throng of surging emotions. "*She* gave it to *me*."

Markel examined his notes and glanced to Mom.

"Where'd you get the money, Mac?" Mom said.

"I saved it from allowances."

Markel checked between Mom and Dad.

Mom nodded. "She gets a weekly allowance."

But then Mom did something I wasn't expecting.

She said, "Although, I thought you'd spent most of it on school stuff, shoes, your backpack." She glared when she said, *backpack*, because she went on, "you know, the one the cops confiscated one point eight three ounces of opiate-laced marijuana!"

"Gemma's!"

"Why did you have it? Why were you giving it to her?" She raised her voice, leaning forward, stiff and accusing in her chair. Dad had slumped and was doing absolutely nothing. His elbow lay lifeless on the arm of the chair, the other hand covering his mouth. Watching.

"I had been holding it, thinking about buying it from her. That's all. I wasn't selling it."

"There are witnesses, young lady, who state otherwise! Who will testify against you!" Mom was yelling at me now, full red-faced yelling.

Markel intervened, sensing Mom was spinning out into a different stratosphere. "We can fight this, but the witness testimony looks bad, MacKenzie."

Mom breathed out and slunk back, coming down off her rabid high. "Jesus Christ," she said, not to Markel, not to anyone, to herself like a tire going flat. More like it was happening to her, and she didn't give one effing eff about me.

After settling down, she said, "So, do you think she's going to jail? I mean, what do you think? What is the possibility?"

"It's an election year. Taggert is running on octane." He shook his head. "The PA's hitting this topic with gusto. You know, like the White House. Nothing's worse than opioids, except possibly illegal immigration. Everyone's up in arms. And since he's the incumbent with a new guy, an attorney from Chicago who has a nice little following, Taggert feels threatened about losing his comfy job." There was a momentary stunned effect after Markel's short lesson about local poly sci.

Finally, Dad spoke, shattering the dead air. He sat forward. "The odds, Mr. Markel." Dad wasn't one for a litany about politics. He wanted facts.

Markel shoved his readers off the bridge of his nose and reread the bill of indictment. "Per RCW 10.31.100; Arrest without warrant. A police officer having probable cause to believe that a person has committed or is committing a felony shall have the authority to arrest the person without a warrant." He paused and said, "That's what the deputy-in-charge did when he brought Mac in. Again, a police officer may arrest a person without a warrant for committing a misdemeanor or *gross* misdemeanor only when the offense is committed in the presence of an officer, except as provided in subsections (1) through (11) of this section." He glanced up at Dad, and continued, "(1) Any police officer having probable cause to believe that a person has committed or is committing a misdemeanor or gross misdemeanor, involving physical harm or threats of harm to any person or property or the unlawful taking of property or involving the use or possession of cannabis, or involving the acquisition, possession, or consumption of alcohol by a person under the age of twenty-one years under RCW 66.44.270, which states, Furnishing liquor to minors—Possession, use—Penalties—Exhibition of effects—Exceptions. (1) It is unlawful for any person to sell, give, or otherwise supply liquor to any person under the age of twenty-one years or permit any person under that age to consume liquor on his or her premises or on any premises under his or her control. For the purposes of this subsection, "premises" includes real property, houses, buildings, and other structures, and motor vehicles and watercraft. A violation of this subsection is a gross misdemeanor punishable as provided for in chapter 9A.20 RCW; shall have the authority to arrest the person." Markel lifted the readers and set them onto a thinning patch of grizzled hair.

"The odds, Mr. Markel," Dad repeated.

"Not *un*likely."

My arms weakened, and my back went hot.

"Good God," Mom said.

"If two people hadn't witnessed MacKenzie here handing the marijuana to the other girl which they then found in the girl's bike bag, well, then . . ."

Mom interjected, "Gemma Painter."

"Yes, Miss Painter's bag, then I'd say unlikely. In fact, highly unlikely. But they're charging on a MIP selling to another minor. And, sadly," he said, and paused on the weightiness of his next words. "Sadly," he said, "that's a felony charge."

28

The Sentence

And that was that.

The judge ordered me to juvenile detention for up to eighteen months. An assistant PA chimed in, saying something about overcrowding at the usual *youth center*, she called it, like it was the Y, or something, and stated they had to *place* me at the Clear Lake County Juvenile Detention. On Google Maps, the detention center listing next to reviews, which, interestingly had zero reviews, shows the facility as *prison*. The title they were using, juvenile rehabilitation is a sugar coating, a nicer term for where they were sending me.

The judge agreed to the change of incarceration. And that was that. At the sound of the gavel striking the wooden block, it was done. The ˶˙˙˙˙ ˶ ˶˙˙ ˙˙˙˙˙k, and they were flogging me with a Cat O' Nine Tails, dragging me down a road, cross on my back to my crucifixion.

They slapped Mom and Dad with a fine of one thousand dollars. Upon hearing the amount of the fine, Mom turned to Dad and said, "I don't have that." Dad ponied it up. He was already pulling out his wallet from a back pocket.

The bailiff and another officer snapped cuffs onto my wrists.

"Mom," I said. She was too busy worrying about the money to notice. Dad made eye contact with me, and mouthed, "Don't worry," like everything was going to be okay. Like he'd make the boo-boo go away. But he wasn't the one wearing handcuffs and being hauled off by officers of the court.

"Mom?" I said again. But she turned and walked off, her hand rising to her face.

The last thing I saw of Mom was her back when she slipped past Dad and booked it out of the courtroom.

29

Do not Leave Town

Before carting me off to juvie, they allowed us the weekend to get things in order. Or, as the judge said, "Your ducks in a row." At the suggestion, my skin crawled, itched as though a million spiders were scrambling under my pant legs, in my sleeves. At once, my skin prickled with tiny nodules pressing out of each follicle. They grew from, what I've heard described as goose flesh, into larger pox-like bumps.

Everyone was busy. The bailiff cuffed and restrained me. Dad signed documents and agreed to bail, if only for a weekend. Great Dad. No bartering for more time? Come on.

The judge's decision for a weekend stay of sentence came late Friday afternoon. No one was available to drive me off-island to the facility, and the judge thought it was easier for everyone involved for me to stay at home. They planned my transportation for Monday morning. The clerk made two phone calls, one to someone who refused to incarcerate a minor at the county jail, the other who refused to make the trip so late in the day because juvie wouldn't admit that late on a Friday night since by the time we arrived, admissions would be closed.

Everyone was diligently working to put me away. It was no wonder they couldn't hear my screams, the horror in my voice, eruptions of blistering hives forming on my skin. They refused to set their eyes upon me, the disappointment—first, because of allowing my sister to be killed, and second, because I was found guilty for selling drugs which, by the way, was a bullshit charge if there has ever been one.

When the hives began to pop, the pain was unbearable and also freaking itched like crazy. I scraped and clawed at my skin until it bled. And when I believed things couldn't possibly get worse, things did. Tiny plumes of yellow fuzz began to emerge from each pustule. As I watched on to my own revulsion, the disease continued to evolve. The tiny yellow plumes grew, exuding, getting longer, wider until I realized, each fuzzy plume was turning into downy feathers.

"Bwack!" I squawked.

Nothing. No one glanced over.

"Bwack!" Again, I squawked and unintentionally caught sight of my reflection and the thing I was morphing into. The interior window mocking me, my mouth enlarged, my lips protracted into a long flat, dark orange beak. My eyes no longer facing front; instead, sitting on each side of my head. My hair, no longer a tousle of mousy brown strands but the smooth head of a waterfowl. WTEffingF?!

I'd become a freaking *duck*.

"Bwack!" I squawked again. I waddled, flapping my wings furiously and reached Mom, who was standing in the foyer of the courthouse waiting for Dad, I assumed. I walked up behind her, swatted her on the back with my right wing, but she refused to turn around. I waddled and fluttered back to Dad, swerving and catching air between other people in the hall. When I caught up to Dad, I swatted him, but he was too concerned about where Mom had gone to notice a duck slapping him on the back, too concerned about the money he'd emptied from his checking account. Mom came hurtling back to him. Angry-eyed, red-faced, she wanted to know exactly why she should spend any of her own money since, for one, they weren't officially divorced, and two, she wasn't getting a dime of child maintenance from him. That he could front the whole fucking thing, she said.

"Not here," he demanded.

I couldn't help but chime in. "Bwack!"

Mom nudged me from behind and into another room, a little too hard and a little too fast, because I

stumbled over a wide set of orange webbed feet and fell
face forward onto the tips of my wings. I staggered
back up, complaining.

"Bwack, bwack, bwack," I squawked, irritated by
the assault.

Nothing.

She kept nudging me, thrusting me into another
room where they placed my feathery ass on a chair and
fitted my right orange ankle with a bracelet (they called
it), a home-*monitoring* bracelet.

I jumped down and Mom shoved me in the back
again. This time, I didn't fall. Her hand felt like the
nozzle end of a rifle against my back, pushing me out of
the room, past Dad, out the door. I flapped and flapped
but couldn't catch a current, the effing bracelet
weighing me down.

"It's your fault," Mom said.

Dad squinted. "How is this *my* fault?"

"You know full well. And if I have to explain it,
then you're even less intelligent than I thought."

Bwack, bwack, bwack. Warm water washed in
under our feet, flooding the parking lot.

"Not here, Uma. Try not to make *another* scene."

We all piled into Mom's car, water seeping in onto
the floorboards, heating up, getting steamy, with Mom
starting the gas and Dad stirring the pot. It wasn't the
first time. I knew the signs.

My feathery butt lifted off the seat, and there I was,
floating in the backseat all alone.

Bwack.

"You son of a bitch." Mom retorted about Dad's *scene* comment.

"That's right. Let's start the name-calling now. Talk about lack of intelligence."

Touché.

Bwack! Bwack! BWACK!

"Stop!" I yelled. My voice suddenly returned, raspy.

Dad turned. Mom eyed me from the rear-view mirror.

"Stop," I said, a bit quieter. "Please. Stop." It was all I could get out before the water began to drain out of the car. Before my butt feathers touched down against the upholstered cushion. Before Mom and Dad shut up. Before . . .

. . . bwack. . . bwack . . . bwack.

And it's funny. I never knew ducks could cry.

30

A Day Trip to Hell

The Clear Lake County Juvenile Detention Building is a seventeen-bed facility for girls that has round-the-clock staff seven days a week with a floorplan similar to a hotel, but the lovely lockdown atmosphere and décor accompanied by a smell I can only describe as something between bleach and cookies.

With all corrections officers and COs being female, we were assured the utmost safety by the San Juan County Juvenile Court Services Administrator—a twenty-something pregnant gal whose name has been indelibly carved into the hippocampus of my brain but whose name I shall never utter because of the lie she told me . . . and at my most vulnerable, no less.

Mom hadn't had the balls to drop me at the sheriff's office for transport to juvie. Instead, Dad drove me. I brought one suitcase of clothing, not knowing they would apprehend it from me as soon they ushered Dad out, so they could *process* me like I was sliced cheese or something. After inspecting my belongings, they confiscated certain items: shoelaces from my shoes, my hairbrush, toothbrush, my 9 mil Glock, my Uzi, and, oh yes, my flamethrower.

Come on. My *toothbrush*?

They also took my jeans and any shirts with buttons. Instead, they gave me puke-green pull up pants and a smock to match. The new outfit reminded me of something you'd see veterinarian assistants wearing, complete with a flattering V-neck.

I was one of two other female detainees being transported. Corrections Officer Andy Corbett, whom they referred to as CO Andy, brought me over from the San Juan County Jail. The county jail is the size of a large walk-in closet with a cot and a tray table that sticks out from the wall, no legs. I guess to prevent someone from breaking them off or either killing themselves, or killing a guard, or maybe both. Anyway, if I were to describe the SJ County Jail's interior design, I'd say stark.

We left early, on the morning red eye ferry. At that hour, the boat is usually pretty empty. That Monday was no different. They transported me in a windowless van, an oversized gray vehicle with the sheriff's logo emblazoned on each side as well as on a metal tambour door which slid up like a garage door in the back of the van.

Once inside, CO Andy used carabiners to clip my hands to a metal bar. He then cuffed my ankles together and clipped my ankle cuffs to a silver floor hook. The bench was a snuggly (grr . . .) metal box but, fortunately, had an inch-thick cushion.

I watched life coming at me through the small window within the dividing wall separating the cab from the back of the van. Shackles held me securely by the hands and feet. What if I needed to scratch my nose? Good luck, bucko.

After docking at the Anacortes Ferry, we made one stop along the way to pick up a detainee—that's how they referred to us. They were holding her at the Anacortes Jail, which normally takes its detainees to Clear Lake County where they were dropping me off. For some reason, they were taking her all the way to Yakima where they kept adult offenders. CO Andy positioned the new girl on the opposite bench and hitched her up the same way he'd done with me.

The van rocked and bumped along the road. She cried the entire time. She sobbed out that she'd been once been a *resident* in Clear Lake.

A few days after Clear Lake processed me, I realized why she'd been crying. That, and she was eighteen, the *age of majority* they called it. She was going to prison. Medium security, but still. She'd hit the big league.

Prison isn't like spending time in camp or at a friend's house. I'd done my homework on the difference between juvie and prison. Plus, Mom and Dad had asked Markel. Prison is a cell with nothing to do except go to the cafeteria in shackles (when they *let* you), go to the gym (when they *let* you), or go to the showers (when they *let* you)—types of transport all considered risky business.

In juvie, Markel had said they sometimes put you in with a *roommate* is how he phrased it. "Your cellmate," he said. He tried to smile. And, from behind a set of coffee-stained teeth, I sensed an edginess, a terror left unspoken.

At dinner my first night inside, CO Madge cracked my fingers when I went for my spork before the command. Everything is timed. You get orders: *One hand behind your back! Sporks up!* Orders so no one can slip their spork into their uniform and spork someone to death.

You see that sort of thing in the movies, but there I was, nursing a set of bruised, swelling knuckles. She didn't break any bones. My pride hurt when other girls snickered. They started calling me Bruiser until all signs of the affront faded.

Of course, my day trip to hell started earlier. After checking in, I ran back to my Dad who was allowed entry up to a point. We clung to each other in a death grip.

He tried not to crumble, but his chin gave him away, quivering out each word. "I wish I could save you from this, Macky. I love you so much."

"I didn't mean to, Dad. I'm sorry." There was no controlling my emotions. I felt raw from the moment Tessa died, through all court proceedings, all the way to my ride into hell.

Two male guards manning exterior areas of the center—one Caucasian, one Samoan—peeled my hands off my father. When I opened my eyes, another stood with hands fisted, arms crossed, baton up, feet planted wide, blocking Dad who was craning to see past him.

"Mac!" Dad called my name.

And that was the last time I saw my father until two weeks later.

Two weeks. Two weeks is a lifetime in hell. Two weeks was what a select few of the *residents* needed to break me down. However, if Dad had come a week later, I'm not sure it would've seemed any different.

It wasn't long after going inside until the beatings began.

I'd heard, like most people, that juvie was awful. However, without a direct accounting, I had no baseline. Awful was this broad concept that morphed and moved like an amoeba. The eighteen-year-old headed for adult prison had been useless. She didn't make juvie sound like a skip through the park. For sure. But with no detail, then the amoeba of knowledge expanded and contracted. The blubbering fool could

barely speak, let alone warn me what to expect once I
got admitted.

31

Everything is Fine – It Like a Big Gym That You Might Find at Summer Camp . . . *Not*!

The Samoan dude grabbed my arm and twisted me toward the entrance. He wasn't rough, but he wasn't exactly sweet about it out either.

When you enter the building, you first enter through an armored kiosk where a high chain-link fence spans off in each direction. After you're let through the security gate at the kiosk, a short grouping of concrete pads lead to a set of double security doors. There's lots of security at this place. ID tags, last names used, orange jumpsuits, empowered guards, juvenile detention professionals, oppressive control, psychologists, and, of course, inmates. But at first, you don't notice. At first, it seems like a big gym you'd find at summer camp.

Spin back for a sec. At the kiosk, a male guard scanned the ID label stuck on my incarceration orders that they issued upon releasing me from San Juan County Jail. The guard was a bored, scar-faced, Italian-looking guy who reminded me of someone just off the set of a *Sopranos* shoot. He was a big dude who'd apparently lived a happy life eating garlic toast and spaghetti. He didn't speak except to say, "After the buzz."

When it sounded, CO Andy grabbed the short space between my wrist zip ties, led me in front of him, pushed me through the gate by the shoulders, closed the gate, grabbed the zip ties again, and pulled me by the ties to the front entrance of the facility.

Once there, CO Andy called back, "In." And the big Italian dude buzzed the entrance doors. CO Andy hefted open one side of the wired glass double doors and led me, this time into the actual facility. Again, lugging me by the zip ties. He nudged me by the shoulders farther inside, this time into a small antechamber where he closed the door. A distinct *click* sounded behind him.

"Fraser, MacKenzie," CO Andy said, bending down to speak into a round silver plate with a series of slots for sound to pass. The plate rested within wired safety glass in front of an intake clerk, a young woman in her twenties named Chrissy according to the name tag on her polo style, white oxford uniform shirt. The facility's

logo was embroidered above her left breast. Her hair
was pulled back tight, and she typed fast on a keyboard
that sat to the right of the window, keeping her eyes
plastered on the monitor as she spoke.

"Number check," she said.

"SJCSO18-2314," he answered.

"A lot for that little place," she said, meaning the
size of our island and the number of people
incarcerated—2,314 in 2018.

"Tell me about it," CO Andy replied. His body
shifted and he gave a small chuckle. The chuckle
wasn't one that would make you think he found what
she said funny—2,314 perpetrators in 2018—instead,
you got the sense that CO Andy found the fact
disgusting.

"Papers," she requested.

CO Andy slipped the papers into a concave pass-
thru in the counter below the glass.

The clerk snatched them up, rolled her chair to a
copy machine, removed the staple from the corner of
the form, slipped the sheets into the copier feed, and
pressed Start. Sheets exuded into a lower tray where she
collected them, stapled the copies, and retrieved the
originals, which she restapled. She wheeled back to the
window and slid the form back to CO Andy.

He turned to me. "This is it. I don't go in with you."
He must have noticed the fear in my eyes because all of
a sudden he became interested in his feet. He shifted his
weight to a more open, steadier stance. He couldn't
seem to find a spot for his eyes to land until he found

the clerk. When he tipped his head to her, she buzzed the entrance door.

"Best of luck," CO Andy said. He spun around and left the building. I watched him as the Italian guard at the kiosk buzzed the gate. I watched him all the way until he got into his van and drove off.

Another buzz sounded, shaking my concentration, and a female voice said, "Fraser?" She'd come in from somewhere inside the facility. I spun around to see a tomato of a woman standing inside this final door. The pale skin of her cheeks stretched tight and thick, contrasting white with yellow strands of blonde-gray hair tied up in a frizzy bun that stuck out like a sprinkler spewing water from under a uniform cap. Through the cap's strap, part of the bun jutted like a herniated colon. Her navy jacket stretched against its buttons. Her thighs appeared as though someone had slipped water balloons inside each pant leg. She was stocky, carried a black gun in a shoulder holster, a baton, and a can of pepper spray through leather loops of her black belt. Her shoes, standard-issue, patent leather black tie-ups, donned a practical heel. Her badge read: CO-23 M. Cuthbert. But everyone called her CO Madge. We called every correction officer CO *Whatever Your Name Is*. That was the rule.

"Sorry," Cuthbert said, "didn't mean to startle you." A slight accent made me think New York City, though I'd never been, only watched shows set in New York. "This way," she said, "I'll give you the grand tour." She grabbed my zip ties in the same manner CO Andy had done and led me to the interior of the facility. Once more, the door shut with the same click, letting me know there was no way out unless the clerk, for some reason, were to buzz me out. That wasn't about to happen.

My chin prickled and shook. A lump wedged deep in my throat. My mouth went dry.

"Now, now," she said. "You're not going to go wimpy on me, are you?" Without releasing my cuffs, she led me to a chair near the door and patted me on the back. "Sit here for a minute. Don't move."

She opened the door to Chrissy's room.

"Chrissy," she said, "get me Fraser's orders and gear."

The printer buzzed to life and swooshed off three copies.

"Thanks," CO Madge said. She exited Chrissy's room with my papers and pulled the door closed, balancing an armload of what I figured was my gear, my new belongings—clothing, shoes, and a hairnet— that sort of stuff. I didn't understand the significance of the hairnet until later. Another click, and CO Madge pulled shut Chrissy's door. Don't dare put Chrissy at risk.

CO Madge shoved my stuff at me, which I took from her, and off we went on our exploration of the facility. "Okay," CO Madge said, "you're not in long. No need to get your knickers in a twist, sweetie. You'll be in and out before you can say supercalifragilisticexpialidocious," she chuckled. "It's a long word, right?" Then, she added, "Let's go. I'll show you where you're living for the next eighteen months." She laughed and scratched her upper lip. "You're gonna make friends fast, by the look of ya," she said. "Just you see."

32

The Facility

The facility, as people called this new hell, had all
the amenities of a small town—residences, a cafeteria, a
gymnasium, and a classroom for ages K thru 12.
Vending machines too. No store.

There are several large meeting rooms intended as
school rooms. High school classes are close in
proximity to the gym but not the cafeteria. Younger
kids' classrooms—those elementary grade kids—are
nearer the cafeteria than high school kids.

When we ventured into the cafeteria, the aroma of
warm, baked bread hit my senses and my stomach
rumbled. Four girls lifted their eyes from playing cards.
They were sitting around a table that could easily seat

eight people. When I made eye contact with them, they went back to their game, a game I recognized as Cribbage.

"This is the cafeteria," CO Madge said.

No, duh. The ice machine, soft drink dispenser, rack of chips, and all those bins of food. those food trays and utensils, did we not just accidentally step into the morgue? Gah.

Of course, there was no morgue, but, come on. Don't I have a nose with which to smell and eyes with which to…?

What does she freaking take me for? A moron?

Thinking better of verbalizing any of this with my outdoor voice, I opted to say nothing.

"Breakfast is at nine, so you missed that, but lunch is at noon and dinner at five," she said. "You also meet visitors here."

Upon hearing the information, I noted how no visitors were blessing this fine establishment, no one wearing civilian clothes.

"Come on," Madge said before she led me back through the wide corridor from where we'd entered, then down toward another room. From a lanyard around her neck, CO Madge used a magnetic card to swipe an electronic keypad set into the door panel. The door clicked and nudged open when it unlocked.

"This is the gymnasium," she said. She pulled me inside and closed the door.

Several girls sat around exercise equipment acting like they were working out. The smallest was a young

girl who couldn't have been much older than Tessa.
The oldest one looked around my age, maybe a few
months older. Their orange gym clothing, cotton shorts,
and T-shirts were adorned with INMATE on the front
and back of the top and only on the back of the shorts in
bold black letters.

"A newbie, CO Madge?" The older one said.

"Chill, Kat." CO Madge rolled her eyes. "She's
trouble, that one," Madge whispered so only I would
hear what she said about Kat.

"Looks delicious," Kat chimed.

A Cheshire cat, if ever. Big stupid smile. My eyes
narrowed. Kat lifted her hands and shoulders to me like,
"What?" The way someone does when they're trying to
appear innocent. Then she puckered and blew me a
kiss. The freak.

"Come on," CO Madge instructed. We turned and
walked back to the door. "Best to work out when Kat's
not in here," was her last bit of advice.

After the gym, she showed me the showers. Again,
she used the magnetic key to unlock the door. When it
burped open, a strong whiff of bleach hung in the
room's mugginess. Down one wall, five completely
enclosed stalls allowed for privacy, complete with a
locking door and electronic keypads. However, set
inside the door panel at eye level were wired windows
the size of letter-sized sheets of typing paper.
Fluorescent ceiling lights shone in bleak brightness,
washing out five sinks and a molded bench situated at

the far end of the room under a high window made of glass that made the pane appear perpetually wet.

"They lock from the inside, but we have the master key," she said, and lifted a set of electronic keys on a coiled, pink stretch band she wore around her wrist. "There's always a bathroom guard too. And every day, three times a day, a CO will escort five to six residents in good standing—referred to as RIGS—to the showers. Morning, eight o'clock sharp, before chow. One p.m. sharp, after chow, and six p.m. after final chow. Residents *not* in good standing—R-NIGS—shower three times a week in the evening after RIGS shower. Got it?"

We started to leave, but before we got out, CO Madge, said, "Oh! I almost forgot. The group bathrooms are the only places with mirrors. Your room doesn't have one in the crapper, for obvious reasons." She made a slicing motion over her wrist. But until she said it, I hadn't considered that someone might off themselves. Another safety precaution. God forbid someone might cut their wrists on a broken mirror.

"Want to see your room?" Her face beamed at the suggestion. Was she really excited for me? But when she noticed I didn't share her same enthusiasm, she said, "It's small but not bad. Your roommate will be gone in a few weeks. Then you'll have it all to yourself until someone new shows up. You have *that* to look forward to. The doors lock but, again..." she lifted her wrist and rattled the electronic keys.

"The master," I said.

"She speaks," Madge joked. Then, "Right. The master with the master."

My room was dimly lit and empty when she opened the door which, by the way, wasn't locked.

"Need to pee?"

I shook my head *no*.

"Well, this is it. Room seven."

Seven, room seven.

Little Tessa . . . seven years old.

"You lock it from the inside. We can unlock it, as I mentioned before, but usually we won't just barge in on you girls unless there's some kind of trouble."

Trouble?

"Trouble?"

"Like, you get sick or there's a fight and the door's locked. Trouble. Come on. Don't be a baby."

I'd said something similar to Tessa not so long ago but didn't understand the sting until CO Madge said it to me.

"I'm not a baby."

"You almost cried."

"I'm in jail. I didn't do anything to deserve this." My words must have amused her nothing short of watching a comedy show because she laughed big and loud.

"Oh man, you have no idea how often I hear that." She wiped her seepy eyes, then said, "Look. I know you think you're innocent, but you're here, aren't you? So, girlfriend, you don't look so innocent. Now, buck up. The baby act is a harbinger of trouble."

"Harbinger?" I said, noting her slight misuse.

"You know, forerunner, portent."

"I know what harbinger means. It's your usage."

"My usage, missy, is just fine," she said. Then, turning away from me, she mumbled, "You little shit." Not quite quiet enough.

It seems I'd hurt ole Madge's feelings. She was the sensitive type about her knowledge of vocabulary. I know the type; however, never thought CO Madge might be the type. Sensitive about intelligence.

So, I dug in. Don't ask why.

"You go to college, CO Madge?"

"Don't get fresh, young lady, or you'll end up an R-NIG faster than you can say potato grinder." On the word *grinder*, a little ball of spit shot out of her mouth and landed on my left cheek.

I wiped it off like it was dirt. "Gross," I said.

CO Madge giggled, then said, "Don't say I never gave you anything."

She was a flipping walking cliché.

33

Let the Beatings Begin

Not long after the four in the gym spotted me, I
learned they went by the handle, the *Bitches from
Riches*. The Bitches began following me, showing up
no matter where I was. Their intent? To harass,
harangue, and hassle.

This virulent gang of four included Kat, short for
Katrin, pronounced like latrine but with a K and no E.
Kat was the one in the gym who called me *delicious*,
also the gang's self-imposed leader. I'll get back to Kat
in a bit.

Second in command was Judith, pronounced
Yudith, but shortened to Yudy, like Judy but with a Y.
Yudy was the odd-man-out member of a strict Hasidic

family. She sported a Marine chop, a short nap of soft black hair that angled into a sharp V of fuzz down the nape of her neck.

After Yudy, came Alexis, then a girl named Crow. Don't ask. I didn't dare. Felt it wisest to simply wonder for the rest of my life how a teenage girl might get tagged with the name Crow. She didn't act crow-like. In fact, she barely spoke. Crow demurred. Followed along. Feared if she didn't, the Bitches might unleash their wrath on her. Maybe she was their tool. Maybe she was the thing they got off on when they couldn't down anyone else. Who knows? But Crow rarely uttered a sound. I only heard her speak once. And it was possibly the most important thing she ever said.

Alexis, known as Lex, fell lockstep in line with Yudy. She was a body double black chick and Yudy's wannabe twin, assuming a black girl and a Jew could be twins. Lex, who other girls called Black Yudy, bleached her woolly, short fro and reminded me of Dennis Rodman. She was tall like Rodman too. The twins, short Jewish Yudy and tall Rodman Lex, were muscle for Kat. Kat's goons, if you will, with Crow as an afterthought of sorts.

At first, when they spotted me, the Bitches only whispered, giggled. They'd eye me, huddle together and laugh, like they all shared some big stupid secret I didn't get to share. An exclusionary tactic. A lame try to make me feel less than. Good Lord. I'd been to high school. I'd already dealt with lower intellects and stupid clique tactics. Excluding me from their freakish group didn't weigh in. I took to ignoring them, not realizing that doing so would heighten their stupidity.

Sometimes, they whistled like scummy high school boys, the ones I'd learned to steer away from. You know the kind? Creeps that get more aggressive when you dis them. Enter the *Bitches*.

But let me back up. If I don't tell you about my roommate, you won't understand. You might understand later, but not now, when you need the information.

Therese, pronounced like Ter-ACE, had been at the King County Juvenile Detention Center since the age of fourteen. She was moved to Clear Lake two years later at the age of sixteen. And in twelve weeks, she would turn eighteen and be free. I envied her on that point. Envied a long life of freedom after being inside for only a few days. And although I wanted to be happy for her—let me correct that. *she* wanted me to be happy about her upcoming freedom—I feared for the people outside. Right now, I couldn't worry about those outside, because I was doing enough worrying for myself.

With my hands clammy at the prospect of meeting my roommate, CO Madge said, "Home sweet home." Her excitement was yawn-worthy, close to that of a eunuch at an orgy.

She swept one arm inside, gesturing me to enter. Then she locked the door, slamming it behind me as it smacked me in the butt, shoving me farther into the room.

The room was smaller and narrower than my room at home. A double bunk bed lined one wall; a desk lined the opposite. There was a closet-sized room that housed a toilet and a sink with no mirror, as CO Madge had stated. A single door allowed for a modicum of privacy, if the word *modicum* meant practically none because the door had no lock.

A thin horizontal window sat high in the wall close to the ceiling. A person would need a ladder to see out. Even so, the window let sunlight and moonlight in if the skies weren't overcast. Otherwise, with no artificial light, the mood in the room remained in a funk.

Once my gaze moved full circle, there she was.

Therese's body took up the length of the lower bunk. She wore a skimpy pair of tight cotton shorts across the firm expanse of her waist and hips. She was all muscle, all brown-as-a-berry muscle. A single, bronzy French braid poked over one shoulder. Her eyes were sable with flecks of silver and gold, as I found out later when her face met mine by a fraction of an inch. The room muddied her sun-washed skin with hints of coral. I couldn't quite make out her ethnicity but surmised her lineage was not Northern or Eastern European. With oval eyes hinting of Asian, African-American, or Latino blood, Therese was a confused bit of ancestry, but one creating an attractive, even if tough, exterior. There was a definite mix of Caucasian thrown in there somewhere, enough to create light-hued eyes. We were opposites in heritage but alike in search of sacred dominion over our own person, for sure, but also inside the small quarters we'd both been thrust into.

"Mine's the bottom," Therese said about the bunks. No "Hello, I'm Therese." No "Nice to meet you." Nothing, just "Mine's the bottom."

I walked the few steps it took in our eight-by-ten-foot cell to the long side of the bunk and began to place my skimpy belongings up on my mattress.

Therese kicked her heel squarely into my thigh, causing me to crumple back. I grappled for something to grab hold of, and not finding anything, I slammed against the wall. Within seconds, a softball-sized charley horse swelled up on top of my leg.

"Never block my bunk again, skank," she said. "The ends, dumbass." She was referring to where I should climb up or down. She had tenure, and I was to bow to her status in our close-quartered hellhole. I pushed away from the wall.

"Use the ends," she repeated. "Block me again, and I'll do worse than kick you. Got it?" She had one hand tucked under her ribcage and was reading a trashy, girl-on-girl, used paperback. She rolled slightly off her side, away from the book, and revealed in her hand a pen she was hiding, one she'd sharpened to a deadly point. Once she knew I saw it, she rolled back to her reading position, covering the shiv. As she flipped to the page she'd last read, she kept her eyes on the book and quietly said, "Say anything about it and you're dead."

That was the first time I cried in front of Therese. My crying was answered by Therese's sharp reprisal.

"Buck up, bitch. It gets tougher, not easier, stupid."

I figured uttering any words would garner another kick, slander, or death threat, so I kept quiet. Who knew what Therese was capable of? Why had she been incarcerated in the first place? As far as I could tell, she might have killed someone.

The softball knot growing under my pant leg ached and tightened against the orange fabric. Scaling the cold metal roll bars at the end of the bed, my quadricep pinched under the charley horse when I climbed onto the top bunk.

But wait. I bunny-trailed away from the original topic. Back to the *Bitches*. Lucky for me, their favorite pastime was harassing new residents—insert sarcastic tone here—and cornering them, feeling them up, punching, forcing, and grabbing their hair—blazing understanding for the hairnet after the first time—in a hold meant to restrain them, then mashing their faces into their boobs. Sick stuff like that. Forceful, ugly stuff.

Later, to the credit of Therese, she told me if they ever got too aggressive, to let her know. Said she'd protect me, but I'd have to give her something in return. You know, barter for her protection. My dad would come through. He could bring chocolate, cookies, clothes. I didn't know what, but I figured Dad could get me whatever Therese wanted. It was crap straight out of *Law & Order*. Unfortunately for me, this time it wasn't TV fictional crap. My opinion of Therese brightened, thinking how I sort of had a friend in her and, if not a friend-friend, a protector.

It was the first night . . . or maybe the second? I can't remember, but I had this dream, a nightmare really, that I was in the car with Gemma's dad, but we weren't alone. His accountant, some guy from a world past, was also in the car. The accountant wore a powdered wig, one of those French-style, mid-thigh-length overcoats, and a lacy accordion-style neckpiece over the bodice.

Very fashionable.

Not.

Anyway, we were speeding along Interstate-5 South toward Seattle with my dad speeding in his truck next to our car, but Dad was driving backward.

I said to Gemma's dad, "Slow down. My dad's driving backward."

Who, in return said, "He'll be fine."

To which I responded, "Not if you speed like this."

Then, "We need to get there. We need to get there," Gemma's dad said twice just like that, "we need to get there."

He didn't slow down until we neared a turnoff into a parking lot of some flea-ridden motel where they apparently needed to drop me. We all piled out of the car near a trellis where this big, fat, green bug was hanging on a plant. The round bug was almost the size of a ping pong ball, and it had long, angular, white spider legs. Thinking back on it, the green bug reminded me of a nuclear-sized daddy long legs, one on steroids. The trellis near the entrance of the parking lot was like the spider's domain or something, its post where it watched people come and go. Guarding the entrance like a gargoyle spider.

Gemma's dad and the accountant led me across the pavement to a miniature set of double doors. The opening in the wall was narrower than both its doors, which made the doors form a V that one could push through to enter the dark confines, but also made it impossible to exit once the spring doors closed behind you. Plus, the narrow opening was so restrictively small, you had to crawl to get in and, once in, you could not physically turn around. You had to back up to get out.

Nevertheless, when they told me to enter, I did. Why? Because I fully expected them to follow me inside, and when they did not, I realized my dilemma. The narrow hallway—if you could even call it that— was barely the width of a large packaging box. The floor and walls were a confused configuration of black rubber squares, tacky to the touch, that dragged against my pant legs. I freaked. I tried to back up, but it was like, *tough luck tuna* because ahead of me the narrow opening got narrower and narrower. And behind me? You'd need a crowbar to wedge the doors back open to escape. Basically, they'd sentenced me inside a suffocating tomb.

My heart pounded like a thousand galloping horses as I gasped awake. It took me more than several minutes to calm down, and when I finally did, I started to cry.

"Shut the fuck up," Therese grumbled, her voice gravelly with sleep.

"I had a nightmare," I squeaked, my voice wobbling, shaky, and pathetic. Sort of expecting some sympathy.

"Go tell Mommy, 'tard. Now, shut up."

But I couldn't stop crying. Not until Therese's foot slammed the underside of my bunk.

That was the second time I cried in front of Therese, but it was certainly not the last.

34

The Incredible Hulk Has Nothing on Me

I didn't see who grabbed my ponytail, because she came up behind me.

All seventeen of us were leaving the cafeteria through what residents called the DMZ, a non-secured corridor, after another crappy dinner.

I fell on my ass, then one of the Bitches dragged me down by my hair. With the force of a street wrestler, she seized me from behind and pulled me backward from under my arms and laid me back in between her legs. Then she steadied herself by planting her elbows against the floor. Doing so, she secured me in a prone position and remained on her stomach in supine.

It was at this point my Salisbury steak threatened to creep back into my esophagus and make a break for it, out of my mouth and onto my neck and chest. Hopefully, with me aspirating on it and choking to death.

Slamming to the floor had knocked the wind out of me, and before I could kick, Lex scrambled to my feet, pinning them to the hard, composite tile floor. She yelled at Crow, "Come fucking help me!" A point of deduction: Yudy was the one who knocked me down. She'd since let go of my hair and had me in a full nelson with her legs wedged under my back and threaded through each of my arms.

Enter Kat. Oh mighty leader.

Fewer guards remained past dinnertime since more cafeteria and custodial workers clocked in for the graveyard shift—an apt term. On one hand, a reasonable person might argue for fewer night guards since most *residents* were locked in their *rooms* sleeping. But other reasonable people might argue the graveyard shift warranted more guards because, as in nature, many predators lurk in the realm of darkness. Predators like Kat.

Kat walked up slowly. She wasn't smiling. She wasn't frowning either. She had a hungry air about her, shoulders down, lower lip wet. Like I was dessert.

She straddled me and plopped down onto my stomach, then leaned forward, placing each of her hands onto each of my breasts.

"Nice," she said. Then, "Nice tits, toots." A statement that made the other three sneer and snicker under their breath.

I writhed, trying to get away. When I did, she leaned back and grabbed my crotch. I froze. I mean, I freaking stopped breathing.

A vision flashed. Tessa pinned under the car even if for only a second. A tear welled and sluiced down my temple and into my hair where it mingled with my hair follicles.

In moments like these, people experience many things, many emotions: shock, embarrassment, how little control they have, wondering how far the abusers will go.

Kat's hand felt like a vice against my pubic bone . . . at first. Once she'd stifled all motion and sound from me, she began rubbing me. I tried to fight, but with the other three restraining me and Kat sitting across my diaphragm, fighting was futile.

"What gives, Kat?"

At first, I didn't recognize the voice. Whoever commented was gnawing on something, something crunchy, lips smacking off chunks at each word.

"Nothing to do with you," Kat barked, not taking her eyes off mine.

"Wrong. Wrong again, ass wipe. That one's mine," Pause, crunch, swallow, "beeotch."

Kat's jaw twitched. She grabbed my crotch harder and squeezed before lifting her hands high off me in surrender. Our eyes still locked.

"My roomie. My girl. Got it?" Pause, crunch, swallow, "bitch." This time she said "*bitch* soft. A red cape fluttering in front of a crazed bull.

Kat glared at me. "That true?"

My eyes flashed to Therese, who ignored me, her hand digging into a sack of potato chips.

Kat caught me, though. "Hey! Don't look at her." Both her hands slammed onto my boobs. "Answer me! Are you? Therese's?"

My head reacted before my mind. I agreed in a rapid-fire series of nods. But that wasn't enough.

"Say it!"

I barely had wind from the weight of Kat on my stomach. "Yes, yes," I said. "I'm Therese's."

"Damnit."

Kat swung a leg off me, a cowhand off a painted pony. Crow backed away and leaned against the wall.

"Let her up," Kat directed to the other two.

Usually, dinnertime offered some sense of relief for me. Everyone was in public view, guards stationed, watching. Juxtapose evenings with the rest of the day when you're constantly checking over your shoulder waiting for the next assault—someone stealing your marker or pad of paper, someone sweeping your feet and dropping you, someone punching you in the kidneys or grabbing you inappropriately just for the hell of it.

But right then, as I lay on the ground after Kat and the Bitches took me down . . .

. . . *Snap! Pow!*

The left sleeve seam of my standard-issue orange jumpsuit split open. Threads frayed under the pressure of my enlarging muscles. Think the *Incredible Hulk* but sans the green skin. Next, the neck-to-pelvis zipper gave way, making a racket like . . . well, like a zipper.

The pain was excruciating! Agonizing when the musculature in my neck exploded into a striated mesh. My forearms plumped out, flaunting a bulge of blue veins pulsing between each sinewy rope of muscle. My thighs bloated to those of strongmen, of strongwomen, of cross country runners and weightlifters. Until . . .

. . . *Snap! Pow!*

Both pant legs burst, shredding the seams and exposing new taut skin and a billowing form. A sheen glistened on my skin. Not from oil, but as if part of my body was glowing as it grew into this newly-created form.

Upon standing, I had to duck my head from hitting the ten-foot-high ceiling. My body hulking out, filling up half the width of the DMZ hall. No *Bitchie* had time to run. Each was still clinging to me when my body transformed from weak girl to not-so-woolly mammoth. Each of them swinging no less than six feet off the ground, screaming like the scared babies they were, scared of *me* and my newfound strength.

I swept past Therese. Thuds from my feet shaking the ground as I walked, knowing I could crush each one of them with my sausage-sized pinkie finger.

After shaking all four Bitches off my arms, they fell to the floor, cowering and sniveling. Such babies. Such

self-absorbed, peanut-headed heathens. Who did they
think they were messing with?

35

On Leave

The facility issued me an order for temporary family leave not long after being admitted. The reason? Gramma Kiki's funeral.

The order allowed me three days out—one day before the funeral, the day of, and another after. The temporary leave ended the fourth day, when I would return.

Kiki's funeral wasn't like Tessa's. Kiki died three weeks after they put me in jail. Mom figured the stress of Tessa's . . . you know . . . and the stress of me going to jail had killed her.

The side of his face flushed after he told me. I gazed past him. Two southbound lanes lay between our lane

and a bank of thick hemlock and cedar plantings
stretching for miles behind a bumper-high, metal
barrier. The trees leaned as though pointing cars to their
destination. Dad flicked the turning indicator up,
checked the rearview mirror, and merged right, placing
a third lane between us. He slowed as we neared State
Highway 20.

"I'm sure she didn't, Mac," he said. "Kiki was old.
Her health wasn't great. Despite her appearance."

Her appearance? You mean that of an old lady?

"Lung cancer," he said. "And Mom has something
else to talk with you about. I'm under strict orders not
to talk about it with you so . . ." He let the sentence trail
off much like horse-tailed cirrus clouds being pushed
southeast, freighting in winter and bitter weather.

I kept my questions deep in the pit of my stomach.
Lung cancer. It was the first I had heard about it. And
as if he knew my hidden question, he said. "Your Mom
didn't want you or Tess to know. Said it was best.
What's the point, and all that." Then he said, "Anyway,
her time was limited."

Isn't it always?

The vision of Tessa's little body broken and bent on
the ground sifted into my mind but spirited away when
I considered poor Gramma Kiki. I wondered if I had
ever been rude to her. Said any unkind words? I
wondered if she was scared. Wondered if Mom was
sad.

Sure. Of course she was. I was. So how could Mom
not be?

The questions boiled in my temples.

Take the safe route. Change the subject.

"How's work?" I asked. A ploy intended to displace images of Gramma Kiki and Tessa.

And . . . snap. Just like that, the conversation changed. We skated over thin spots, precarious layers where deadly ice breaks, where deep, frigid waters will swallow you whole.

I'd learned the craft of small talk during my short time on the inside . . . and how to avoid eye contact. Avoiding eye contact, as with small talk, is big with visitors who don't know what to say, because saying what they actually think might be too injurious to the prisoner. Here's an alternate theory designed to connecting small talk and eye contact: people choose to avoid deeper conversations because deep conversations require eye contact and visitors don't want to make eye contact with us because when they do, they see the horror in our eyes. Eye contact becomes a direct download from a resident's brain into a visitor's brain.

Before checking out, Chrissy had placed a monitoring bracelet on my ankle. It matched great with my prison-issue shoes, orange gym shorts, and tunic. They encoded the GPS location for Mom's house into the bracelet, along with those for Gramma Kiki's funeral service.

"It's cold out," Dad had said, seeing me in my shorts.

"I'll be inside the car."

"Still," he said. Then he unsnapped his plaid flannel quilted jacket, pulled it off and threw it over my shoulders. "There."

"Now you're cold."

"But I'm rough and tough and hard to bluff," he said.

"You're shivering, *He Man*."

Dad giggled and it was all I needed right at that moment. A friendly smile, one without a price tag.

At the funeral, I recognized a few people. However, none of them were eager to greet me. If we made eye contact, they acted like they didn't see or recognize me. Some gave side glances, some whispered behind their hands. All kept a safe distance, like whatever I had might be contagious.

A few people attending were Mom's friends, but most were Gramma Kiki's, and too old to care. Two of Gramma's closest girlfriends sat next to Mom. They sidled down the pew past me, trying hard not to let any part of them or their clothing come in contact with me, like I was a leper or something.

The tall one, a strict-faced woman whose name I can't remember, patted Mom's arm in condolence, her expression all melty and kind. She whispered something into Mom's ear and patted her again, then glanced over to me. Her soft demeanor froze to the original creviced scowl, offering no sympathies my way.

Thankfully, this lady hadn't attended Tessa's funeral. Other than Gramma Kiki, mostly locals were at

Tessa's funeral. Dad's parents didn't show. They had been pretty much AWOL for the last five years. Both had disabilities and lived on the far side of the country in some old folks' home, as Dad referred to the place. At least they were still together, still alive.

My first day back, Mom had voiced a dark thought, one of the few words she'd spoken to me during any of the three days staying with her. She'd said, "I far expected Claire or Carl to die first." Dad's parents. Then silence. I knew not to speak. You learn not to say anything from being inside, where speaking to someone about their despair, their grief, their joy—even if you were sympathizing with them but doing so without being asked directly to chime in—would land you on the concrete floor of a basketball court getting kicked and punched until a warden moseyed in to break it up. A fact I learned fast.

I brought inside wisdom home with me for my time outside. Didn't utter a word. No "I'm sorry, Mom." No "She's in a better place." Nothing.

Before, when Dad dropped me at Mom's, I fully expected Walt and April to race up and greet me, but only Walt showed, all dog-happy and waggles. Mom adored Walt. Called him Little Man and Waggy Walt. He was her third child. Our *brother*, she'd say. April was mine. Mine all mine. Although, on the rare occasion, I'd loan her out to Tessa.

But April didn't show. I figured she was probably asleep under my bed as usual.

My breath caught when I opened my bedroom door. Mom had emptied the room from all its belongings, my belongings. Again, I didn't comment. Didn't ask what had happened. Because why would it matter? What's done is done, and belongings are the things of free people. It wouldn't have mattered to learn where she'd taken my stuff. It was only stuff. I mean, it's not like misplacing your sister.

I turned the knob as if entering a sanctuary and pushed the door closed in a whisper behind me. Inside, leaning against the door's sturdiness, I tried to acclimate to the room's ambience, its stark desolation— the sheetless mattress, the uncluttered desk, my posters torn from the plaster.

Shame replaced every inch of the room, floor to ceiling, wall-to-wall. My room. My shame.

A faint trace of bleach and furniture polish hung in the air. The nap of carpet void of footprints. My green tea kettle wallpaper stripped, replaced with a coat of white paint.

Most of my clothes had been stuffed unfolded into three black landscape bags and stowed deep inside my closet. So they looked out of place when I noticed swinging on three hangers a black pair of slacks, a white dress blouse, and a black jacket. I assumed the outfit was meant for me to wear to the funeral. On the floor, she'd set my favorite pair of black urban boots. The stash box where I hid money was gone. She'd likely bagged, given away, or tossed everything else—

my flutophone, a soccer ball, the chess set Dad gave me.

"April," I said softly.

Bending down to scan the space below my bed, a place I'd often find April *and* Tessa hiding, the carpet stood at full attention. I kicked off my shoes and pulled the black plastic bags out away from the corner of the closet. But April wasn't hiding there either. I left to check the laundry room, thinking maybe she was using her cat box but, no, she was not.

Then, I noticed a strange smell wafting within the house and a hazy film in the air.

"April, kitty?" I called again. I didn't hear her yammering voice answer. Nor was she trotting out from some hidey-hole upon hearing me call.

I tried again, "April? Kitty, kitty!"

Then Mom spoke out, calling to me. Saying something, something with zero emotion, like the lilting voice of an orator from propaganda radio. A matter of fact, no nonsense tone. Information only please.

And I thought I understood, but her creepy tone made me feel out of sorts, unbalanced, dizzy.

"What did you say?" I said.

From the kitchen, she said, "Your cat," she said, pausing, "she's not here."

I moved closer to the kitchen. "Where is she?" I asked. I was walking to the kitchen entry when I froze. Mom was sitting at the table staring out the window, taking a drag off a long, slim cigarette. Next to a cup of coffee sat a bowl, one from a set Tessa and I used to eat cereal out of.

"You're smoking?" It wasn't a question. It was a challenge.

She blew gray fog from between her lips as a precursor for the letters, words, and phrases next to topple off her tongue. "I gave her away."

I covered my ears.

"What?"

She didn't respond. And, with another drag and another exhalation of filth flowing to the window, she slumped back against her chair. Like she had tired of our discussion.

"Who did you *give* her to?"

We were now back to the point at hand, my cat.

"I'm not doing this," she said. "Talk to your dad about it."

She snubbed out the cigarette into the cereal bowl and slid her chair back. With her hands pressing against her knees, she got up, wiped ashes off the stomach of her jeans and pushed past me. I tagged after her, railing question after question at her until she disappeared into her bedroom and locked herself away.

I slammed my own door behind me and continued to scream profanity-laced questions at her from inside my room until I could no longer form coherent sentences.

Resting my head on my arms, elbows high on the windowsill, I watched rain frizzle out back. Clouds scudded by, invigorated by a steady wind that flattened grass, bent reeds, and shivered bare tree limbs. For three days, my room was another jail cell. Pain on the outside stemmed from a different set of rules but hurt just as badly as the rules inside the detention center. How many ways would I be punished for my crimes? How many bad luck rolls were in store? And how in the hell was I ever going to get April back?

36

Finding April – Day One

Mom insisted on burying Gramma Kiki on the island at the Saint Francis Catholic Cemetery. A convenience not lost on me. She made Dad buck up half the dough. Mom had been dipping into a small savings fund that she had all but drained. Plus, the cheaper route, cremation, was out of the question for Kiki, who'd once told Mom that she didn't want her body burned to ash in an incinerator. That was the weirdest talk I'd ever been privy to. Tessa was there. She bawled her eyes out because it scared her so much. She was only five, for crying out loud, and Kiki decided to talk about bodies being burned to crispy critters right there in front of the grandchildren?

Really, Gramma? Decorum, please. Think of Tessa, you beasts.

At the funeral, we were sitting graveside after a so-so attended church service when I turned to Dad.

"Did Mom give April to you?"

He shushed me. "After," he said. Which meant we'd never ever get back to the matter.

I couldn't blame him. The three of us were sitting in folding chairs right next to Kiki's casket after all. The casket, for some odd reason, had been hoisted into the air above the hole where she'd soon spend her days in eternity. Suspended on a yardarm sort of contraption by a series of commercial-grade straps that reminded me of appliance belts used to dolly around refrigerators or washing machines. These straps were much thinner, though, compared to ones used for appliances. Plus, these seemed a tad worn and dirty from decades of wear and tear in and out of deep sixers. Mud caked the bottom of a frayed strap slung under the casket where I imagined Kiki's feet lay.

I wondered if she was wearing shoes. She loved her royal blue pumps the best. I wondered if Mom had remembered to give the mortician her blue shoes.

"It's just…" I said to Dad, making sure to keep my words whispered so only he could hear. But at that very second, the priest, Father Don, began his sermon. Dad shook his head and lifted his hand for me to stop.

"Dearly beloved," Father Don said.

Dad reached over and snuck my hand off my lap. He held my arm under his arm, sort of wrapped with our fingers interlaced, and more to control than to console.

"Dad," I whispered, "is she with you?"

Mom nudged her body into mine.

"She's with you, right?" I was using my quietest-ever whisper. My lips smacked a little, but honestly that was the only sound I was making.

See, the thing about a graveside service is that no one makes a peep. Sure, people cough. Some sniffle. But, given on a day like that day with not even a hint of wind, everyone watches, and everyone can hear the slightest utterance from the dearly departed's family. I imagine there must be a rule book somewhere at one of the major online bookstores for graveside service etiquette. One that states, "Upon a family member's death, family members and attendees must remain motionless and deadly quiet so as not to detract attention from Dearly Departed, the priest, or the casket hovering precariously over the hole held up by rotting appliance straps." There'd be other rules, I'm sure, but that rule might be the number one rule of funeral etiquette.

The number two rule of funeral etiquette might be, "Attendees must look appropriately distraught to show sympathy for the family members of the dearly departed."

And understanding there might be either written or unwritten rules—perhaps both—once again, I turned to Dad, leaning in so near his ear that I could feel the tiny bristles of hair on my lips. I was about to comment about that fact to him followed by another question about April when Mom placed her thumb and index finger on the underside of my upper arm and pinched me so hard that I squealed.

Etiquette Rule number one—broken. Multiple times.

The temple veil rent. The walls moaned. And, oh my holiest of Holy cows. Did I just feel the earth quake? *Gasps* and *tsks* spun around behind us—from all those judging lips who stood and sat alike. I felt their scorching eyes tearing off Kiki's casket, lasering a path to where we sat, and boring burning glances into the back of my head. Even the priest shifted his head up from his Bible and frowned. Judgment, my good man. Judgment.

Mom's eyes slammed shut. I rubbed the underside of my arm after making an audible *Gah!* Dad acted like he was choking to stop from laughing. He covered his mouth and coughed twice into his fist. As if to say to everyone watching, "See, I'm really coughing."

Nobody bought it.

I let out my disapproval with a *tsk* and glared at Mom like she'd committed child abuse, like it was the cruelest thing she could ever do. But I was wrong. Because the cruelest thing she could ever do was give away April.

Before I wrenched my eyes back to the priest, like wind bending a tree in half during a gale storm came an earsplitting creak from in front of us. But the earsplitting creak wasn't coming from any bending trees.

Pre-stated fact: no wind today.

No, the earsplitting creak emanated from the *grave*.

Heads swiveled from me and back to Gramma Kiki. The priest jerked back and juggled his Bible, nearly dropped it into the hole, but secured it before sinning.

Mom, Dad, and I jumped up, knocking back our folding chairs when we tried to retreat from the horror show happening before us. The end of the casket, the one I hoped was housing Gramma Kiki's blue shoes, tipped suddenly.

Then, all hell broke loose.

The earsplitting creak turned into the lamenting of all things Biblical-gone-wrong. And the lamentation, into wincing in pain.

Then, *Pop! Pop! Pop!* One, then two, then three of the straps split. And boom!

The casket dropped feet first into the hole, effectively standing Gramma Kiki up on end, in a way that if she so desired, she might simply push the casket open and slip on out.

However, per the Federal Trade Commission (I know. The priest told us later), caskets are *not* required to lock because locking a body inside a casket actually speeds up the rate of decomposition. *Ew.* So, the lid snuck open ever so seductively, causing several people now standing watching this freakshow, to lean both forward and back, glued to the scene and praying Gramma Kiki wouldn't crumple out of the casket, but also possibly hopeful for Gramma Kiki to make a final appearance.

At this point, Dad found his voice again and decided to speak. "Shit." Which, for a nanosecond, took attention away from Gramma Kiki and her tightrope act, which had taken attention away from me, which had taken attention away from Father Don.

Thank you, Gramma Kiki.

However, before unveiling Gramma Kiki and all her glory, things smoothed out—or shall I say went back to their normal depressing state—after the pallbearers and two burly crew hands from the cemetery raced in, leveling out Kiki's casket and setting the box onto a set of board planks that had been used as a staging platform. After the crew hands retrieved a set of newer, more stable strapping, they finally skipped further ceremony and lowered Kiki to her final resting place. At that, the service ended. The priest appeared unhinged. Some might say *verklempt*.

We lost a few attendees who left mortified. No pun intended. Others stayed out of respect for Mom but weren't good at trying to hide their obvious amusement. Kiki's friends tried to console Mom, who had gone white like she'd seen a ghost. And I almost said that very thing, but then Mom started to cry. I knew, without reading anything on etiquette, not to crack a joke when Mom cried.

I did, however, think of a more rounded-out set of rules, adding Etiquette Rule number three, which might state, "At all costs, try not to let the casket plummet six feet into the grave." And Rule number four, "If the casket *does* fall into the grave, never, and I mean never, let the body fall out."

Needless to say, the funeral lacked all the markings of a traditionally successful one. But, when you give it some thought, what funeral has ever been a successful one? Certainly, not for the honored.

Mom was heartbroken. "She was going to miss Kiki," she had said earlier that morning, "like the dickens."

If Mom might only apply those same emotions to me, because inside, I really needed her. I missed Mom too. Like the dickens.

37

Finding April – Day Two (My Last Day on the Outside)

Of course, I couldn't leave the house because of the flipping ankle bracelet, so after having a great big fight about my cat with Mom, I locked myself in the scrubbed and desolate room that was once mine. The only differences between my bedroom and my jail cell were the carpeting, the lock on the inside instead of the outside, and the mini blinds instead of wired glass windows. Although, I noticed Mom had replaced the handle with a lockless doorknob during my weeks away.

It didn't escape me that she didn't give Walt away. Probably because of his *soulful* eyes. *He* was still here.

So, her giving away April was another form of
punishment for me, as if jail wasn't enough.

Because she'd taken away my laptop and iPad,
Mom gave me a notepad and a few ballpoint pens.
Using a real pen felt awkward since they only allowed
inmates the use of thick markers in an assortment of
colors at Clear Lake Juvenile. No pens. No pencils.
Markers because they don't want to find us penned to
death, sliced open at the wrists with the nub or the lead
of a pencil, or find we've killed other inmates. Still, I
don't think they considered us jamming an eye out with
a marker. One sharp blow with the felt end, and you'd
lose your eye, if not your life. Death by marker, straight
to the eye socket. It makes me wonder how Therese got
the pen she fashioned into a shiv.

I'm thinking all of this amid background noises—
the backdoor to let Walt out, a car roll by outside, a
toilet flushing. That's when the phone rang. Nothing
unusual, except this time, Mom burst into the room. I
nearly crapped my pants because at that very second, I
was penning a boiling, venting note to the very woman
who now appeared inside my door, phone in hand.

"Gemma," she said, "No more than five minutes, or
else."

She set the phone face down on the desk and
walked out, shutting the door behind her, almost in
slow motion.

"What." It wasn't a question.

"Hey," Gemma said. "Heard about April. That
bites."

"What bites is that I'm there and you're not."

"I told you, Mac. I tried. But Mom refused. She says if I say anything to anybody, I'm not going to college, first because I'll be sent to jail, second because they will use my college fund as a down payment on a new house, and thirdly, they would be charged themselves and need to abscond to a different state."

"Like before."

"Shut up," she said.

"I'm surprised my mom didn't hang up on you. Look, I can't appreciate your troubles right now, nor do I care to. If you haven't noticed, my situation is a little dire. They put me in a cage! A god-awful cage. I shouldn't be there. I didn't do anything wrong."

"Except get caught," she quipped.

"You know what, Gemma? Fuck you." And with that, I hung up.

What she said reminded me of what Markel said when he told us they don't typically charge a minor in possession unless they're selling. But I wasn't selling. *Gemma* wasn't selling. It was a bogus charge and a majorly effed-up situation where no one was guilty, but everyone was, all at the same time.

38

Visitations

Back at Camp Dread and Loathing . . .

"Where is she?" I said . . . about my cat.

With my hair up in the net, a split lip, and a yellowing black eye, Dad had demanded an explanation. I told him I ran into a *door* and refused to give further specifics about who the door was or if the door got in trouble for affronting me, then turned the subject back to what I really wanted to find out from Dad during his visit.

"Honey," he said, "just forget about April. She's gone. She's with another family who adores her. Stop worrying. She's safe. They don't let her go outside.

They love her. It wouldn't be fair to yank April out of their lives."

Mom refused to visit. After two months, I stopped asking Dad when she might show.

We sat at a round eight-man-table as close to the cafeteria entrance as possible. He sat straddling one of three curved benches attached to the table base, ready for flight.

Kitchen staffers had already begun cooking for dinner and it smelled like another Salisbury steak night. Thrilling. Through the high-set series of windows trimming one side of the room, I could tell the sun was setting into a flame of pink. The sky reflected off a long maze of patchwork fluorescent ceiling lights that made everyone look two seconds away from dead. But Dad, given his tan from working at the stone yard, looked arguably healthier than the rest of us insiders. One hand rested between us while I used the other to snack on a bag of nacho tortilla chips Dad brought me. He tried to grab my free hand, but I pulled away and stuffed it between my thighs, my mind hard-wired on the topic du jour.

"Just tell me who. I mean, what do you think—I'm going to walk out of here, pop over to the island, visit the people who now have *my* cat, and, like, I don't know, stalk them until I find the right time to snatch April from them?"

"God. You're as persistent as your mother." He shifted on the bench as if he were thinking about getting ready to leave.

But it was too soon. I didn't want him to leave, so I changed the subject.

"Why was Tessa crying that day?"

His face darkened. "Crying? What day?" He honestly seemed confused.

"The day before she died. She stormed down the hall in tears. You and Mom were fighting, *again*, on the phone."

He wiped a hand over his face and looked at the chips I'd shaken out of the bag. Then he looked at the wall to his left, looked at his lap.

"I don't know," he said. Then, in an attempt to recover, he said, "How could I know? I wasn't there."

"Don't play me, Dad. Something you said upset Tess. What was it?"

"How am I supposed to remember something your mother and I talked about six months ago?"

"It's a pretty important timeframe. I remember every single detail from days before to days after. Even up to now. How come you lost specific memories about Tess. You're her father, for *eff's* sake."

"Language, Mac," he said. "Look, your mom and I were talking about our separation. That's all. Nothing diabolical. Are you trying to pin Tessa's . . . you know . . . on me?"

"Just trying to put two and two together is all."

"Well, as far as I can recall, two and two sometimes don't add up. Look, all I want to do is get over it. Move on."

"Isn't that convenient?"

"Oh my God. Straight out of your mother's lips."

I stuffed a chip into my mouth, fearing another judgment might fly out and push him away, but he'd already decided to leave because he dismounted the bench.

"Now, I'll see you next week. Try not to get beat up."

"How am I supposed to not get beat up?"

He shook his head and lifted his hands like *I don't know*. Before he walked out of the door, I felt my heart clench. And as if he could feel it, too, he turned back, blew me a kiss, winked, mouthed the words, *I love you*, blew me another kiss, then knocked on the door for the guard. A buzzer rang behind me at the same time the guard opened the door for Dad. CO Madge entered the room, placed her lousy hand on my shoulder, and escorted me back to my cell. The exact same reverse order of how she led me to the cafeteria when Dad arrived.

39

Paybacks Are a Bitch

"Are you a cat person or a dog person," I asked
Therese, my voice floating up and off the ceiling above
my bed, each letter swirling like fireflies in the dark.

"Shut up with your stupid girl stuff."

"I'm a cat person, I think. I mean, I love dogs, too,
but cats are so cool and easy."

"Pussy," she whispered. The insinuation not lost on
me.

I ticked a cricket with my tongue and the fireflies
dissipated from sight.

Sleep and exercise had become my escape from
further confrontations with the Bitches. Also from
Therese, who continually reminded me that *I owed her*.

Like owing Therese was a date token or something she could cash in whenever she wanted. Or needed. The place sickened me.

Lights out came five minutes before. The cell was a tomb.

Outside, wind knocked trees around, playing leafy shadows like sign language off the frame of our window and ceiling. Someone, a guard most likely, had a TV program buzzing on low volume. The electric whir and louder commercial breaks of inane insurance commercials, mattress store jingles, and beer ads wafted through the building like a lullaby.

"We need to talk," she said.

I knew what she wanted. She wanted me, and I didn't want to talk about it. I wanted it to just go away, to have her forget about it. I had successfully avoided the matter up to now.

"God, Therese. Come on. You're not my type." I tried to laugh but instead it came out sounding like a hiccup.

"I can *be* your type." I barely heard her.

"Please go to sleep. Don't say stuff like that. Jeez, don't think about it. I'm not like that. I like boys. Anyway, Dad can bring cash and, I don't know, cigarettes. Isn't that what prisoners like? Cigarettes?"

She groaned and said, "The horror."

"Cigarettes?"

"Boys."

A tense vibrato jittered from our laughter and she seemed to give up on the idea.

"I like money," she said.

"I can get you twenty dollars each visit."

"He won't suspect anything?"

"I'll tell him it's for snacks and stuff."

The guard must have heard us talking because she yelled, "I said, *Lights. Out!*"

"Screw you," Therese whispered and giggled.

I knew Therese expected me to pay her back. I knew what the payback entailed but hoped I could dissuade her with money. Because if I didn't pay her back in some way, shape, or form, then she'd mark me free game for the Bitches.

"I'll give you another week," she said. "I can't promise anything."

Relief from being given a week respite sent a wave of relief through my core, warming me and helping me relax. In this place, every second felt like a year.

But a few minutes later as I was drifting off to sleep, my bunk lurched, and I awoke with Therese's hand over my mouth. She had climbed into bed with me.

When I struggled, I felt a sharp jab against my side. The shiv.

Her mouth was wet against my ear, and she said, "Make a sound, and I'll shove it straight into your liver."

40

A Short Note on the Seven (or so) Stages of Grief and Loss

On grief: It's not *how* you feel but what you *do* when you're feeling what you feel that counts. Or so psychologists will tell you.

The problem with emotions is that they are tricky imps if left on their own. One minute you're feeling happy; the next, you're scraping cat shit off your shoe. Metaphorically speaking, of course.

Either way, The great *they* have delineated seven stages of grief and loss. *They* say a person may experience some or all of these stages (sometimes at once) during the course of grieving, and they go on to say that few people ever experience none. Anyway, the visiting therapist, Deborah Grout, brought copies of an article from recover-from-grief.com entitled *The Seven Stages of Grief: Through the Process and Back to Life*. The article charts out the following:

1. SHOCK & DENIAL
2. PAIN & GUILT
3. ANGER & BARGAINING
4. DEPRESSION, REFLECTION, LONELINESS
5. THE UPWARD TURN
6. ACCEPTANCE & HOPE
7. RECONSTRUCTION & WORKING THROUGH

With the last two somewhat *interchangeable*. I wonder how they came up with that little tidbit. I wonder how much of this crap is simply psychobabble hoo-ha. An idea from some doctoral student's dissertation papers or was it from hard facts— information populated by human studies. Because you see, a person on the inside, someone who has to live through each step of this *so-called* process while incarcerated, deals with their own brand of loss and grieving. Erase all this sage info and consider one whose grief has multiple layers: her parents' pending divorce, her sister's death, being ripped out of her home, going to jail, the real possibility that incarceration will cause her to never get into college, and being beat up and raped on the inside. These stupid therapists don't have a clue but, oh yes . . . at least I have this lousy article to give me comfort.

41

Suspension and a Sense of Dread

I rested my head in my left hand. My elbow was propped on the table where I sat lingering in the cafeteria after breakfast, after *not* eating a plate of two *poached* eggs or two pieces of toast. Three other people remained behind who weren't either kitchen staffers or guards: Crow, who sat alone, and two other girls from the far side of the residency whom I'd seen over the course of two months but didn't associate with. You tended not to get to know people here for fear of getting beaten, raped, or shivved. The two together sat mantled over empty plates and spoke in a low humming conversation. Crow sat a room's length away against

the interior plaster wall. I sat sort of in the middle of the
room, nearer the kitchen where everyone could see me.

CO Linnea stood post outside the entrance with the
door closed. I watched her talking on a cell phone for a
time, then I went back to swirling designs into my food
on the plate. The eggs looked like a battlefield bombed
by crazed hens. Oozy yolks had gash marks of egg
whites where my fork cut through the yellow. Toast
crumbs speckled the mess of eggs and the edges of the
plate. Crumbs littered my lap and the edge of the table
from a single half-moon bite out of a corner of a slice.

I loathed runny eggs. Made me want to puke
looking at the food. To make matters worse, today's
cook wasn't Susanna, the nice, youngish, busty, short
Latina who owned *Susanna Q's Catering* and always
wore her hair maxed out in a long net which she
attached to her head in a series of spangly, emerald
crystal clips. No, today's chef was another Latina,
Elmie, from *Susanna Q's Catering*, but not nice and not
attractive. This girl was a stubby, pock-faced little troll
who never smiled. She cooked like she'd learned to
cook at a zoo and acted like she was doing her own
time in hell by working two mornings a week at the
detention center kitchen. Why didn't Susanna just fire
her?

A dark purple gob of loganberry jam covered both
slices of my toast. Today's troll never toasted the bread
long enough. A better description would be she tanned
the bread after brushing on an SPF50-level vegetable
oil that glistened in spots before slapping on jam with a

tablespoon. I wanted to gag but wasn't sure if it was because of the slimy mess on my plate or because of what Therese had done to me the night before. Who, by the way, sat ridiculously close to me, nudging me like we were having a great time together while she scarfed down her breakfast before leaving the cafeteria for her scheduled shower. CO Madge was assigned today's morning shower rotation.

The lights pooled a ghostly spotlight onto my skin. Was blood even flowing in my blue veins? I felt dead, humiliated. Wrung out. And I still had sixteen months left to suffer this nightmare. None of which was my doing. The only thing I was guilty of was being in the wrong place at the wrong time.

How in the hell had this happened? How in the hell!?

My thoughts burst out of me. "Fuck!" I shoved my plate across the table with the strength I had left. It clattered to the floor. A battle of hens spraying across the composite tile, baby chicks splattered with their entrails under the upturned plate and bleeding out in whites and yellows and purples.

The two girls sitting alone gasped, springing to straight posture. Crow didn't react. Hardly fazed. The only motion she made was when she lifted her eyes in my direction. They appeared dreamy, as if she was stoned. Then she fell back into her thoughts. She chewed slowly on a piece of underdone toast.

CO Linnea charged in, her eyes fuming, her brows pinched and angry.

"What is going on in here?" She was headed directly to me. I didn't say anything and stood to face her when she reached me. I don't know why I said what I said but with us face-to-face like that, I called her stupid.

Then I said, "If you can't see what's going on in here, then you're denser than everyone says you are!"

And I pushed past her through the door, headed back to my room.

As I closed the gap to get to my, *our* room, I neared the bathroom/showers, knowing at some point probably sooner than later, I was going to catch hell for the outburst at breakfast. But, honestly? I didn't really give a flying you-know-what. Let Elmie clean it. Her cooking was shit. Maybe we'd all be better served with Elmie as part of the cleaning staff.

I wasn't being quiet about my mood. I let my anger, my humiliation, froth out. I was rattled and talking loudly to myself. Saying things like, "What's going on here?" Repeating CO Linnea's comments, letting the whole scene replay in my head and not stopping it from coming out of my mouth. I stomped as I neared the corner just before reaching the showers, when I heard a woman's voice say, "Shh!"

My feet nearly screeched to a halt and threw my body forward when I stopped. My body had taken on a life of its own, acting outside rules Mom had trained about good behavior. Throwing food, calling people stupid, running away, all felt like a cowardice of self-preservation, the opposite of self-control.

However, stopping so suddenly when I heard the woman's voice told me a few of my faculties remained in place.

I figured behind the wall was Kat and the gang of *Bitches*, less one freakishly-disturbed-looking Crow, who was still scarfing down food in the cafeteria, last I witnessed.

I flattened my body against the wall a mere two feet from the corner. I barely breathed before hearing, "They must've gone back." And then, "Coast is clear."

Thank God I heard their feet padding quickly across the slick tile away from me and not toward me or else I would've had to scramble back toward the cafeteria and face the wrath of CO Linnea and Elmie for my egg mess. I'd have to force my eyes to look apologetic at anyone remaining in the room.

After I was sure they were gone, I slinked up to the edge of the corner and peeked around. All action felt slow, like there was no gravity. I had no sooner snatched a glimpse around the corner when I saw CO Madge escorting Therese down the hall and Madge giving one lingering slap onto Therese's ass. A slap that made me choke. When I caught my breath, they both spun around, but I had already flown down the hall in the direction of my Come to Jesus meeting with CO Linnea.

42

The Biggest Cats on the Planet Eat Humans

The next time, Theresa said, "That wasn't so bad, now, was it?" She slid her naked body off mine, my face wet with tears. "Fucking baby," she said when I whimpered. "Make a noise, and that bitch guard'll be in here so fast, you'll be the one who looks guilty. Trust me. She'll think it's you."

But I wasn't moving. I wasn't planning on moving. The only thing I wanted was to curl up and die. I turned to the wall, hoping to corner the pain, to hold it in. Therese had pinned me by the arms with her knees as she forced herself into my face. Her knees gouged deep, bruising my forearms just below the elbow. Arms that were still bruised from the first time. Plus, her weight stopped the flow of blood to my hands. Minutes later, the tingling stopped and feeling returned to my fingers. I set both hands against the cold, flat surface, let a trickle of blood ooze down my throat from where Therese had applied the shiv.

I always thought I'd rather die than be raped, but I was still alive. And for now, I had to live with guilt and shame that was new and unrelated to the guilt and shame I already felt for Tessa's death.

The wall was safe. The remainder of the night, safe. Sleep, safe. For now, anyway. Tomorrow would bring its own new terror. But for now, I had the wall and its stable, cold plaster. The constant white. And as my hands kept moving over the wall's flatness, I felt my body falling forward off my bunk, but I didn't tumble to the floor. I tumbled through the plaster, between the studs, and came out the other side where giants lived. Giant, human-like beings twenty feet tall with gangly long legs that reminded me of stick-people. They drove stick-shift cars, built homes they'd sketched from charcoal pencils and lived inside their charcoal-pencil dwellings. In Stick Land, stick dogs and stick cats ran in and out and grew to the size of Volkswagen Beetles. All of Stick Land was white except for the line-drawn forms. The stick cats were enormous. And before I could sneak off, one cat spotted me. I was still lying against the base of a stick home, my face smashed into the white of the stick wall.

When the cat lunged, I scampered along the base of the house like a mouse trying to find its escape hole. I'd

seen the horror of April after some poor rat or
chickadee to know my days were numbered if I didn't
find cover. This massive cat would kill me. After
suffering quite enough humiliation already, the thought
of being batted around by a large carnivore gave me no
comfort. None whatsoever.

Instead, the strangest thing happened. Out of
nowhere, Therese showed up. She had tracked me into
Stick Land and was standing between me and the cat.

Her focus was on me when she said, "Hey, pussy!"
She laughed when I spotted her and she said it again,
"Pussy!" Taunting me.

And when she did, the cat seemed to lose interest in
me and became incredibly curious in Therese. The cat
rose up on her haunches and was about to attack
Therese, who dwarfed in stature next to the cat. But at
that point, Therese hadn't seen the bus-sized cat and
once again said, "Pussy!"

Courage, albeit misplaced courage, was not in short
supply for Therese, but luck had thumbed its nose at
Therese when the cat, from behind, swiped down on
Therese with one large stick paw.

Therese blinked. At first, it only appeared to be a
flesh wound, but when half her face carved away from
her skull and Therese dropped to her knees, I knew the
situation was more dire than a flesh wound. The next
swipe dealt a killing blow and severed Therese's head,
sending it soaring down onto the stick grass where it
bounced up next to a bubbly-drawn stick bush.

The cat bounded forward, giving chase to Therese's head as if it were one of those plastic kitty toys with a jingly bell inside. She knocked it under the bush, snagged it with a single claw, lifted the severed head, and tossed it into the air where, once more, she would tackle the head, rinse, and repeat like a game of soccer.

But nearer to me, Therese's body had slumped forward and landed face down. As the cat toyed, jumped, and batted Therese's skull, I snuck away farther down the wall and scrambled into a thick shadow of charcoal on the opposite side of the house where the sun wasn't shining. There, I remained huddled in the dark until at some point I must have fallen asleep because I startled awake the next morning to the bell inside the detention center going off for everyone to *rise and shine*.

"Get up, bitch," Therese said in her special, loving way. "Remember, say a thing and you're dead."

"You died last night," I said.

"What?" Her face crunched. Of course, she thought I'd lost my mind.

"Stick cat got you," I said, my voice raspy with sleep.

"Whatever, freak." She flashed the shiv, brought it up so close to my nose I felt the sharp point. Then she withdrew it and wagged it at me like some lame high school band baton twirler and pocketed it inside her shirt.

43

Plodding Through the Seven Stages of Grief:

1. SHOCK & DENIAL

The sudden onset of this stage is un*deniable*. Get it? Yeah. A total grumbler.

Look, all I wanted was people to leave me alone. Shock and denial both flood your brain so fast that when the next stage occurs, you hardly remember experiencing the shock or denial. You remember parts of going through the first stage because you say and think things like *Wow, I was blindsided*—about the shock, and *Man, I was totally oblivious*—about the denial.

Huge gaps exist. After watching Mr. Pauling's car run my sister down, flash! Enormous blanks fill the pages of my memory card. Mr. Pauling is huddled on the road. His face is bleeding. Then, flash! Gemma pulls me away from Tessa. Then, flash! The deputies are questioning people. Everything about that day, and moments after exist in flashpoints.

I'm home.

Mom takes me to the sheriff's office.

We go to a lawyer.

I can't remember crying. But I must have.

We go to Tessa's funeral.

Did I cry?

I end up in juvie.

I don't remember crying. Not until new horrors started occurring.

I tried to force back specifics, but it's like I was attacked by some big brain eraser. Trying to recall certain aspects exhausts me since Tessa died.

One might argue that with each type of loss, each stage of grief, a person might experience longer or shorter spurts of memory lapse. With the suddenness of Tessa's death came a sudden shock. Anger followed on its heels. Bill Pauling was the target of my anger. Rage billowed. Shock skipped away when anger found cleats to run with and flared so virulently that in some of the reports I had scared witnesses at the scene. At least, that's what the prosecutor said at the bench trial. It was only when the APA talked about it, that the ice started to break and memories began to melt in. None were clear, and because something was jogged inside my head from a mere suggestion, it made me question the validity of the memories at all.

I wondered how Mom's loss felt. We'd gone through one type of loss when Dad moved out. A gut-wrenching experience for all of us, although probably much harder on Mom. But for Mom and the loss of Tessa, her baby, I can't fathom what that feels like. Can't wrap my head around that pain. Losing a sister was the worst thing I had ever experienced. But losing a child? No. My synapses won't fire on the loss of a child. I can't imagine the pain she must've experienced. Is experiencing still.

Then we must consider the loss of an innocent. How differently we feel when someone as innocent as a seven-year-old is stripped of life.

After Therese the night before, I skipped breakfast, lunch, and dinner the following day. I skipped a shower.

A day later, I made my way down for dinner, snagged a dinner roll and a pat of butter, then absconded with them back to my bunk.

The day after, Therese had the decency to leave before I woke up. She returned after I had fallen asleep. I don't know where she went, but I was relieved she'd stayed away.

It was the eighth day before I was eating three squares again. I took a shower once during that time because I couldn't stand my own smell.

It was the day before Dad showed up to visit. Up to that point, I hadn't seen him for two weeks. His excuse—a big job. He couldn't get away. Needed to finish the job. Had to work weekends.

"You okay?" he asked.

"Stop asking me. I told you, I'm fine."

"You look upset."

I shook my head. I hated his stupid questions. "I'm in fucking jail."

"Hey," he said. "Don't use that kind of language with me, young lady."

"Or what? Gonna send me to my room?!"

That was the end of our *talk*. I bolted out of the cafeteria. I hate when people see me cry.

The remaining stages of grief and loss work this way:

2. **PAIN & GUILT** - My stomach ached as though a football-sized tumor were growing inside me. I figured I somehow caused my plight and that I deserved everything I was getting.

3. **ANGER & BARGAINING** - I was pissed off at everything and everyone. I got thrown into a *time out* room, basically solitary, for a week. They don't call it solitary because solitary confinement was banned, but that's what it is. They put me in after getting into CO Madge's face about not wanting to take showers. Told her I didn't need one, with her responding by saying, "You stink like a dog who just rolled around in deer shit." When people laughed, I ran at her, but she coldcocked me with the baton, making me go down like

a sack of bananas right there on the cafeteria floor. And, yes. In front of everyone. At lunchtime. Good times, right? While inside solitary with nothing at all to do but contemplate the existence of my belly button, I found myself on my knees praying, begging God, asking for forgiveness for, like, everything—Tessa's death, Mom and Dad, getting myself into a position where I'd found myself getting raped. Everything. The pot. Not being observant enough about Tessa when Bill Pauling's car bowled over her tiny body. I confessed every sin I'd ever committed. I offered God a deal. Asked Him to get me out sooner than later and, if he did, I'd never stray from the straight and narrow. I told Him I'd even go to church. God forbid.

4. **DEPRESSION, REFLECTION, LONELINESS** – This stage occurred the first day after being released from solitary. No surprise, but I realized how not one person from the outside had tried to fight for my release. Not Dad. Not Gemma. Duh. Of course, not Mom. Not my pathetic piece-of-shit lawyer. This stage lasted longer than one might suspect. Exile, banishment not only from one's home and family but also while in jail is its own special form of punishment. I didn't want to do anything but sleep. Because if I wasn't sleeping, I cried. There were several reasons to be depressed, which I've laid out before: Mom and Dad's separation, Tessa, the unwilling loss of my virginity. Life had tanked, turned to shit in less than six months. The attacks by Therese on and off up to the

time she got sprung. And afterward, by the Bitches, Kat mostly.

Then, after six months I got a phone call.

"Mom told me I should call first." It was Gemma.

"What about?" I didn't care either way if I ever talked to her again. She was an outsider now. One of *them*. A civilian. I was a war-torn soldier.

"I thought, I mean, I was thinking . . ."

"Get it out, for fuck's sake," I said.

I heard her take in a quick breath. "Well, you probably don't want me to, but I thought maybe I would come, you know, there, uh, to see you?"

"Do what you want." At that, I hung up. Why? What should I have said? "Oh, pretty please, will you? I'd *love* to see you. It would make the next twelve months *so* pleasant!"

Bullshit on that. Seriously, what should I have said?

By Saturday, Therese was gone. The Bitches took over where she'd left off. For a blessed, but short two months, however, I had the room to myself.

The guard knocked at three p.m. On Saturdays we got CO Linnea Kearsh, the perky guard who was studying criminal justice at UDub, getting a degree in justice studies with an emphasis in juvenile corrections.

CO Linnea was a small-framed, petite, blue-eyed blonde, with an athletic build. Cutesy, barring no other description. She always wore uniform blues, although the facility also issued drab khakis which some other COs preferred like CO Marge, the fireplug. CO Linnea

kept her hair in a tight ponytail under a cap with the
name, CO KEARSH embroidered on her breast pocket.
She slept in a truck on-site and came in to pee but
basically, she lived out of her truck there at the facility.
A true believer. A rarity. Someone who thought they
could change juvenile detention for the better. Held
classes on the subject of prison rape reform. I went to
one but left early when she talked about 2018 stats and
how prison rape was on the rise. But CO Linnea wanted
to implement a proven plan to reduce rapes, that the
way to reduce the frequency of rape was to tell COs
about anyone you knew of —which included
yourself— getting assaulted. From what I knew, change
wouldn't come anytime soon.

"You have a visitor, Miss Fraser," CO Linnea said.
Her fresh skin shone like the joy in her eyes. I wanted
to punch the joy right out of her. Wanted to tell her
about the rapes but knew if I did, they would commit
far greater abuses and with much more frequency. And
I wanted to tell people who wanted to visit to leave me
alone, that visitors were kryptonite.

"Tone down the happy, please," I said. "Who?"

She ignored my comment. "Some young woman
named, um…" Glancing at a sheet of paper, she said,
"Miss Gemma Painter."

Wipe that stupid smile off your face for fuck's sake.

"You know her, right? She said she's your best
friend."

"I don't have friends."

"Now, Miss MacKenzie." She sounded like a slave speaking to a slave owner. "Don't say that. Just because people don't call or come around to see you doesn't mean they aren't thinking about you or praying for you. They're just afraid. We're all afraid at some level, wouldn't you agree?"

Oh, this sugary bullshit. Stop already.

What I was afraid of? The next time those freaks rape me, you senseless boob. What are you afraid of? Getting a *D* on your next exam?

"Fine. Please. Don't speak," I said. "I'll go." I slipped off the upper bunk. I hadn't yet made the move to the lower one, the bunk of tenure. I didn't want it. Didn't want to sleep on the same mattress Therese had occupied.

Lethargy pulled me across the floor. I slogged to the door where CO Linnea stood. After exiting, she pulled the door closed but didn't lock it, in keeping with her mantra *we need to trust more and fear less*. A motif she repeated. She had a freakishly optimistic attitude.

Gemma looked nervous. I could tell she was loaded when she sat down. I peered through a cutout of wired glass inserted above the handle in the cafeteria room door. Observing her sitting there amid several residents—some with visitors, some without—and each one eyeing her tender form. I chuckled. I thought it would be nice to leave her there a few more minutes. See if she could handle it.

Kat and the rest of her gang of pukes huddled together as usual. But suddenly, Crow arose and walked out in what I might describe as a huff. *Weird Crow*, I called her to only me. Weird Crow.

After a few blessed moments watching Gemma all alone in there with the Bitches, watching her unravel, I strode in. CO Linnea followed and stood centurion at the door.

When Gemma spotted me, her face lit up, its strain melted. Her shoulders dropped, untensing. A physical reaction I'd also seen with my father that first time he visited. It's funny. On follow-up visits, guests act like they're all up in it, like they're used to it. Like they're tough. Right. Spend a stint inside, and you'll soon find out you don't know tough.

But Gemma wasn't going to come back. Her pity came with too high a price.

She held open her arms, but I avoided her chummy hug and instead sat down three feet away from her. Her face soured. Kat chortled. I flipped her off.

"What do you want?"

"Jesus, Mac. I'm your friend? Remember?"

"Really. History might argue."

"Give me a break. Please."

"Why should I? My sister is dead. I'm in jail. You're living outside. I don't know you anymore."

"Mac. Can we please just talk?"

"Isn't that what we're doing?"

"Actually, you're talking. You're blaming me for everything."

"Well, aren't you to blame? I mean, it was your pot. You kept pressing me. So, who else? Me? Tessa? She

was a baby, Gem. A fucking baby and now she's dead."
I couldn't control my mouth, my pain. I was in on a
bum rap, one Gemma should've been serving.

Gemma cried. Handily, she'd thought about
bringing a wad of tissue. It made me wonder if she'd
left any in the box. She collected four sheets and
offered them to me.

"Wipe your nose," she said. Then blew her nose
with four of her own.

"Why do you always use four at a time?" I said, my
voice shaky with tears.

"Do I?" she asked.

We both laughed.

"Every fucking time," I said.

"Oh man. I do, don't I?" She laughed harder. I'd
pay for it later, too, we two sitting there crying like
babies. She straddled the bench, slid closer, and pulled
me into a hug.

"I'm so sorry, Mac. For everything. Everything
flipped on its head. I'm so sorry."

When I let go of Gemma, I spotted CO Linnea
wiping her dweeby face. What a loser. I shook my
head, like, *really*? She held up her hands, surrendering,
and shrugged her shoulders.

I said, "Need a tissue, CO Linnea?"

Everyone in the room looked over and started to
laugh.

"Real funny," CO Linnea said. "Thank you, no."
She reached into a pocket and pulled out one of those
blue car-window-washing paper towels. "Have my

own." She blew into it, wiped her nose twice, and pressed it back into her pocket. Gross.

"Can you help me?" I said to Gem. "I can't remember."

"Remember? Like what?"

"About the day. Tessa . . . you know . . . like, I can't remember crying. I mean, the details come in flashes, but there are huge gaping holes."

"You cried all right. I called you every day, and every day you were crying. Or cried to me, anyway, on the phone."

"You called?"

"Oh, God. Mac. Every. Single. Day. You don't remember?"

"It's all big blanks," I said.

"Look," Gemma said. "I came to visit but also to bring good news. But I can't promise anything," she said, and paused.

"What?"

"Well, okay, but don't get your hopes up. Okay?"

"What," I demanded. I was tiring of the back and forth.

"I found April."

I closed my eyes and let the words flow over my tarnished skin. The sweetest thing I'd heard in months. April's face, her fur, her form danced in a vignette for me alone. A gift. Gemma had come bearing one gift. A salvation. She found April.

I opened my eyes. Gemma wasn't smiling. "How is she?"

"Well, they say she's fine."

"You don't believe them? Who the hell is *they*? You don't have her?"

"I just found her." She sounded defensive. "They really love her, Mac."

"She's my cat, Gem!"

"It's been six months."

"I don't give a flying fuck if it's six years. She's mine. My dad will keep her with him. I want her back!" I stood. Slid a hand over my hairnet. Gemma's hair was so pretty and loose, light, flyaway like always, matching her freckled skin. Her hazel eyes shifted to the others around the room, checking if anyone noticed. Her irises shone glassy, the whites veiny.

"You're high?"

"I couldn't ask them to give her away."

"Why not? You *scared*? You fucking baby. You should be in here. Have a gang of girls attacking you on a regular basis!" I let visual settle upon her. I refused to release our gaze.

And when she placed a hand over her mouth, I knew she realized what I meant.

"That's right. It's been a real picnic. Call me a punching bag for sluts."

I guess the information startled her because she bolted up and ran out the door. And what stays with me most about her leaving is that not once did she glance back before letting the door close behind her.

PART THREE
the end

"Grief is the price we pay for love." —Queen
Elizabeth II

44

The Upward Turn
MacKenzie

Solitary confinement is its own special kind of hell.
Even so, sometimes the solitude can be freeing. Other

times, the walls constrict around you. You feel so claustrophobic, you think you'll suffocate.

Four windowless walls make rooms in solitary. Word around the block is there are as many solitary rooms as there are beds in the facility. Just in case.

Guards deliver three meals a day through a slot in the door that lifts inward. They place the tray on a ledge outside before pushing it through the three by twelve-inch-wide slot.

At first, I didn't eat. Not because I wanted to protest in some fast, due to inhumane conditions or injustice. No, it was nothing like that. I just didn't have the stomach for food. I lost weight within three days. My baggy uniform told the tale.

The fourth night, I thought I saw Jesus. I know. I know. A spiritual message? But the sighting wasn't all that holy. He was standing there, glowing amid the darkness of my room, kitty-cornered to my cot, and downing a can of beer, slurping and belching the same way Mr. Painter did once when he took me on a ride around the yard on his mower.

Jesus even offered me one. It was Heineken, which brought up many questions. Like, really? *German* beer? But then he spoke, and my question fizzled.

"You have to eat something," He said to me. I capitalize the word *he* because He's Jesus, for Christ's sake. Then He added, "Beer's got nutritional value. They used to drink it on long-haul ships across the Atlantic to the *new* world." He put emphasis on the word *new* and rolled His eyes in a most Un-Jesus-like and sardonic manner.

"What's wrong with new?" I asked.

"Like they thought they were traveling to heaven," He said.

And if anyone could read someone's thoughts, Jesus could. Right?

Which made me say, "Can you read my thoughts?"

"What do you think?" He chuckled, sipped more beer out of the can. Burped.

"What do *I* think? Can't you just suck the answers out of my brain? Don't you already know my thoughts before I ask them? Anyway, I'm tired of talking. Let's do this whole Q&A this way: I will listen to you, what, telepathically, right? And you listen to me so neither of us need expend any energy. Okay?"

"Sure. We can play it that way, I guess. But, in my experience…" He paused and took another swig of beer, burped again, and went on. "Humans don't remember what they think about as much as what they say."

"Well," I replied, "you're most likely some hallucination I'm creating in my brain anyway, so, let's do a Q&A with *me* thinking up questions and *you* answering them aloud. How does that sound, Jesus?"

He crouched down in the corner, the glow from his body sliding down with him. He placed his beer on the floor, settled down next to the beer, and crossed his legs—Mahatma Ghandi style.

"Go," He said, prompting me to begin my questioning.

"Why the hell is this happening to me?"

"Why shouldn't it?" He asked. "Are you better than anyone else?"

"I hate that philosophical notion: Why NOT you? It doesn't help my attitude. I'm not amused."

He lifted his shoulders, tipped his head. "You asked. Sorry if it offends." Then He said, "Next?"

"Why did Tessa have to die"? But before He could say, "Why shouldn't she?" I thought, *Don't go there with the why shouldn't she crapola, Mister.* "The bigger picture answer, please. That's what I want to know. What good was there in Tessa dying?"

"I'm not authorized to reveal big picture concepts to humans."

"Oh, give me a break. Like your dad isn't going to forgive you. After all you've done. The crucifixion and all."

He squinted. "I remember how I died."

I rolled my eyes.

He answered after giving my question about Tessa some time. "Tessa's death was a stop-gap measure. Her purpose had been fulfilled."

What the hell is a stop-gap measure?

My hands began to shake. I sat up in bed and leaned against the wall. My legs mirroring Jesus' position. Before I could cry or yell or pound my fists, Jesus spoke again. "Look, if you can't handle the answers, we can quit. You wanted to know. That's the answer."

I cried anyway. Jesus got a little uncomfortable. I think, because He downed the beer, crumpled the can, and set it on the floor.

Then He arose, came to me, sat on the bed, rubbed his hand across my forehead, and I fell asleep.

Near morning, the creaking of an outer door somewhere in the solitary facility caused me to stir. Through sleep-filled eyes, I spotted the beer can in the corner of the room but only momentarily until a dark-haired woman in a long, gauzy frock appeared. She wore a headpiece that looked something like a nun might wear under her habit. The frock cascaded to the floor and whooshed as she walked over to the can. She stuffed the can deep into a fold of her frock, glanced back, smiled, then walked to an exterior wall, slipped through it, and disappeared as easily as she'd appeared.

"This is nuts," I whispered.

"You say something, Fraser?" CO Madge had taken to calling me by my last name for my time in solitary like it was an added assault to call me by one name like a number.

Like, *you say something zero-zero-zero*? An apropos name for the opinion I had of myself.

"My hands are full. Pull open the slot," CO Madge said.

I looked through the narrow opening partly obscured by a plate of ham, eggs, toast, jelly, and a two-inch wide pouch of OJ.

CO Madge squinted. Still, I could make out a veiny redness in the whites of her eyes.

"You have to eat," she insisted. Her eyes flared, the red veins growing. Moisture trimmed her lower lashes. She repeated, "You have to eat."

"Aw," I chimed, "it's true. You *do* love me."

She clicked her tongue, shook her head, rolled her pathetic blood-streaked eyes out of my line of sight, and walked off.

45

Acceptance and Hope

Jesus didn't bother visiting again. But on my last day of solitary, someone knocked.

The clock mocked me. It wasn't time for breakfast, lunch, *or* dinner.

"Yeah?" I called through the door but got no answer. I called out louder. Again, no answer.

I grumbled and got off my cot, "Come on . . ."

My mood swarmed from gloomy impatience to mild irritation.

"I said come in!" I lifted the metal tray flap. The ledge was empty, as I'd suspected, and no one was there. When I pressed my face against the opening, I could see each side of the door clearly but not below the ledge. That was the only possible place to hide, under the shelf.

"Okay," I said, "cut it out."

But nothing happened. No one jumped up in surprise. No one said anything, because no one was around. I almost spoke again when I spotted CO Linnea peeking through another door into the larger room where solitary confinement rooms are located. From my vantage point, she was only now sticking the key into the lock. Because when she entered, she called out, "How long have you been there?"

It could've been my question. Instead, I said, "Is anyone else in here?"

CO Linnea made a 360-degree scan of the room.

She shook her head in an I-don't-know-what-you-mean way. "Why?" She approached my door and fumbled with the keys.

"No one's under the tray shelf?"

She stepped back. "Here?" she said, pointing down at her feet.

I nodded.

"No. If they are, I'm standing on them," she replied and tried hard to hide her confusion. "What's going on? You okay?"

I stumbled to the cot. My knees shook. My hands shook. When CO Linnea entered, she rushed to me.

"You're totally white." She placed one hand on my forehead. It felt heavenly to be touched in kindness. I began to gulp in big sucking pockets of air. "Hold on." She lifted her walky-talky, depressed the call button,

and said, "Solitary three. Stat." She released her thumb
from the button and clipped the walky-talky back onto
her belt, then grabbed my left wrist and checked my
pulse. "God. Your heart is racing. What happened?"

Footsteps thundered outside the solitary ward.
Several locks unlatched and a herd of feet slapped
louder as they neared my cell.

CO Makeela and CO Cammy rushed in. CO Linnea
moved out of the way but kept her eyes pinned on me.

CO Makeela carried a white and red medic bag.
From it, she pulled a stethoscope and blood pressure
cuff.

They began talking with soothing voices. "Okay,
Mac. We gotcha, kiddo. You're okay now." And,
"Let's just get this cuff around your arm. She was
pumping up the cuff, tightening it around the lower part
of my upper arm when my head began to swim.

"Her eyes," CO Linnea warned.

"Shit. She's gonna crash," CO Cammy announced.

And that was that.

Next thing I recall, I awoke in the infirmary hooked
up to an electric blood pressure machine that checked
not only my BP, as the nurses said, but also my heart
rate and temperature. Every so often, the machine
dinged. As my eyes began to adjust to the surroundings,
I spotted CO Linnea sitting in a chair against the wall.
She was poking around on her cell phone, giggling at
something.

"FaceTiming?" I asked. My throat felt stiff and
raspy.

Relief flooded her eyes and her cheeks lifted into a dimpled grin. "You're awake."

"What happened?"

"You passed out. Scared the shit out of me, Mac."

"You're not supposed to swear."

"Yeah, well you're not supposed to pass out." CO Linnea came to my bed and stood by my right side, then placed her hand in mine. "I'm just happy you didn't puke." She giggled and her smile filled her face from cheek to cheek.

"Me too."

"So, what happened?" she asked.

"Jesus. Someone."

I wanted to tell her but knew how stupid it would sound.

"Someone what?"

The Jesus part was lost on her. She was prompting me to finish when CO Makeela walked in.

"You awake?"

"I think so," I said.

CO Makeela carried an iPad. She punched something into it, then continued to talk. "You gave us a scare, girlfriend. Scared my butt good."

"I didn't think anything scared you, CO Makeela. What, with all those rings on your fingers. A bejeweled set of brass knuckles, they are."

"Gotta husband 'at adores me. What do I do?" She winked.

"I'm just surprised. What with the blood-and-guts job you all have," I added.

CO Makeela glanced at CO Linnea and shook her head. "Blood-and-guts," she said. She went back to checking the monitors, punched the face of her iPad a few more times. Then said, "Blood pressure's almost back to normal. Heart rate, too." She freed a hand, placed it on her round hip like she was the queen of the infirmary. "What got up in your head that made you fall down?"

"You sure have a way with words, Makeela. And I don't know what happened. One minute I was awake. The next? Not so much."

"It's CO Makeela, by the way. So, why're you not eating?"

"I ate breakfast—eggs, toast, the usual."

"You dehydrated?"

"I don't think so. Maybe. I drank my OJ."

She squinted. "You pregnant?"

"What!?" I rolled my eyes. "Now, how the hell am I supposed to get pregnant? Immaculate conception? Last I heard, you need a sperm donor for that. Have things changed so much since I've been inside?"

CO Linnea laughed at me and my outburst.

"She's feeling better, Keela," Linnea said.

"Damn right she is." She uncuffed the BP machine, "Think you can sit up without keelin' over again?"

I pressed against the mattress into a half-sitting, half-lying position to make sure I wouldn't get dizzy. "Yeah. I think so."

"Need to pee?" Makeela asked.

"I can try. It'd be nice to wash my face."

"K," Makeela said. "But you're not walking. Gotta get you to a toilet in a transport chair. Can't have you falling over again. It'd make me look bad."

"God forbid," I said.

"God forbid is right." She leaned in and pressed her lips against my forehead, and whispered through the kiss, "Scared the shit out of us, girl." She pulled back, her eyes glassy and soft.

"You ladies sure cuss a lot. And in front of the residents? Tsk. Tsk." I waggled a finger at Makeela.

"Wait here," she said. "I gotta get that chair. I'm also bringing you another OJ and a 20-ouncer of H_2O. I want you to drink both before we get you to the bathroom. Deal?"

"Deal . . . Keela." We were never supposed to call the guards by their names.

"I'm gonna mark you up for that." Makeela winked. "Next time," she said. Then she walked out.

Linnea scooted the chair over to my bed and patted the shin of my leg through the covers. She was giving me a big toothy grin. Then she got up and followed Makeela out.

And although I felt better physically, I couldn't shake the eerie feeling, wondering who had knocked at my door.

46

Reconstruction and Working Through

"Oh," she said, "I almost forgot. Your new roomie," she was saying all of this with the door closed between us. "She'll be here," she checked her watch, "in three days at 1600 hours, checked in by 1630, so pick a bunk between now and then."

"What?" I asked. "I thought she wasn't coming for another *ten* days." My whiny tone lingered.

"Family issues. Needed early entry." Then, she added, "Happens. Be ready."

I wasn't sure if she meant make room for her or ready yourself for a real creep, but when I asked? Crickets.

CO Madge was on to the next room, knocking on that door, calling for my neighbors, "Breakfast!" Then she tracked back to me and said, "And make a bed for her! Better sooner than later!" Her words trailed down the hallway, dissipating as she walked out of the residency, followed by the telltale heavy clack of the door as she headed toward wherever the hell CO Madge went next.

Right after, CO Linnea knocked. "I thought you might like this book," she said as she popped her head inside my door and handed me *Help! Thanks! Wow!* by Anne Lamott.

Which, after reading the back-cover blurb, I said, "Christian stuff?"

"Lamott is a Jew but promotes some great Christianity in her work."

"Oh, good gravy. No." I shook my head and tried to hand the book back.

I hated everyone's newfound attention for me. All this Jesus-God stuff was beginning to freak me out. But Linnea refused to take the book back, so I tossed it to the foot of the bed onto a slope of blankets.

"Actually," she said, "not a choice. It's part of your recovery. Read it and report back by Tuesday next week. If you hate it, fine. I don't really care. Whatever, you know? But something tells me we're more alike than not, and I sort of wanted to know what you thought about it."

"I get out of here in two weeks. How about I send you an email?"

"Funny. Real funny. Read it, or I'll sit in here and read it to both you and your new roomie for the next week."

Linnea was halfway out the door when she turned back, touched her watch, and mouthed, "One week." She got a serious look on her face, pointed her fingers back and forth between her eyes and mine like she wasn't messing around. Then she said, "I mean it, Fraser. I'm going to be checking on you. You and your status, asking questions. Got it?"

"Fine," I conceded.

"Oh," she added, "you have a guest. She's waiting for you."

"Who?"

Linnea lifted her shoulders. I didn't rush to find out. Most likely Gemma with an April update on how well my cat is doing with her new family. Instead of going to the cafeteria, I flipped the pages of the book to the first chapter. It read:

It is all hopeless. Even for a crabby optimist like me, things couldn't be worse. Everywhere you turn, our lives and marriages and morale and government are falling to pieces. So many friends have broken children. The planet does not seem long for this world. Repent! Oh, wait, never mind. I meant: Help.

Linnea popped back into the room, interrupting the next line by calling from the hallway, "She's waiting!"

"Fine. What do you want from me? Read? Or visit?"

"I want you to put some hustle in it. That's what I want," Linnea instructed.

I guess she wanted to walk me to the cafeteria. Plus, I think she was still a little worried I might faint again. We'd gone to calling my little fainting spell an *episode*.

She wore her hair pulled back in a knot high atop her head. I studied the hues, banded as if she'd thrown it up in a rush and ran out the door. I examined how each section changed colors, how the colors seemed lighter than I remembered, how gray had found its way from the crown of her head to her temples and ran along the trim behind her ear like spun silver. It was as if the edge of her hair was beachfront and her pink-toned skin was the waters spilling off in all directions away from the changing sands.

"You going in?" Linnea questioned. All proud of herself and sporting a shit-eating grin.

I didn't move. Didn't speak. I wanted to remember this moment for the rest of my life, taking in the cafeteria smells—grilled cheese sandwiches and something sweet, perhaps cherry pie. Yes. Cherries, in cherry syrup and sweetened pie crust. My stomach danced with the aromas but went vacant and sick, thinking about putting anything into my mouth. Maybe she had intended to stay and eat with me. And as the notion crossed my mind, she straightened her back and placed one hand onto her stomach. A mom tell. She could *eat a horse*.

The sun sashayed in and out through a series of elongated windows that easily stretched four feet tall from top to bottom and two yards wide. Nice airy windows, green tinted with standard-issue wire hatching through each pane and backed up by bars outside. Shadows from the bars darkened and lit as clouds passed in front of the sun. The bars were a constant reminder that there'd be no escapes from the everyday hell here at Camp Dread and Loathing.

"Mac," Linnea whispered, "you can't just stand out here all day. She's waiting to see you."

"Why?"

"Why?" her voice rang back, incredulous with impatience.

"Why now?" I clarified.

"Who knows?"

"I do," I said. "Guilt. That's why."

I turned to leave, but Linnea grabbed my upper arm. "You'll regret this decision every day of your life."

"How the hell do *you* know!" I didn't care who heard. And sure enough, Mom turned to the door. "After seventeen months? Now she shows up? Screw her." Our eyes met through the tiny door window. Then I broke away, wrestled my arm out of Linnea's grip, and left.

My life had been altered unchangeably. A cage will do that to a person. I had needed a mother. What I had gotten was her absence.

47

The Showers Make Me Feel Dirty

I arose before dawn with a sinister vibe curled around my throat. A foul mood snuck in and tightened my chest when the image of Tessa running down the hall crying woke me.

Why? What did Mom say to make her cry?

My vision was still blurry but managed to see every item I owned—a brush, standard-issue shoes with no laces, the jumpsuit, even the items in the sink. Each lay precisely where I'd placed them the night before.

I'd started my period and placed a twenty pack of tampons and a plastic sack of mini pads in the sink. Starting your period in here is a true blessing because no one will bother you when you're ragging. The iodine odor told me I needed to change my tampon. Added protection of the pad helped me not mess my sheets— a trick, a bit of Mom wisdom.

After cleaning up and brushing my teeth, I wiped a hot washcloth over my face and called it good. After slipping out of my pjs and back into my standard orange jumpsuit, I sat on the lower bunk and chuckled, thinking how pissed off Therese would be to see me on her bed.

A knock at the door and CO Madge snarled out, "Breakfast, Mac."

"Whatever," I said in a most half-hearted way.

In the room adjacent to mine, a loud thump vibrated against the wall. They were at it again—Vannice and Torrey. Most likely the fight before raping Vannice again, a way to get a good hungry on for breakfast. I'd be able to tell by the look on Torrey's face when I saw her. Vannice's too. This place was disgusting, and no one cared enough to change it.

One particularly nasty go with Kat, I said I'd out her to CO Madge. Kat's response was, "CO Madgey's my sugar momma. What she gonna do but give me that pudgy love she give so freely." I have no idea why Kat insisted on talking like some hip-hop star, seeing how she was Caucasian, but she did.

I had been keeping my distance from the Bitches and, thank Jesus himself, they'd left me alone for once. Guess they were gearing up to see the new girl. That poor unsuspecting simp.

Dad brought *The White Deer* to me on one of his visits. Said Mom was clearing out some things. Trying to forget how Mom was reaming out Tessa's room, probably like she had mine, I decided to read Tessa's favorite book.

"Have you read this book?" Dad had asked.

"Tessa's." I reached for the book. My hand quivered. I checked to see if Dad had seen.

"Your mom's going through her room. She said she doesn't want it to become, as she put it, '*Some shrine to a poor little dead girl, like some crazy parents have who've lost a child.*'" His eyes glistened.

I changed the subject. "A long time ago," I said.

"What?" He'd forgotten what he asked me.

"The book. I read it a while back. Once."

Dad pinched the brim of his nose, "Well, it's yours now. She always brought it with her. Read it all the time."

I replied, "Every. Single. Night."

He chuckled. "At home, too, huh?"

I nodded. "I miss her so bad." I wasn't sure he'd heard me because he didn't speak right away. He shifted his leg over the bench into his usual straddle. Then, nodding, he touched his heart and mouthed, "Me too." No voice. No breath. Only sign language. He knew the rules. No emotions. Not here. Not in front of other residents.

"Your mother and I have decided…" and he was about to go on, but I couldn't bear to hear that they were planning to finalize their separation and file for divorce. Not right then.

I shook my head, stood ready to sprint, stuffed the book under my arm, and walked off, not waiting for him to finish. My heart couldn't take another strain. I felt like the world was barreling down on me.

What I really wanted was to hide away and read a little. Back in my hole, while standing at the door, I tossed Tessa's book onto the top bunk. I decided to reclaim it. But I threw the book harder than I thought. It hit the wall and slid down behind the lower bunk and landed on the floor under the bed.

"Good fucking crap." My randy mouth was getting randier with each passing day.

Dropping to my knees, it appeared to be stuck flat against the wall, so I lay on the floor and slid my body as far as I was able under the bed, but my head was too big to fit. So, while wrestling my hand around fishing for the book's spine, I cut my hand on something sharp.

"Shit!" I yanked out my hand. My little finger had a slice in it an inch long and was bleeding. "Shit, shit, shit." My teeth clenched with the pain.

I struggled to get up and ran into the bathroom. The cut required two bandages. Retracing my steps, droplets formed a trail like a sign pointing *THIS WAY* to the bunk beds. I wasn't about to reach under there again, not with whatever the hell cut me still so close to the book. Instead, I muscled the metal bunks out from the wall, giving me a foot, and picked up the shiv. It shone in my hand like the Holy Grail. But when the door clicked open, I snapped the book closed and hid the weapon. Then, I pushed the bed back against the wall and did quick work on the blood trail. I still had a wad of paper towels in my hand when . . .

"Breakfast!" CO Madge's fat face was wedged between the door and the jamb. "How many times do I have to tell you to get your butt up and to the cafeteria?"

I snuck my hand behind my back and stuffed the paper towels into my waistband. "You said to clean the room."

"Don't lie to me. You were reading." Her eyes dropped to the book in my hand. I lifted my hands in a surrender gesture. "You don't get your butt outta here, I'll confiscate that thing. When I tell you to do something, do it. Now, get your butt to the cafeteria. Pronto!"

"Yes ma'am," I said, grabbed Tessa's book—shiv and all—off the bunk, stuffed it under my armpit, and raced out the door before CO Madge had a chance to snatch it. With Madge, her moods turned from loathing to lust in a flash. Action was key with Madge. If she pinned you in somewhere, you were meat. Her meal for the day.

I was sprinting down the hall when she called out. "You can't run from a shower, young lady, and yours is tomorrow morning. I'm on." She giggled. Her voice turned syrupy, beckoning like a wanton woman. My feet slowed to a skip as I got away from her.

With the shiv.

"You look like a wet cat," CO Madge declared as she opened the shower stall.

I spun to see her lascivious mouth dripping with saliva. I tried to cover myself, but how do you cover yourself with nothing but a bar of soap and a washcloth? I slung the cloth over my breasts. My hands formed a fig leaf in front of my crotch, knees bent, feet flared.

"Get out!" I barked.

"Now, now, little one." She unbuckled her belt and stepped into the stall. Wrenching my hands back behind me, the washcloth dropped away, and CO Madge slipped the belt around my wrists.

"Let's give a taste, shall we?" She slipped her hand high between my legs.

Her touch was rough and cruel. She went further than Therese ever did. I felt something tear inside me. The pain buckled me. I cried out, but had no fight left and dropped to the floor. Water from the shower curled off my wet hair and mingled with my tears.

When she was done, she issued a warning. "Don't you say a word. Understand me? You do? It will be the last thing you ever say."

After she blotted the front of her uniform with my towel, she closed the stall door but waited in the bathroom.

I forced myself up and out on legs that felt stringy and weak. CO Madge was sitting near the door, eyeing me. I was a cornered rat ready to scurry off across the floor, and the ugly, fat cat sat steadying itself, muscles shivering, ready to pounce. I managed to towel myself off and slip into my clothes.

"Come on, cookie. Let's get you back to your room." She sounded almost normal like she'd done nothing wrong. Like it had vaporized from her memory bank.

I didn't cry on the way back to my room, and thank God, the new girl wasn't there.

"Remember what I said," Madge reminded me, "Say a word, and . . ."

I clambered onto my bunk and pulled Tessa's book from under the pillow. "Madge," I said.

"That's CO Madge, resident!"

"CO Madge," I corrected myself. "Therese," I said.

"What about 'er?"

"She left me a present."

"Aw. Now, wasn't that chummy of her."

"Wanna see?" I said as if I liked her and wanted to get to know her better. Like I wanted to be her pet.

CO Madge walked in, leaving the door agape, closing the distance tentatively between us. She didn't trust me. She was the one who shouldn't be trusted, but maybe by then, Madge was feeling a little leery herself, sensing that I might have become indoctrinated to this place, learned some tricks to survive inside this holy hell.

"It's okay," I said. I sort of smiled. Sort of flirted with her. The snare was cast. The trick worked because she sauntered straight up to the bed and leaned against it to see my gift, Therese's gift to me.

"It's in here," I said, and opened *The White Deer*.

Time slowed. Became 16 mm film not quite up to speed. I grabbed the shiv too fast and nicked my palm but didn't care. The pain was exquisite compared to what I'd suffered in the showers.

I raised the shiv fast.

Madge's eyes plated open.

Before she could react, I jammed the point into her cheek. She screamed. Fell backward, grappling to hold together the loose skin on her face. To stop the blood flow. She fumbled for the emergency buzzer on her pager.

I knew I was dead. Assaulting an officer would land me into an adult facility. There was only one recourse, and I took matters into my own hands. I steadied the shiv, took one deep breath in, and jammed the blade into my arm once, twice, three times. A spray of warm blood released, and with it flowed all the horrors of juvie.

Madge began to scream. She said, "Help!" Over and over.

I slumped low onto my pillow and closed my eyes. I felt the shiv slip out of my hand to the floor and shatter, its shards mixing with dust and blood on the floor.

48

Call 9-1-1
CO Linnea

CO Linnea raced into the room. "What the hell?"

Blood trickled between each finger pressed against Madge's face. She held a sharp object in the other hand.

Blood everywhere.

Mac lay in the top bunk unconscious.

Blood. Everywhere.

Mac's arm hung off the bunk mid-air as though begging for alms.

Linnea strained to keep her voice steady, her lips pressed against the speaker, the walkie-talkie shaking. "Call 9-1-1. Stat! Room seven!"

She checked for a pulse. It was faint.

At some point before Linnea arrived, Madge had noosed a pillowcase around Mac's bicep immediately above her elbow to help stop the bleeding.

"Mac, can you hear me?" Linnea said. She placed a hand onto Mac's brow and smoothed down her hair as she examined her. "Why is her hair wet?" Linnea asked and checked her pulse again. The question went unanswered. She glanced over her shoulder. Madge was sitting on the floor against a desk. She knelt down next to Madge. "You okay?"

Blood. Everywhere.

She assumed the blood on Madge was from Mac but then saw more blood seeping through Madge's fingers. When she lifted Madge's hand from her face, Linnea gasped. The skin on her cheek was flayed open. Pink and white flesh lay gashed open, showing like white rice and tomato sauce.

"Jesus!" Linnea cried.

Madge's eyes were glassy. She needed to get back to Mac, but Madge needed attention too.

She jumped up when she heard the door into the residencies unlock and creak as it opened. A drumbeat of feet approached Room seven, and EMTs filled the small quarters.

The lead ordered Linnea and Madge out. Madge tried to stand but slumped back onto the floor. Linnea helped her up and guided her to a chair outside the room. One of the EMTs followed. The other, the lead, tended to Mac. The male EMT examined Madge and tended to her wound.

"You're gonna need stitches. This will stop the bleeding temporarily." He swabbed the area with quick-drying povidone-iodine, then peeled sterile packaging from a thick, shiny swatch of gauze and pressed firmly. Madge winced at the pressure against her cheek. "Sorry," he said. "Can you walk?"

Madge nodded and reached for Linnea.

"Take her to the ambulance," he said. "Seat her. Do not lay her down. The right-side bench looking in. We'll be there momentarily. If she starts to bleed, apply pressure. I have to help with the girl." Linnea assisted Madge, holding her by the arm as she led her down the hall.

The small girl from Kat's group had shown up. Linnea glanced at her and wondered if she'd ever heard her speak. Was she mute? Crow, she remembered. With a name like that, you'd think she'd be chatty. The girl stood as though glued to the wall, pressing one thumb between her teeth. "Nothing here. Go to your room," Linnea said.

The girl dropped both hands to her side but didn't obey the order. She was glaring at Madge.

"What the hell happened?" Linnea asked her fellow guard.

Madge wasn't responding. She was in a limbo of shock. Linnea had seen it before. Shock affected people in different ways, and Madge had gone dull. But Linnea asked again, pressing her, "Madge." She jerked her arm and spun Madge to face her. "What happened?"

Madge lifted a hand over her cheek. Her fingers danced over the compress. "Is she going to be all right?" Madge said.

"I don't know. There was a lot of blood." She asked again, "What *happened*?"

Madge squinted but winced. The lines around her eyes spread like spider legs that twitched her cheek and stung her wound. "Shit," Madge mumbled and pressed her hand flat onto the compress.

"This is the last time I'll ask, Madge, and then I don't know what I'll do."

"Stop pushing me," Madge demanded. Her shoulders jerked, she started to cry, then wrenched her arm out of Linnea's grip.

But Linnea wasn't having it. She pressed Madge against the wall, trying to keep her voice low. "What the *fuck* happened in there, Madge?"

"I don't remember."

"Bullshit. Her hair was wet. Why?"

"I guess she washed it."

"No residents go in or out of the showers without a CO. How did she get into the showers?"

"Maybe she washed her hair in the sink."

Linnea frowned. Didn't believe her. "How did you get hurt?"

"She freaked out and stabbed me. How the hell do I know what set her off. She's loony."

"If I know anything about Mac Fraser, I know she's *not* loony, Madge." Linnea pulled Madge off the wall and led her closer to where Crow was standing, nearer the residency exit. Linnea's hand was reaching for the doorknob as they were passing the small girl. And they were nearly out of the residency when the girl whispered. Linnea caught only a shred of her words, but it seemed Madge heard everything.

Madge flew at her. "Shut up, you stupid little bitch!" Madge said.

Linnea wrestled Madge's arm back and stopped her from reaching the girl. "What did you say? Crow, right?" The girl nodded. "What did you say?" Linnea said again.

"She's a freaking liar!" Madge said, trying to drown out what Crow was saying.

"Quiet. Or I'll arrest you for cause right here. Right now," Linnea threatened.

Madge demurred. Her breathing picked up. Tears welled in her eyes.

The girl, Crow, repeated quieter than before, but to Linnea her words resounded like a bullhorn.

"Madge showered her." Crow's thumb returned to her mouth. She couldn't have been older than thirteen, fourteen maybe. The slope of her shoulders owned a memory of preadolescence, her breasts forming bumps. Her carbon hair straight. Freshly washed but drying. Her skin showed no signs of acne with peach tones shimmering under a light fuzz. Not a drop of teenager oiliness around her nose or forehead, not a sign on her chin. And yet, her black eyes smoldered with a knowledge well advanced of her age.

"Showered her?" Linnea said. Madge protested, interrupted. Denied and yelled over Crow's words.

"Shut up, bitch!" Madge blurted, her jaw bending under her wrath. "You'll pay for this, you little sniveling piece of shit."

Crow's eyes filled and overflowed. "It's true!" she said. Then what seemed like years of pent-up information came spilling out. "She. Showers. Us!" Tears warbled her words. Pain lacing each syllable. "She did Mac this morning."

"Liar! You little bitch."

"I saw you. I saw!" Crow slumped to the floor and tucked her knees tight into her chest, then laid her head onto the dips between her knees and bawled.

Linnea glared at Madge. "You. Come with me." She jerked Madge toward the exit of the building and out front where the ambulance was parked. The doors hung wide enough to fit a gurney, two EMTs, and a visitor into the back. Two long metal benches ran along opposing sides. Linnea assisted Madge inside the ambulance and seated her where Madge began to crumple.

"Need help?" A voice from the front beckoned and an ambulance driver slid open the window between the two sections of the vehicle.

"I got it," Linnea said. And he slid the window closed again. Linnea reminded Madge, "Don't lie down. Do, and you'll bleed out."

Madge leaned into the corner. "I feel woozy," she said.

"I don't give a flying you-know-what." Then she decided against what she was going to say, and said, "Fine. Lie down. Bleed out for all I care."

"I'm hurt and you're being mean."

Linnea shoved her face so close to Madge's she could smell the onion on her breath from dinner the night before.

"You did something to Mac. You have *me* to contend with now."

"Yeah?" Madge mocked Linnea. "You going to beat me up. You and that scrawny little ass of yours," she chortled.

Linnea didn't think she had it in her. Never thought she could intentionally harm someone, but at that moment, she grabbed Madge by the arm, pushed her flat, then gouged a knuckle into her injured cheek. Madge belched out in pain. Blood blossomed under the patch.

"Worse, Madge," she said, "much worse than beat you up. I'm gonna have your career." With that, Linnea yanked Madge back up into a sitting position. "Oh, dear." Linnea scrunched her nose. "Looks bad. You're bleeding again."

A loud crash sounded at the entrance and the doors flew open. Both EMTs jogged, rolling Mac to the ambulance. Linnea stepped out and said, "She's bleeding again."

"I was afraid of that," the male EMT said. He jumped inside and helped pull Mac's gurney in. Then turned to check Madge's face and began fussing with her while the other EMT readied Mac, strapping her down for the drive.

Madge glanced past the EMT's shoulder and before the female closed the doors, Linnea's eyes locked onto Madge's, and she mouthed, *you're busted.*

49

Realizing You're not Perfect
Uma

Gemma's words garbled through an uncontrollable stream. Uma could only focus on the girl's curls, the carrot color of her hair, which appeared shorter since the last time she'd seen Mac's friend.

God. Was it already nearly two years since Tessa died? Mac's time in detention would be up in, what, one or two months? Uma had experienced moments where she'd lost track of time. Today, standing there looking at Gemma in her doorway, she thought of how she'd also lost track of the daughter she still had. Gemma looked more mature but still had a childlike drama to the words spilling out of her mouth.

Uma interrupted her, "Good lord, Gemma. Settle down. Your drama isn't appreciated."

Gemma flinched at the insult but repeated herself. "But you have to *do* something!"

Uma stepped away from the door, leaving it open for Gemma, and walked into the kitchen. It was no surprise Gemma followed her inside.

"Shut the door, Gemma," Uma called over her shoulder.

Gemma pushed the door but didn't let up. "Mrs. Fraser," she continued, "you *have* to do something."

"What do you want *me* to do?" The request came out insincere. Uma swallowed, suppressing her anger. Gemma stood a few feet away and close enough for Uma to tell she'd been smoking pot. Her clothes were saturated with the smell.

"Talk to somebody. The prosecutors," Gemma rambled on.

"And what do you think I should tell them? That Mac is unhappy. She doesn't like jail so much. Come on." Uma rolled her eyes, then went on, "You girls think you're so smart. You think you're adults. You have no idea. You've barely started your periods, and you think you know everything about everything. About everyone. Well, guess what, young lady, the world doesn't rotate on your ridiculous immature whims and wishes. It's filled with real human problems. It's not a game you download on your phone. The world is filled with sadness. Shit that grabs you by the neck and drop-kicks you in the ass. Knocks the life right out of you. And you know the worst of it? You don't die. That would be too easy. No. Instead, you just keep on living. Which, by the way, doesn't mean you don't *want* to die. That you don't want to take a knife and shove it into your stomach to stop the pain. That you don't want to jump in front of an oncoming truck. Hang yourself from a tree. Because," Uma paused, took in a deep breath of air and screamed at Gemma, "You. Do! You want to die! Every *fucking* day!"

Gemma's eyes reddened. Pools of tears leached onto each shaft of her lashes, turning them a ruddy orange shade. She didn't dare blink. Losing equilibrium, Uma grappled behind her for something to steady herself. Then she turned away, leaned against the counter and tightened her arms around her waist. After a moment, she turned back to Gemma, who was wiping her face. She reached out, but Gemma balked. Uma took her by the shoulders, then pulled Gemma in.

"I'm sorry, Gem." Uma said. Her chin next to Gemma's ear. "I'm so sorry."

"Mrs. Fraser," Gemma begged, "you have to understand." Uma held her tight as Gemma spoke again. "None of this is Mac's fault. You have to know the truth. It wasn't Mac's fault." She paused then said, "It's mine."

Uma's brow furrowed. She pushed Gemma out of the embrace and stared into her eyes, searching them, trying to understand. "What are you talking about?"

"We didn't even see Mr. Pauling until it was too late."

Uma lifted her eyes to the ceiling in frustration. "You were making a drug deal. Mac was selling you pot laced with opium. Isn't that how she got the money?"

Gemma was shaking her head no.

"No?" Uma questioned.

Gemma continued to shake her head no and lowered her face.

"What?" Uma was demanding an answer now.

But Gemma froze, went silent.

"What, I said!" Uma grabbed her shoulders and shook her hard enough to make Gemma stumble back. "Tell me!"

Gemma toppled into a kitchen chair. "No. They got it wrong."

"Who got what wrong, Gemma? Stop screwing with me or so help me God, you're out of here."

Gemma's shoulders began to quake. She began to moan then pulled in a silent pocket of air and cried with no sound. She breathed out a tumbling set of words through a tidal wave of sobbing. Uma dropped to the floor in front of Gemma.

"Okay, Gemma, settle down. Settle down. Tell me slowly."

Uma got up, poured tap water into a tumbler, and wrapped Gemma's hand around it. "Take a sip and calm down." After she drank, Uma pressed her. "Now, from the beginning. Slowly. What happened?"

Gemma took two more sips then downed the entire glass of water. She wiped her mouth on the sleeve of her sweater. Uma softened. It was a girl's sweater, a waffle-weave cat sweater with dogs chasing the cats around a cream background over a series of green stripes. This girl in her kitchen was years away from being an adult.

When her gaze met Uma's, Gemma shook her head again, this time adding, "Mac wasn't lying. She was telling the truth." Her face crumpled and her shoulders jerked again with a suppressed sob. "The pot was mine. Well, Mom and Dad's. I didn't know it was different. I just grabbed a bag and was giving it to Mac to try, but she decided she didn't want to and was handing it back when everything happened. When Mr. Pauling…you know…" She placed both hands over her mouth as though she'd just revealed a national secret.

Uma's heart thumped. Her breathing went shallow. Her hands felt cold all of a sudden, colder than if she were standing in a snowstorm. Her blood seemed to stop flowing. Every thought seemed to catch on a craggy fragment like a jagged stick. A guttural squall melted out of her.

Knowing what was coming, Gemma pressed her back against the chair and closed her eyes when Uma slapped Gemma's face. The force of the strike caused a droplet of spittle to fly from her mouth. Then Uma struck her again.

50

Confronting the Perps

"Now, Gemma. Get in!" Uma commanded. She leaned over from the driver's seat and pushed the passenger door open.

"But my bike."

"Later. Now, get in! I'm taking you home."

Uma craned the steering wheel hard and left. The car recoiled off the curb and bounced each passenger to the right. When she squealed to a stop, the car sat half on and half off the front lawn and driveway of the Painters' home.

Uma killed the engine and faced Gemma. "Don't you dare say a thing," she said.

Gemma's face was red. If Uma needed a picture of fear, it was sitting right in front of her.

"Get out," Uma instructed, "and remember, if you say anything, you'll never see Mac again, so help me God."

Gemma ran to the door and disappeared inside. Uma could hear her mother calling her name. Deeper inside, a door slammed shut. Gemma's bedroom door, Uma figured.

Bob Painter showed up and stood behind the screen door. He scratched at the stubble of one cheek. "Stefi," he called to his wife somewhere behind him. When she showed up, he used his thumb, directing his wife's attention toward Uma, who hadn't yet gotten out of the car. Bob slipped out of sight, leaving Stefi behind the screen. After a few seconds, she raised her hands, like *what's going on?* When she lowered them, she wrapped her arms around her narrow torso.

Uma unbuckled her seatbelt, exited the car, closed the door, and leaned one hip against the front panel. The heat of the car soaked the cotton of her blue skirt.

"So," Uma finally spoke, "you could've told the PA but decided to do nothing?"

Stefi's face paled and she glanced back and grabbed the door as if she were about to close it. But Uma charged forward. By the time she reached the porch, Stefi had closed the interior door and snapped the lock.

Uma fumed. "You did nothing? You let them charge Mac with something she didn't do!" She yanked open the handle of the screen door and pounded on the door. "You talk to me, dammit! You talk to me!"

Finally, Stefi spoke, "Leave us alone, Uma." Her words were muffled, but Uma heard her clearly. The door couldn't drown out the fear in her voice.

"You still could say something. Tell them Mac is innocent. Tell them." She paused.

And Stefi interrupted, "What exactly? Huh? Tell them that it was my daughter's? Send my own daughter to juvie?"

"Where'd Gemma get it, Stef?"

"Go home, Uma."

"You fucking lowlife!"

Suddenly, Bob interrupted. "Hey, Uma. Enough." A few seconds passed. Then he said, "Look, if you don't get off our porch, I'm calling the sheriff."

"You know what, Bob?" she said, "You just do that. Call them. Right now. I'll sit here and wait, and when they get here, I'll tell them that you have opiate-laced marijuana in your possession. Probably a little coke too. Right, Bob? You do that. Call the cops. If they haul me away, they'll arrest your ass too. You'll lose everything and then what will happen to your precious *innocent* little Gemma? So, yeah . . . please, Bob. Call the cops, you sonofabitch."

But then a neighbor called out, "Hey, is everything all right over there?"

Uma charged down off the porch to see him. He was an older man who owned a gift shop in town. "It's none of your concern, sir. Go back in your house." She charged back up to the door. Bob had opened the interior door. Uma grabbed the handle of the screen, but it didn't budge.

"Uma, this is our life, our neighbors. Please. Just, please, go home."

"Your life? You want me to all of a sudden give one flying fuck about *your* life when my life has been ripped apart at the throat?" Tears burned her eyes, but she refused to give him the satisfaction of seeing her cry. Her words shook with anger. "You and *your* drugs have destroyed my life." She pounded a fist into her chest. "Destroyed us. And you think I care about *your* life?"

A distant siren let out two short bursts, *blip, blip,* and was approaching fast like it was coming from Court Street. She had less than a minute to get out.

"You call the cops, Stef? You bastards."

As soon as the words escaped, her cell buzzed in her pocket. She ran back to the car, opened the door, and checked the display. It was Skagit Hospital. By the time she sat down, she'd missed the call.

"This isn't over," she called to them. "You'll pay for this." Uma slammed the car door, jammed it into reverse, bumped back onto the street, and drove in the direction of the siren. When she made the first turn, Undersheriff Zac was cornering the Painters' road. She lifted a hand in recognition. Zac waved, and Uma pulled the steering wheel right and drove toward home.

51

The Second Call
Ben

When she answered, Uma's *hello* sounded tight. That's how Ben would describe it later. Tight, a tinny void of air sound echoing inside his truck from the hands-free setting. He could tell Uma was in her car. "Something's happened," he said. He ground a knuckle into his jaw. The kitchen counter supported his weight. He needed support.

"Why'd they call you?" Uma's voice was still tight. Rattled even.

"They're taking her to the hospital," he said. Then, "I don't know. Maybe because I visit."

The heat from her breath seemed to steam through the phone.

"What happened?"

"They're taking her to the hospital."

A pause delayed her next words. Then, she said, "What. Happened?"

He knew how she felt. That this couldn't be happening again. Uma's serious tone took on a grimness he hadn't heard since Tessa had been killed.

"I'm not sure," he said. "They didn't offer much but to say they'd meet us at Skagit Hospital."

"Is she alive?" There was fear in her voice.

"Far as I know."

He glanced out the window and noticed everything looked ordinary. The world wasn't ending. Birds flitted through the air, landing on perches. The wind tossed branches of trees. A ferry's horn echoed from the harbor in the distance. A car drove by, slowed, and turned. Life churned on as usual, with or without him wanting it to. With or without his children. His stomach gurgled. Pain shot through his gut. A surprise gasp escaped his lips, followed by a short moan. He choked it back, held a fist to his mouth but couldn't control his emotions. His daughter's life hung on a bough swinging between life and death.

He couldn't lose another child. No. He *wouldn't* lose another child. What kind of human being allows his child to die? A surge of weakness overwhelmed him, dropped him to his knees. And he screamed.

"Please God. Don't let this happen. Please. I'll do anything you want. *Anything*. Just please don't let Mac…" His voice shook when he whispered, "Die."

Her voice brought him back. "I'm heading to the ferry," she said.

"Un," he cleared his throat, "where are you now?"

"Turning back from Golf Course Road," she replied.

"Come here. I'll drive us."

"How will your love interest take that?"

"Uma." His voice shook from the jab. "Stop," he said, "just get here."

"Fine," she said, and a vacuum absorbed the space within the car, leaving him deaf with fear.

52

Flying
Mac

My body tingles. I float on a wave when they lift me off my bunk and place me flat onto a gurney. A man in a uniform cinches a rubber tourniquet around my bicep. On the bony side of the opposite hand, a woman wearing the same uniform sticks a needle into my vein. I know it should sting, but I don't feel it prick me. She props up a metal support and hangs a bag of fluid on a hook, then fiddles with the end of the tubing until it's attached to the needle in my hand.

"Got it?" The male asks.

"Ready," the woman replies.

The gurney bumps over the threshold and down the corridor as they run.

The gurney stops. The female stays behind, steadying the bag hanging on the metal arm while the man unlocks the door.

Crow is huddled near the residency entrance crying. I zip over and put my face next to hers. She ignores me. "Everything will be okay," I say. But she's still ignoring me. I zip onto the gurney and ride with my body after the man returns.

Away we go! Down the hall toward the main entrance.

CO Linnea is getting out of the ambulance when we arrive. CO Madge is positioned on a seat just inside the door, fear emanating around her like a ball of energy. Lots of fear—quivering lips, watery eyes, pale.

The legs of the gurney fold under itself when the bars hit the ambulance. Bump. Another bump and I'm fully inside. CO Madge is staring out at Linnea. I've never seen Linnea angry until now. It radiates from her like the fear from CO Madge—devil brows, red cheeks, glassy eyes, snarly lips.

The man is trying to stop my bleeding, applying a *pressure pack* over my leaky wrist. The woman places a mask over my nose and mouth. Oxygen floats inside the mask.

The driver asks, "Set?"

"Set!" Both EMTs speak at once. My body jostles with takeoff.

We merge into traffic along I-5. The sirens squeal, sounding distant as they bounce around inside the ambulance. Red and white lights flash overhead, flooding each corner of the ambulance. I sit on top. My hair straight up, side-to-side, all over, wild, slapping my face with the wind. Medusa hair.

"We're losing her," the man says.

"Eyes glossy, unresponsive."

Another alarm sings. "No pulse," the man adds.

"You take the chest. I'll bag and count."

"One . . . two . . . three . . . four . . .five . . . six . . . seven . . . eight . . . nine," the woman EMT counts. "ten, eleven, twelve, thirteen, fourteen, fifteen, sixteen, seventeen, eighteen, nineteen, twenty, twenty-one, twenty-two, twenty-three, twenty-four, twenty-five, twenty-six, twenty-seven, twenty-eight, twenty-nine, thirty."

"Bag . . . one. Bag . . . two."

"Repeat."

"One, two, three, four, five, six, seven, eight, nine, ten, eleven, twelve, thirteen, fourteen, fifteen, sixteen, seventeen, eighteen, nineteen, twenty, twenty-one, twenty-two, twenty-three, twenty-four, twenty-five, twenty-six, twenty-seven, twenty-eight, twenty-nine, thirty."

"Bag . . . one. Bag . . . two."

"Pulse!"

They stop.

The man listens with a stethoscope. "Weak. Thready." The dinging of the blood pressure monitor continues. "Pressure's too low."

The driver speaks into a handheld device. Gives details to the hospital relayed to him by the two taking care of me. A distance falls between their voices. CO Madge butts into my consciousness. She wants to speak.

The driver says, "Female. Sixteen. Laceration left wrist. Tourniquet. Fluids." Repeating into his handheld.

CO Madge sputters. "I didn't do it. You have to believe me."

"Ma'am, please." The female EMT acts in sharp motions. Irritation paints her face. She doesn't believe CO Madge. Here's what her disbelief looks like— narrowed eyes darting to my arm and then the male EMT, shaking her head in a way only the other EMT (and I) can see, pursed lips.

CO Madge quiets when the male EMT checks her face. He says, "You're going to be fine." His tone professional. No hint of the accusation roiling in his gut.

The female has a child around the same age as Tessa. She hopes her son never experiences anything like this. Self-lacerating. Cutting. The trend of child self-maiming. Suicide.

I lift off the gurney, silver blanket hanging—a magic trick as I levitate.

"Her pulse," the male says. His tone serious. His eyes on the monitor.

Again, they perform CPR. I see the male for who he is, a father with four children, ages eighteen, twenty, twenty-three, and twenty-seven. The twenty-seven-year-old from his first wife. His second wife and he had the others . . . plus three cats—Mittens (he didn't name her), Spike, and Crawler. The eighteen-year-old will leave for college soon. The male is having an affair with someone he doesn't love. He thinks about the woman who has become increasingly desperate to see him. He needs to cut her loose. Guilt, torrential waves hit his gut every few minutes.

The drive to the hospital is twenty minutes. He notices the female EMTs eyes glisten within the bright fluorescent confines, strobing under the red and white emergency lights.

"Shannon," he says. His words jar the female. "It will be what it will be. Pull yourself together."

"Dammit," Shannon whispers.

"She gonna die?" Hope swells in CO Madge.

"Ma'am, please," Shannon, the female EMT articulates. The anger helps her. She fiddles with the tube dispensing fluids.

I tremble.

"Heart rate?" The male asks.

"111. BP 70/60. Temp 95. Cover her. Her skin." She's angry. "Focus, Jim. Where's your head?"

Jim packs me down with a bristly wool blanket sporting an embroidered red cross that lands across my thighs this time. My heart pulses in my ears. Warmth descends into my skin.

"Temp 96," Shannon says.

I float off the gurney. A monitor whistles.

"She's crashing again," Jim announces.

They work fast. More pressure on my chest.

A penlight flicks on. "Eyes glassy but responsive."

The siren whines. I try to focus. Their faces fade in and out. Again, Jim lifting my eyelid. Shannon checking.

Tessa pops in. "What's up, buttercup?" she says. I giggle.

"Check her airways," Jim orders.

"She's breathing. Her chest."

He glances to my ribs after Shannon's comment.

My little sister's face is nothing short of joyful. Here's what Tessa's joy looks like—rainbow eyes, rosy cheeks, lips so wide they make her rainbow eyes squint, giggling.

The driver chimes in, "Turning in 500 feet."

Shannon and Jim brace as the ambulance bumps over the curb. CO Madge knuckle-grips the metal bench. We shimmy to a stop in front of a double sliding ER door.

The driver jumps out. He runs to the back doors. They fly open.

Shannon presses a print button on the monitor and a receipt-size report spits out. She tears off the report and pockets it.

"Ma'am," Jim says. He directs his comment to CO Madge, who tries to stand. "Stay where you are."

"Take me first," Madge insists. "I'm still alive."

"We have to get the gurney out, then you."

But CO Madge won't have any of his orders. She bolts out, misses the step, and falls onto her hands and knees. Her cheek dribbles out blood. A nurse rushes out with a wheelchair.

"Ma'am!" the driver yells. His name is Sven. He's a black dude with a bald head. "We told you to wait!" Sven's face fills with anger. He helps CO Madge up, her face actively bleeding.

"Jesus," Jim barks. Shannon and Jim get the gurney out of the ambulance, past CO Madge. They roll me through two open glass doors where nurses and interns await. An LPN assists with additional equipment, more supplies, another bag on a wheeled pole, a tray table.

The ER doc rushes up. Shannon hands him the printout. "Get her to ER 117," he says. "Stat."

He's the doc who will stitch up my arm. The nurse will continue feeding other people's blood into me until my empty light goes off.

"What about this one?" the doc says to Sven.

Sven placed CO Madge into a wheelchair. "She needs some serious stitches for her face. Check her knees and wrists for fractures. She fell out of the ambulance."

The doc yells for the head nurse, "Who's resident tonight?"

She walks to a whiteboard with a blue marker and locates the resident on staff. "Fagan. Dr. Fagan," she says.

"Call Fagan for this one in the wheelchair," he says to the nurse behind the counter. "Come with me," he orders the nurse.

53

Patching Madge
CO Madge

She noted a Latina nurse assisted the doctor. At least it wasn't the big black eunuch who tossed her into the wheelchair.

The Latina stood at the head of the examination room table applying pressure and holding Madge's cheek together. Dr. Fagan was tall and black, youngish. Madge estimated his age around thirty-five. His shaven hair gave a President Obama sort of appeal. He snugged a surgical cap onto his head and spun on a swivel rolling stool toward Madge. He covered his nose and mouth with a face mask, then slung a stretch band over his head to hold the mask in place.

Next to the examination table, a tray held suture equipment. A curved needle strung with thick, dark thread reminded Madge of a rug needle. Next to the needle lay a series of extra lines of thread, four folded gauze squares, and three mini packs of povidone iodine. One mini pack was torn open with a moist red square pulled halfway out. Fagan removed the square and wiped Madge's cheek to disinfect it before he started working on her.

"So, you work corrections at juvie?" Dr. Fagan said. *Bedside manner chat* Madge supposed.

"Mmhmm," she grunted.

Madge had long forgotten a man's warmth and intimacy. She'd hopped the gender preference line six years after beginning work in juvenile corrections. The reason, she argued, seeing so many naked girls. Some so young she had to look away. She knew what she felt for these children was wrong. Hated it yet couldn't seem to quarantine her urges. And, boy, had she tried. She took the requisite vacations, dated one man during a break who stole fifty dollars from her purse the night she'd finally asked him to sleep over.

Fagan concentrated, deep in thought while he stitched her face. His knuckles and fingers blocked some of her sight while he worked, the needle rising and falling with each stitch. His eyes followed the pattern, a slow sewing machine seaming Madge's face back together. She expected the result to appear ghoulish—a needlepoint with black thread zigzagging the flap of skin with jagged rows of tiny Xs.

"How long?" he asked a few minutes later.

"Hmm?" Madge mumbled, having already forgotten the line of questioning.

"In corrections?"

The nurse applying pressure was preventing her from talking, so Madge held up both hands, fingers wide and pumped twice, then held up her index finger.

"Twenty-one years?" he asked.

"Mm-hmm." Madge rolled her eyes.

"That's a long time," he said. "You don't like it?"

Madge lifted her shoulders and frowned.

"Not much?" Fagan said.

"She can't say much, Dr. Fagan." The nurse's nametag appeared upside down, but Madge could see her name was Aura. And lying there, with her upside down and the light glinting above her head, Aura did seem to glow. Her pretty face focused between the doctor's work and Madge's eyes. Madge winked at her and she grinned.

"He always does this," Aura said. "Talks and talks. Asks questions too. Like, *Hey, doc, how the heck am I supposed to answer you*? Right, Madge?"

Madge couldn't grin with Fagan's hand on her face, but she wasn't feeling any pain from the six injections of lidocaine he'd administered before starting.

"Sorry. I didn't mean to make you smile, dear," Aura, the nurse, said. "Try not to. You do, and you'll have a catch in that stitch. He's not a cosmetic surgeon, you know. We call him the butcher." She laughed, then added, "Not really. He's good. He's doing a good job.

You'll probably have a thin scar, but he's making each of these stitches really smooth and close together. You're going to heal up like nobody's business," Aura said, her tone reassuring.

Madge still couldn't keep tears from draining down her temples.

"Oh honey, don't worry," Aura said. "Shh, shh. Everything will be okay."

But she knew it wouldn't. She knew nothing would be okay. Her job was on the line. Hell, her freedom was. What she had done was criminal. Not just that they were children, but rules state COs can't have relations with inmates. The irony hung thick. She could be charged and sentenced to jail.

Even with Aura's cooing, Madge's tears would not stop.

54

Coming Clean After Getting Dirty

My eyes barely cracked. Both of Dad's hands clutched my right forearm. His head rested on his hands. His head moved slowly, answering no to the question asked seconds before I fully regained consciousness. I didn't speak. Wasn't sure if I could.

"I didn't care if she wasn't my own," he said. "I loved her as much as I love Mac."

Broken out of my stupor, it seemed he was speaking to himself.

Now, the fingers of my left hand tingled under someone's death grip. Alertness came on in slow, steady clicks like cogs on a gear. But before I could turn, a doctor entered the room behind Dad. The death

grip on my left hand ebbed. Dad rose and stepped away
to allow the doctor through.

"Hey, MacKenzie," he said when he saw I was
trying to open my eyes, "I'm Dr. Boyden. You're in the
hospital."

Dad shot a look past the doctor across my bed, his
eyes fraught.

"She's awake?" Dad said.

Dr. Boyden ignored the question. "How you feel?"

I shook my head. "Sleepy," I said, my voice barely
a whisper.

"I need to ask you a few questions about what
happened. You feel up to it?"

I nodded.

"Good. Good," the doctor said. "Do you remember
what happened?"

I shook my head that I didn't.

"Okay. Well, you tried to hurt yourself. Do you
remember cutting your arm?

My eyes shifted to the ceiling panels of acoustical
tile arranged in a patchwork. Electrical conduit ran
down the wall behind my bed and disappeared. My
gaze moved to the blood pressure cuff wrapped around
my right arm. A bag of blood hung from one of two
metal hooks, both hooks attached to the rack that
looked like something you could hang your coat on.
The other hook held a bag of clear fluids with the label
reading: LACTATED RINGER'S.

Memories flooded back. Madge's face exploding in red. The searing pain of Therese's shiv entering my arm.

"No," I muttered.

"I'm sorry. Did you say no?"

I cleared my throat and swallowed. "Water?" I said. The doctor indicated to Dad to retrieve a cup of water. The sound of chipped ice sloshed inside the plastic pitcher. A plastic cup appeared in Boyden's hand. He held the cup while I sipped.

"You don't remember what happened?"

I closed my eyes. "No."

Dad shifted up to Boyden's shoulder, still standing behind him. He glanced past me to the other side of the bed. I was turning my head when the doctor demanded my attention.

"Let me tell you why you're here. Okay? Maybe it will help you remember. You have a laceration on your left wrist."

I turned my head to my arm. And there she stood. Mom. Pity filling her eyes. I wanted to puke.

"Why, Mac?" she said.

When I spoke, it wasn't to her but to the doctor. "Get her out."

"Can you both step outside?" the doctor requested.

"Not him. Just her," I said.

They each exchanged a look I can only describe as pathetic.

"Ma'am," the doctor said.

Mom let out a weak sniffle and walked out.

"Okay, she's gone." He wrapped one hand around mine. "Can you talk about it?"

I nodded.

"Good. That's good." He hooked one foot around a rolling swivel stool, pulled it close and sat down. He never let go of my hand. "So, what happened?"

"CO Madge?"

"She'll be fine. But you got her good, MacKenzie."

Dad chimed in. "We call her Mac."

"Mac," the doctor said. "Sorry."

"It's okay," I said.

"So, about Madge. What happened?"

"I tried to kill her."

My dad seemed to lose strength. He backed away and sat down in a guest chair. "Jesus, Mac," he said.

The doctor held up a hand to shut him up.

"It's all very upsetting for your parents. For me. I'm sure you can understand hearing someone say they tried to kill someone else is, well, startling, Mac." He paused, his eyes resolute but filled with sadness. "Why do you feel that way about her?"

I turned to the wall, to a void where Mom had been standing. My arm was wrapped in a sleeve of white gauze. My thoughts? A confetti of fluttering letters, words, sentences spinning in a tornado of emotions.

"Take your time, Mac," he said.

I answered immediately. "Have you ever been humiliated?"

"Often." A silent chuckle followed his wry look.

"No. I don't mean, like *Oops! I accidentally farted* humiliated. Humiliated like you were reduced to shit on the bottom of someone's shoe and you had no chance of ever getting scraped off. That kind of humiliation."

"Ah," he said, realizing the error of his response. "I'm sorry. No, Mac. Never like that."

"She's the reducing factor. I'm the shit."

"Your mom?" the doctor asked.

I sighed and shook my head.

"Who is *she*?" Dr. Boyden inquired.

"CO Madge," I said.

Dad's shoulders began to quake.

"What, Dad? Can't take it? Cause if you're not man enough to hear it now, to hear it all, then leave."

He wrapped one arm around his stomach and pressed the other over his mouth.

"Mac," the doctor said, "look at me. I'm here. I'm listening. Do you want your dad to leave too?" After a second, he said, "Yes or no?"

"I don't care either way," I said.

"All right then. Can we get back to Madge?"

I nodded.

"How did she humiliate you?"

"Not just me," I revealed.

"Okay then. How did she humiliate you *and* others?"

"She likes to," I paused. My eyes burned. I took in a breath and when I exhaled, I said, "*shower* us."

"Oh God." Dad slumped in his seat.

The doctor's eyes were searing but focused on me. "She was doing something to you in the showers?"

"Something?" I said. "*Everything*."

"She sexually assaulted you?"

"Yes." I said, nodding.

"And others?"

"Lots. And because of her doing it to some girls, they turn and take it out on other girls. It grows, exponentially."

"Did someone else take it out on you?"

"My roommate."

Dad moaned. The doctor spun toward him. "Mr. Fraser, sir. If you cannot control yourself, I'm going to have to ask you to leave."

When he started crying, I said, "It's okay. He's okay. He didn't know."

"You sure?" the doctor asked.

I nodded.

"You said she did this to others in the showers?"

Once again, I nodded.

"Can you tell me who?"

"My roommate, Therese. She's gone now. Kat. Probably Crow, 'cause she's the weakest one. CO Madge likes the weak ones, small ones who are barely showing signs of the female form. Tender skin, she'd said about Therese. Something CO Madge had been complaining to her, that she no longer had tender skin like when she was sixteen and seventeen. I guess the younger they are, you know," I paused, "she likes it better."

"It's not your fault. You know that, right?" Dr. Boyden declared.

"Hell, yes. I know it."

"What she was doing is illegal, a breach of trust, not to mention despicable. If they can prove it, she will go to jail for this, Mac. Would you be willing to testify against her?"

"Are you a doctor or a lawyer?"

"Let's just say, I've seen this sort of thing before. I know what will happen if people speak out about it. The bad guy goes to jail and the good guy tries to heal. Sometimes they do. Sometimes they don't, but the odds of healing are greater when people recover from sexual assault by confronting their abusers. Okay?"

Dad was a knot of anger. His hands clenching and unclenching. His face, tortured. Both jaws twitching. His eyes a million miles away like he was in a dark, narrow alley meeting up with CO Madge. Taking out his anger by bashing her face with his fists.

"Yeah. Okay," I said, agreeing to speak out against my abuser.

Dad was wound so tight I thought he might explode.

"Dad?" I said, "I'm sorry I——"

He raced to my side. "Shh," he said, "you didn't know what to do, baby. Don't blame yourself. I love you, Macky. You know that, right? Love you more than life itself."

After he kissed my forehead, he asked the doctor, "So, what next?"

"Well, she needs to heal. We'll keep her on suicide watch for another week. The rules. Then broach the mental issues. She'll be here in Pediatric Psychology for a full two weeks, and after, she'll have to return to the facility, where they'll keep her on watch."

"How long?" Dad said.

"Up to her. Ultimately, a psychologist will determine that."

All I heard was *the facility*. And that's when I flipped out. The doctor pressed the nurse's button and two orderlies and a nurse ran in, saw me in panic mode, and administered a sedative. And that's when I calmed down and drifted off to La La Land.

55

A Forced Reunion

The nurse was replacing my bandage when Dad walked in. "She wants to see you, Mac," Dad said. Dad somehow managed to get me to do what he wanted. His sweet way always won me over. And no way could I refuse those blue eyes or his compassionate tone. I decided right then to someday marry a man with blue eyes.

Today, however, those eyes were fractured. He hadn't slept. Told me as much. Plus, his beard took on an unmanicured shabbiness.

"You look tired," I said. I reached up and rubbed one finger under his chin. I wrinkled my nose at the stubbled patch.

"You don't look so great yourself," he chuckled. "You know you can tell me anything. I love you. I'm your father. I could've helped."

"I didn't know what to do, how to tell you." My wrist throbbed under the gauze. I shuffled my body to allow Dad more room on the bed to sit. He adjusted and snugged in closer and grabbed my good hand. "You know…" I said, "I heard."

Dad's eyes dropped. He understood. "Everything's gone haywire."

"Tell me about it," I laughed. Not because it was funny, but to lighten his mood.

"We hoped—"

I cut him off. "That's why Tessa was crying. She overheard you two talking about her."

"Jesus, Mac. We never wanted you girls to find out. It's nothing anybody needed to know."

"How did you keep it quiet all these years? I mean, the rumor mill."

"Look. I promised your mom." He paused at my reaction. "No," he said, "don't roll your eyes." He waited until I was ready to listen. "Like I was saying, I promised your mother I would never say anything about it to you girls."

"So, we were just never supposed to know? What if we got DNA tests? We'd know then."

"Look, if you're going to get upset, I'm not going to talk about it any further with you right now. Anyway, by the time you could afford to get a DNA test, you'd both be adults." He scratched at his cheek. "I mean, this whole thing can wait until—"

"No," I said. "Not until anything. I want to know *now*. It's gone on long enough. You have to come clean, Dad. Tell the truth."

The breath he took was big enough to fill up a gallon jug. "Well, only if your mom is involved."

"No," I exclaimed.

"This is the deal. I made a promise to your mother not to say anything to either of you. If you can't abide by us telling you the whole story together, then we're not telling you at all."

"It's her fault, isn't it?"

"Do you want to hear what she has to say or not?"

And although I didn't, I agreed to allow my mother back into the hospital room. But only to explain everything.

56

The Funny Thing About DNA

Dad slipped out of the room. Several seconds passed before Mom emerged from the hall.

Guilty as charged.

When Dad didn't follow her in, I knew he'd pulled one over on me.

"Where's Dad?" I asked.

"He thought it best for us to talk alone, Macky."

"Don't call me that. Dad can call me that, but not you."

"I don't blame you for being angry with me," Mom said.

I refused to say what I wanted to say and turned my head to the wall.

"I should've come to see you."

"Dad!" I called. "Dad!"

"Do you want to know about Tessa?"

Right then, her name acted as a trigger because something inside me uncorked. I could barely speak. My body convulsed. I could hardly form words before I whispered my sister's name.

Mom's eyes filled, but she stood strong. Like she'd done after Tessa's accident—resolute, stoic even. If I ever saw her upset, she became a statue with tears. She pressed on. Had to work. Dad was long gone by then, and she had to make a living. She had to clean the house. Wash our clothes. Fix dinners. Attend to funeral arrangements. Put her youngest daughter in a hole in the ground.

So, she wasn't about to let a little teenager's snit break her. She sat stiff-backed on my bed and put her hands on both cheeks over the trickle of silent tears. If she were to keep what was left of her family intact, she needed to stay in control. She said her name, "Tessa," as though she were saying anyone else's name . . . with no attachment. The tears didn't warp her words. They simply drained out.

Even so, all I wanted to do was kick her off my bed.

"Go," I said.

Mom shook her head, refusing. "Not this time. No," she said. "You're going to listen to me."

"Dad!"

I didn't want to know. After everything, I realized that nothing mattered. I didn't want there to be anything between Tessa and me that wasn't different from anything I already knew. I wanted fiction not fact. Feed me a lie. I'll go on my merry way. I yelled for Dad again. Nothing. He wasn't going to get me out of this.

I closed my eyes and felt my mind whisk me away to the rooftop and my paper wings. To a land where no one knew me. Where I was Superwoman. I flew through branches and clouds. Buzzed Walt and made him bark like the crazy little mutt he was. My wings felt heavy as they pulled me up. My arm was healed and so was my heart. The wind bolstered me higher into the air. Soaring. Soaring. Higher until—

"Mac!" Mom said.

My body stalled midair. Puttering down. Dropping me back into the bed.

After unclenching my eyelids, I saw Mom through the slits . . . still there. My arm was still wrapped. My heart? Still broken. I was back in a Godforsaken land where my family made up stories to mollify. Back to the land of lies.

"Please. No," I said. "Please don't."

"It was an accident," she said.

"Mother. Stop." I tried to get out of bed, but she held my legs.

"I got pregnant."

Then, the strangest thing happened. Her composure cracked. She clenched her eyes and at the same time her hands tightened around my shins. She lowered her face and her shoulders quivered.

"It was so stupid." Her words jumbled. "So, *so* stupid. Oh Jesus," she said. She breathed in deeply then continued. "What was I thinking? I was infatuated."

"With Dad?" I said.

She shook her head. "No," she admitted.

"Who then?"

Mom's strength began to falter. She tipped her head back and let out a long sigh. "It doesn't matter, honey. What matters is I caused so many people a world of pain. We had to sign a nondisclosure agreement. I thought he loved me. Oh my God. What a fool. I was so enamored with him. He had money. Lots of money. And he wanted *me*. I knew he was married, but I thought maybe he could take me away, divorce his wife."

"This was when I was eight? Right? God, Mom. What about Dad? What about *me*? Didn't that matter?"

"I was only thinking about you."

"Obviously not," I said.

Her head bobbed. "Yes. I was. I worried about giving you a better life. It was hand to mouth with your dad, and I was tired of struggling."

My throat tightened. She made me sick. "That's disgusting."

"I was twenty-nine."

"Jesus, Mother. Freaking no excuse." I wasn't giving her an inch. "You just throw out your vows?" I paused, then said, "for *money*?"

"Trust me, young lady. I've done my penance."

She tried to grab my hand, but I wrenched it away.

"How does your arm feel?" she said.

"What do you fucking think?"

"Mac—"

I cut her off. "Look, *Mom*," I stumbled for words, wasn't sure what to say next. Too many options, each sardonic, accusatory. I pushed her off the bed with my foot and she almost fell. Her eyes widened. How could she imagine I could forgive her? I didn't want to see her surprise or hurt expression. I didn't want to *chat*. I didn't want her there any longer than necessary. "Look, *Mom*, anything I say to you…" I stopped. "Just go. I'm not interested in your apology."

"Mac, please."

"No. Get out. I have nothing to say to you that is nice. If I say what I want, you'd freaking explode into a million pieces."

"Mac." Her tone was pleading, nauseating. "How can I make things right?"

I laughed. "Are you serious?" I let out a puff of air. "No one can make any of this right."

That seemed to shut her up. She laced her fingers and let them fall in front of her pelvis, prayer-style. She opened her mouth to add something, but by then I was finding the wall ultimately tons more interesting.

Before she left, I threw out another barb. "Don't forget, *Mom*. You gave away my cat!"

I didn't look at her right then. I waited until I heard her steps toward the door. She had dropped her head. She placed a shaky hand onto the doorknob. And, thankfully, without saying more, she pressed the door open and let it fall closed behind her.

In the hall, I heard Mom and Dad murmuring. Next were footsteps fading down the hall. Mom's, of course.

Such a fighter, Mom. Always up for a battle. *Not.*

Dad poked his head in. "Can I come in?"

I shrugged.

"She's trying to make up with you."

"So not gonna happen."

He glanced to the door then back over to me. He swiped one hand through his shaggy hair. "Man," he said, "everything has turned to shit, hasn't it?"

"Truckloads," I agreed.

He covered his eyes with both hands. Then, his shoulders caved. His voice warbled when he spoke. "It's all my fault."

"What?" I said. "No, Dad. None of this is your fault."

His head bounced in quick succession. "Yes. *All* of it."

"Good Lord. Is everyone in our family a drama queen?"

"It's not funny, Mac. If I hadn't left, if I'd been stronger and stayed. Shit. If I'd forgiven your mom, let it go, none of this would've happened. With Tess. With you."

I'd never seen my dad cry before. It crushed me. I scooted up into a sitting position. "Dad, sit down." I patted the mattress. Thankfully, there was always a box of tissue on the bedside table. I wheeled the steel tray next to him. "Don't cry, Dad. Take a tissue," I said.

After taking in a couple drying breaths in and wiping his face, he composed himself, but all his strength seemed to drain away. His shoulders slumped and he sat there silent for several minutes. I didn't know what to say. I simply touched his forearm, and he let out a long sigh. I figured the best thing to do was change the subject.

"So, have you heard any news about April?"

He clenched his eyes but didn't speak, then shook his head that he hadn't.

57

The Upward Turn Revisited

After my week under suicide watch and psych counseling, an additional requisite week of therapy began. CO Linnea attended each group session with me. Daily.

"The way to kill your demons is to confront them head-on," Deborah Grout, the therapist, stated. Deborah Grout wasn't tall, fat, or oily. She wore her hair in a low, loose ponytail that trailed between her shoulder blades. The white smock she wore sported a nametag that bore her credentials: PhD in Psychology. Deborah insisted on being called Debbie. Debbie's natural shade of gray-blonde hair made me think she was older, but then the bright smooth skin around her eyes made her look younger, not fifty, maybe forty.

Debbie assigned daily homework—reading and writing exercises. Some writing exercises were fill in the blanks and multiple choice. Some were *first-memory* exercises. It's surprising how many first memories the subconscious stores up.

But not a day passed that CO Linnea wasn't at our group settings and, usually by my side. At first it worried me.

"I assure you," she said, "what is said in these sessions will die with me."

How could I not believe her? She was trustworthy.

Even so, that first session, I hadn't expected her.

"I can leave if I make you feel uncomfortable," she'd said.

Surprisingly, her presence calmed me. I was all nervy that first time, my skin crawling. I'd never gone to a therapist before. Felt skittish about what was going to happen. Would I sit there and bawl my eyes out the whole time? Would any of the other girls? There were seven, including me. One tried strangulation as her way out. A few others had their wrists in bandages too, left and right arms like bands of companionship. The rest sat dumbfounded from attempts at overdosing, their eyes sunken and drawn, raccoon-ish.

No one cried. Thank God. I'm wasn't sure if all that tension and control could be blamed on CO Linnea being there or if the blame was simply because a new person—me—had been inserted into the mix. Maybe it was both.

You can't make someone believe, someone who has tried the same thing—tried to off themselves—that your attempt was any more meaningful than theirs, can you? No. And although listening to everyone's story felt close and devastating, still, no one dared shed a tear that first day.

The first session was more of a *get to know you* meeting.

"Barbie. My name is Barbie," the girl sitting to my right said. "I live in Edmonds. Mom musta heard, 'cause she got there right after I kicked the step stool away. She screamed and cried. Lifted my body to loosen the knot." She shook her head. "I still don't know how she heard. The floor has carpeting. Fuck." Barbie stopped talking, and I felt her pass the intro off to me.

"Mac. I don't live at home right now."

And although she had all the goods on each of the patients, Debbie asked, "Where do you live right now, Mac?"

I couldn't believe it. The others weren't exactly criminals, just hard-time girls, troubled, who had gotten tossed into juvie for whatever reason. All were girls wanting to die. Like me.

"Really?" I asked.

"If we're each going to get through this process, we must be totally honest, not only with other people but with ourselves. Anything less falls under the category of denial."

I tried to make a joke, but failed miserably, when I said, "Like in Egypt?"

Some girls giggled. I grinned around the circular set of chairs at the others.

Debbie said, "Humor is a mask to hide your real feelings."

Kicking her right then sounded like an awesome option. One way to show my real feelings.

Then she said, "How about we attempt honesty?" She wasn't rigid but matter of fact. Like: These are the rules, ladies. We must abide by them. The problem? I didn't want anyone to know about juvie.

"No," I said. "Honesty bites." And I got up and nearly made it out of the room when CO Linnea body-blocked the door from the outside, making escape impossible. That is, unless I wanted to deck her. And I did not.

"It's part of the deal, Mac," she reminded me. "Part of your mandatory agreement. Like everyone in here."

"Ohmygod. Seriously? That's freaking wack."

Everyone was staring. Except Debbie, of course. No, Debbie's hand quickly penciled something onto her notepad. Then, she stood and joined us at the door. Her voice was more than a whisper but still stern.

"Let me," Debbie said. "Mac, I'm not trying to humiliate or embarrass you. But honestly, you're not special here."

I blew out my rejection of her analysis and leaned against the wall.

"You feel different, don't you?"

I nodded and rolled my eyes, then crossed my arms over my chest.

"Each of the others feel different too. You have to believe me. I've been doing this kind of work for fifteen years with girls like you. Some live at home, some don't." She tipped her head to let me know she wasn't going to out me. "The one thing each of you have in common, the *only* thing each of you have in common, is that you feel different. To explain why you feel different is part of the healing process."

So, I blurted it out right there by the door. "Okay!" I said. "Fine! So, everyone. I'm in juvie. Okay? Everyone happy?" I pushed past Debbie and headed back to my seat. The chair skidded and clattered when I sat back down.

Debbie followed, then stood in front of her chair and said, "See? That wasn't so hard, now, was it?"

Everyone burst into laughter. And I did, too, but then I'd wound myself up into such a bag of nerves, tears came out through the laughter. Debbie let what happened next happen.

The other girls acted like I was some sort of antihero, asking me things like, "Is it really as bad as we hear?"

"Yes," I said. "It really is."

"Are there girl gangs?"

I nodded to that too. "Yeah." No need to say more.

But then one girl, Olive, one who'd tried overdosing to a place called *nowhere land*, said, "Is there rape? I heard from my uncle that bad girls get thrown in and raped by other inmates. Is that true?"

I shot a glance as if to say, *Quiet!* Just to shut her up.

"It's okay. You're safe in here." She patted my bandaged arm.

"I got raped. And then," I said, and I showed them my arm.

Gasps hushed from the other girls, except for Olive. She stood and ran to me. She fell to the floor, put her head on my knees and cried. When we finally made eye contact, she said, "My uncle raped me. Has since I was seven."

Seven. Seven-year-olds are only babies. I know.

My words didn't form anything recognizable when I tried to say, "I'm so sorry."

God. How my heart broke for her. She was different, had a different horror story to tell. But Debbie was right. We weren't any different because we were all damaged. When I glanced up, some girls were crying. Others were trying to hold it together.

Then Debbie broke in. "I cannot tell you how awesome this is, and on a first day! You girls are going to be so strong. So strong. I'm not worried about your futures. No. Not in the least. You're going to be okay. Okay?"

Then Debbie rose to help Olive back to her chair. "All right," she said, "let's get to work. Let's make you all strong, amazing women."

58

The Spring . . . And I Don't Mean the Season

Dad walked me out the gates of juvie after getting sprung. I liked calling it *getting sprung*. Made me sound dangerous.

"Your mom wanted to come," he said.

It had been eighteen months since I'd stepped through the facility's front doors by my own strength. It was late spring in early June, sunny but chilly. A shiver spilled through my bones, and I held myself.

"Here," Dad said. He slipped off his work coat.

"No, Dad," I said. "I want to feel this. Anyway, it smells like dust."

I faced the sun. It was almost noon. The disparity of cold and warm made my soul glow. The facility's

landscape crew had just mowed the fields around the
grounds, and the scent transported me to Mom's house,
to a time before Dad left, a time before Tessa died,
when Dad mowed the yard every Sunday unless it
rained. "Smells like home."

"Come on," Dad urged. He wrapped an arm around
my shoulder and tucked me in tight. His chest was like
a heating pad. Warm enough to make my chill
evaporate to nil.

He turned to me. We were still sitting in the car in
his driveway. He turned off the engine.

"I got all your stuff," he shared.

"What happens with school?"

"You can either go back and get your high school
degree, or you can get a GED. Up to you."

What to do? What to do? All over my face, I'm
sure.

"Macky, you don't have to figure everything out
right this second. Give yourself some time. Give
yourself a break. Will you do that for me?"

His big goofy face melted me. Made me happy.
"You're right. Okay." Plus, I was home.

The room he'd prepared was smaller than mine at
Mom's but had all my stuff like Dad promised.
Everything except one sad dog, Walt. And no more
Miss April.

Dad's cell went off in the tone he used for Mom
calls, for my sake. Beethoven's Fifth.

Dun, dun-dun-dun, DUN! He answered and I chuckled. A finger rose to his lips and he stepped out of my new crib.

"Yep," he said to Mom. "So far . . . not right now. We're going to eat . . . whatcha want for lunch, Mac?" he said, obviously from Mom's prompting.

"Whatever," I said.

He walked off down the hall and their conversation walked with him into the kitchen.

My new room had zero artwork on the walls. But he'd bought me a new bed, which felt like lying on a cream puff. A scarred wooden desk sat opposite the bed. Dad was excited to tell me that he'd bought it *on the cheap* from San Juan Island Buy, Sell, Trade on Facebook.

The desk chair reminded me of an old-fashioned school chair with its plastic seat fanning out from the back to the front and its aluminum frame. That was the decor. At least the bedspread was colorful, a polychromatic floral pattern with lots of sunny yellow, orange, and peach. The matching shams told me Dad had gone above and beyond his talents, probably with the help of a salesclerk.

He walked back into my room telling me something I was already aware of. "That was your mom."

"No doubt," I said. He didn't seem to understand how I knew, so I said, "The scary music?"

"Ah. Yeah. Well. Ha! Tuna melt sound good?"

"Sounds awesome!" I said. "Hey, nice pick on the bedding, Dad. You did good." I was all smiles and cheery.

"No, your mom picked those out."

I couldn't fly off the bed faster if there'd been a snake inside the covers.

"You're going to have to forgive her someday. At least before she dies," he said. "Come on. Let's get some food." He put his arm out and led me into the kitchen.

"You have any other bedding I can use?"

"Jeez, Macky," he said. "Yeah. I'm sure I have something. Now, come on. I'm starving. All this springing you from jail has made me hungry."

59

Twelve Stepping It—Forgiveness

Dad didn't want me to go to Mr. Pauling's, but I disagreed. Told him, "Debbie says it's part of the healing process. Confront your monsters." How could he argue a point made by a professional, right?

Although, Debbie had never said anything like that, but we did study the *12 Steps of Addiction* because she explained, "People who have been abused, if unchecked, suffer similar qualities of addicts and tend to perpetuate similar abuses if they don't conquer their fears and offer forgiveness to their abusers." She handed out empirical evidence, studies we all read from. And while I wasn't ready to make a trip to the women's facility at Walla Walla to forgive CO Madge —who had been stripped of her standing as a

Corrections Officer, by the way, and was now simply
Madge—I'd had a ton of time to consider what I might
say to Bill Pauling once I was out.

Not only did I deserve it, but so did Mom and Dad.
So did Tessa. So did Pauling. A real face-to-face
between the victim's family and the criminal. A come-
to-Jesus moment, for sure.

They'd let him out early. Health issues, good
behavior. Took his license to drive away permanently.
Made him go into rehab and drilled in him the 12-step
program. Made him take three weekly pee tests. Made
him wear an ankle bracelet keeping him on house arrest
for five to seven years. He was allowed to go shopping
but with restriction orders—no alcohol, no cigarettes.
He was allowed to attend religious services. He was
allowed to do most everything with exceptions
administered by the court. Absolutely no bars or
restaurants that served alcohol. Absolutely no alcoholic
beverages, the pee tests making certain. Or . . . back to
jail he'd go.

The thing is, when Dad dropped me off in front of
his house, my hands started to sweat. My heart thumped
into a trot. My feet cemented to the sidewalk.

"You don't have to do this," Dad said. But the
comment knocked me forward and next thing I knew, I
was knocking at Pauling's door.

"Yes?" Pauling said when he opened it. It took him
a minute. His face worked through a sequence of
changes. At first, he didn't recognize me, and I didn't
offer my name. After a few heartbeats, he realized who

this girl was standing in his doorway. "Oh my God," he said. Then, what came next threw me for a loop. "Are you here to punch me?"

"What?" I said.

"Go ahead. Take your best shot." He stuck out his chin. The folds in his neck were filmy. His eyes cloudy and laced with an angry fear. I knew the look. When I didn't hit him, he said, "Not the chin? Well, then, how about here?" He patted his stomach and pooched it out.

"What's the matter with you?" I said.

"So, now I don't deserve it? You certainly didn't have any trouble the day of . . . you know."

And then a scene like a tidal wave of that day bowled over me. I covered my eyes. Shame is like that. Makes you want to hide. I bent forward.

Dad called out. "You okay?"

I put one hand up behind me, still bent over. A series of silent tears rocked my shoulders.

"Are you okay?" This time it was Pauling asking.

I shook my head no, still standing in a bent position.

"Here, let me help you," he said. And he helped me up over the threshold.

Dad called out. "Wait a minute!" I heard his truck door opening.

"Dad, I'm fine." My face streaked wet.

"You sure, Macky?"

I repeated that I was and walked inside Pauling's house.

Brewed coffee overran any other aroma inside. The coffee maker burped in the kitchen. He kept the

smallish place clean and airy. Not what I had expected.
An open floorplan displayed a pitched ceiling; a lone
sectional sat diagonally across from a small HDTV,
much smaller than the one Dad had insisted on buying.
A box of Ritz crackers sat open next to a plate of cheese
on the kitchen counter. A frying pan still on a burner
had remnants of egg baked onto the side. He'd set a
wooden silverware box on an end table next to a chair
that sat across from the couch.

He kept the carpeting and linoleum floors clean. No
clutter. No mess, except for the pan still on the stove,
but I forgave him that sin since it was only eleven in the
morning.

"Want a glass of water?" he asked. When I didn't
answer, he said, "Coffee?"

I lifted my eyebrows and nodded.

"Sugar? Cream?"

"Both. Please," I said.

He pulled a small carton of creamer from the
refrigerator and set it on the counter along with a five-
pound bag of sugar from a wall cupboard, followed by
a spoon and a mug. "Help yourself," he said. "I'm a
black coffee drinker." The eye contact between us
fluttered between pity-filled and embarrassment,
discomfort and needing to vomit.

He allowed me space on the couch and took the
chair by the end table, pulling it closer to the coffee
table that separated us.

The coffee was strong, much stronger than my
parents made.

"Is it okay?" he said.

I nodded and my eyes danced around the room trying to land anywhere besides his face.

"So," he said. "You wanted to see me?"

"Did I hit you?"

He chuckled. "You have a hell of a right jab, young lady. The left's not so shabby either." He paused. "You don't remember?"

I shook my head, our eyes connecting finally.

"You took doubles at me, double punching. I hadn't seen anything like it since Nam. You should enlist. You'd make a great soldier under fire."

His joke was lost on me and my eyes filled. He must have sensed an onslaught of tears coming because he reacted. He jumped up for a box of tissue and handed them to me.

"Now, wait. Here. You had every right to kick my ass. Look," he said. He arose and took a step toward me. I shrunk back. "It's okay. Look," he said, and bent down pointing to a scar over his left eye. "See that?"

"Jeez. Ohmygod," I said. "That was me?"

"You are with me always, young lady. Your scar is my constant reminder to stay clean. So don't feel bad. MacKenzie, isn't it?"

"Mac," I said.

"Mac, you're one of two reasons I'm clean. You and . . ." His words trailed off.

I knew what he meant. "Tessa. Her name was Tessa." Upon saying her name, my strength swelled. I would not succumb to his kindnesses. I wouldn't be duped by the sweet old man routine. I set down my coffee and leaned forward. "She was only *seven*," I said.

He placed his cup down, too, and lifted his gnarled and dry hands over his face, scar and all, up to his fading hairline. His shoulders jerked once. I sat back and watched him cry. I didn't offer forgiveness. I just watched. I felt my strength surge out of his remorse.

My dad's truck rumbled, and I heard him pulling away. I spun to the window behind me. Bill Pauling sniffled.

"He's leaving?" Pauling said.

He straightened his leg and pulled a handkerchief out of the pocket of his pants. I jumped off the couch and ran to the door, but Dad was turning left toward town, a mile from Mr. Pauling's and another three to Dad's.

I pulled out my cell and texted. "WTF?" The *shwing* of him reading it jangled. But he didn't text back, never while he was driving.

"I can walk you home," Pauling said.

"I'm sixteen." So irritating.

"Still," he said.

"I gotta go." The air was chilly but had warmed since Dad had dropped me off. I zipped my hoodie up to my neck.

But then a *blip-blip-blip* of an incoming text alerted me. It was Dad. He wrote, "I'll B back."

"He says he's coming back."

"When?"

I shrugged. "Not sure."

"Come back inside?"

He stepped out of the door, allowing space for me to enter. I returned to the couch and to my coffee. He stood and sipped from his mug, then sat down and placed the cup between both hands.

"Tell me why you're here, Mac. What did you expect to see? A drunk? A slobbering pathetic old man?

My words had fallen prey to a fishnet in my mind. Where should I start? There were millions of things I wanted tell him. How much I hated him. How I felt forced to forgive him. How I wished he were dead. How many times a day I cry missing my sister. How he destroyed our family. How I missed the way we were. How all good had been lost, burned to ashes because of him.

But he forgave me instead. "It's okay. I deserve whatever you want to say. I won't ask for your forgiveness. I don't deserve it. I deserve your wrath. So, give it to me. Let me have it. I forgive you for it. Been expecting it. I relish your ire. You know why, Mac?" When I didn't respond, he said, "Because I know I deserve much worse. I deserve the harshest punishment."

He got quiet afterward. Sat back. Let the moment settle.

I searched his face hoping to find a fitting word but found none. I closed my eyes and thought: *God? What do I say?*

And when I looked at him again? I knew.

60

Double-teaming Conspirators

"Meet me there," she said.

Ben hadn't thought what was right or wrong. He was acting on autopilot. On instinct.

He cranked up the air to a warmer setting, switched the fan on stronger. Autumn had laid a bridle path of yellow, orange, and red leaves across the road as he drove south on Mullis. It curved into Cattle Point and passed the house of the family that owned the movie theater. Next, the road bent west past Golf Course Road to a new building, next to Terry and Linda's business park. There, he pulled into the newly graveled drive, slowed, and put the car into park and sat in his car outside the front of the caretaker's house. Dy, the caretaker, was a lady known as the *Mobile Groomer*, a sweet gal from Minnesota with a precious little dog, a black and white one named Kiwi. A spot of a dog, really. One maxing out at seven pounds, maybe.

"Hey, Ben!" Dy said. She was out deadheading potted roses on her front deck.

Ben waved and lowered his window. "I'm waiting for someone. Is it okay that I park here?"

"Sure. I have to run, but feel free," she said.

She turned, swept petals and spent rosehips off the porch, then got into her car, and pulled out. He watched her car rock over the uneven driveway, and when she was gone, he settled into his seat and waited.

The evergreens around the grounds were taller than the ones in Uma's front yard. He missed that house. Missed his family. So much that he wanted to die some days. And he'd thought about it. Thought about climbing the Douglas fir in the back and jumping. Free-falling. Ending everything. It would be so simple. But landing mangled on the ground wouldn't end with him killing himself. It would kill Mac. Uma, well, he didn't know if she would care. He sensed she would, but it would feel different for Uma than for Mac.

The trees around Dy's place rocked with a surge of wind from the south. Rain was coming. South winds always brought rain. He spotted mountainous clouds lurking out past Griffin Bay, southeast from where he sat. The sun blinked on then, off from errant clouds scudding through the sky. Each time it shone from behind a cloud, warmth panned over his face. It was a welcome warmth, but he also welcomed a change of seasons. Getting to sleepy days of fall and the hibernation of winter. Not too long after that, crocuses reemerged under thawing snow. Next, early spring daffodils, then May tulips, and here we go again. Another year is gone. Seasons clicking off time.

He checked the rearview mirror. His temples had gone gray but before he could ponder life's mysteries and speediness to get to the end, his eyes brightened. Another car crushed over the gravel drive and pulled in next to the passenger side of his car. And when the driver's window rolled down, he lowered his so they could talk.

61

Thanks for the Memories
Bill Pauling

Bill Pauling felt numb and a little nauseous. But he also noted a sense of relief, as if someone had finally lifted the plastic bag from over his head—a bag that had been noosed around his neck for the past two years.

He only remembered sketchy vignettes of running down the little girl. His drunken stupor erased much of the actual accident. But with the help of deputies, witnesses, and now Mac, the scenes were beginning to fill out.

Only on occasion did pieces of the accident bubble up. Those times were the hardest, making him want to grab a bottle, to douse the memory entirely. The agony of wanting to drink was a vicious cycle, and now the dead girl's sister sat in front of him, telling him about her own pain, the family's loss, feelings of her own guilt. So much of it was new. The story of how the girls were there in the first place—to meet up with Mac's best friend, now her former best friend. The little sister was along only because her mom didn't want to be saddled with her while she cleaned. He mourned for the mother also. Knew she bore her own guilt. The *what-if's* of grief. He mourned for the dad. Couldn't imagine losing a child.

He was staring miles away, considering everyone's loss when Mac broke the uncomfortable silence.

"But that's *how* she died. *You* know that." Emphasis on the word *you* not lost on him. She lifted her mug and downed the remnants of her coffee. Then she said, "Want to know how she lived?" Her lips spread wide. The kindness extended by her face gave him hope for even a shred of forgiveness.

Through the telling of her story, Bill found himself amused and devastated. Sometimes he would offer his take on things, a philosophical spin in hopes of quelling her sadness. Mostly, he listened to Mac like anyone might during a chat between friends.

It broke his heart when she cried. But embarrassment about emotions had taken a back seat to their honesty, and both were speaking freely.

62

Thanks for the Memories, Part Deux
Mac

"Gemma Painter rolled the joint like a pro," Mac said. "She was bobbing her eyebrows because it was the first time I'd ever smoked pot. Making me, like, the last Mohican in high school when it came to smoking pot. I was a sophomore; practically everyone else had tried it by then. And, well, since pot was legal for adults, what were a couple of years give or take? Right? Anyway, what harm could come of me trying it? That's what I was thinking.

"Tessa was riding her bicycle in big loopy circles, sweeping by us, and then circling around and sweeping past Roy's. Big circles. I yelled at her to leave us alone, that this was big kid kind of stuff, and not to come over by us. 'Cause I didn't want her to know about the pot. I told her she would find out soon enough in her own time. But then I said, 'Get lost, creep.' Gemma and I laughed, then Gemma repeated it to Tess. We were so stupid.

"Tessa's face went red, you know. Got mad but not really mad, got her feelings hurt, and sped her bike back to Roy's. I remember her bike skidding, making the dog race behind the lady. Gemma shook her head and rolled her eyes, like 'kids these days.'

"We were messing around across the street from Sunken Park and the gazebo. It was Saturday, and Mom said she wanted to clean the house in peace. She was on a tear—*in a mood* Dad used to say—and she told me I had to babysit Tess. I was so pissed. But something major was up Mom's butt, big time. Any argument with her wasn't going to end well for me. Kids know these things about their parents.

"Anyway, Tess rode her bike between lanes two and four, then up to the board and batten building of Roy's, behind a woman ordering a coffee. Tessa's wheeling around antagonized the woman's yappy little dog, which pulled its bright red braided leash to its length. After that, I remember weird details like the dog baring its teeth, clear and white, offsetting the pallor of your car's paint. The bike's glittery paint outshining the gray weather with its vibrant lime green shades, the handlebar ribbons, playing cards from the night before still in place snapping the spokes.

"Tessa wasn't paying attention. She was straining to see what me and Gem were doing. At the same time, your car cornered the road. Tessa didn't see you because she was still focusing on us, trying to catch a glimpse of what we were up to. It was like she knew about the pot and was trying to stop me from taking a hit off the joint. I started to choke. And spun around to see if she saw. I hope she didn't. I hope that's not her last memory of me. That thought haunts me.

"Anyway, how could I yell? I was choking and couldn't scream *watch out!* My throat had clamped shut, paralyzed by alien fumes entering my lungs. But I'd gone stiff with fear by what I saw was about to happen.

"It was then that my legs freed up. By then, the impact of your car . . . well, Tessa didn't have time to respond. A freak accident, they called it. Coming out of nowhere. Strike like a rattlesnake. An IED. Boom. Sayonara. No last words. Nothing. Just gone.

"Your car rolled up and over Tessa, pinning her chest to the ground for a split second, then rolling off. They said her back had been pierced by one of the handlebars, and the triangle-shaped bike seat creased her back. When your car bumped off her, it lumbered away sharply to the right and almost hit the dog. But the woman was screaming. She'd seen everything and had already pulled the leash tight. Thankfully, they dodged in time for you to miss them. Your car ended up facing the wrong way and rolled out and off the drive-thru, buckling the fence behind Roy's.

"Tessa looked so lonely lying there. Like she decided to lie down for a sec while events happened. She was collateral damage, same as the fence. You know, this is weird. I remember thinking how it looked like someone had posed Tessa. I also remember thinking *someone slapped her* because her head was twisted away from Roy's. The underside of her skull was crushed too.

"As I stood over her, I saw that her gray and white striped sweater blurred when blood began sponging into it. But after seconds, it began to pool out in a pattern left by your tire treads. Which is crazy, right? I mean the treads were stamped into her sweater."

Mac covered her face. Pauling had placed a hand over his mouth and was silent while he waited for more information of the tragedy he had caused. It was his comeuppance. Mac didn't care. He needed to hear it. But she assumed it was something he'd been waiting a long time for. He wiped his nose again and went for his coffee. The mug shook as he lifted it and sipped.

Mac drew in a deep breath and started again.

"Like I said before, Tess was riding all over the place, up and down the ferry lanes, down into Sunken Park, around on the basketball court, then busting it up the hill toward the road. She'd hit the sidewalk, bump over it, then fly across the street back over to Roy's. The ferry had left a half hour before, so I figured no big deal, right? No cars. But," Mac said, and chuckled, "that poor dog freaked out each time she came flying by him. Those streamers whizzing straight out from the

handlebars. After the first couple of times seeing the
dog lose its mind, Tessa began to do it on purpose. Kept
edging closer. The dog's leash was straight out like a
cane. The dog was some sort of spotted mutt. It had a
long nose and skinny tail that spun like a windmill each
time Tessa rode by. I guess they were both having their
own special fun. I started to ignore Tessa and the dog.
That was when Gemma cupped her hand around the
joint and took the first drag.

"'*Like this*' she said, and then drew in a deep breath.
'*Hold it,*' she told me. Her voice got all croaky while
she held smoke inside her lungs. I was so nervous. My
hands got all sweaty and shaky. I glanced back again to
see if Tessa might see, but she was spinning circles,
terrorizing that silly dog who, by the way, was going
ape crazy. I ducked my mouth behind Gemma's hand.
The joint felt hot on my lips, but I took a small drag. Oh
God, it was awful. The smoke scratched. I coughed and
coughed. Couldn't stop. I thought I'd choke to death.
Sometimes, I wish I had."

Pauling glanced at the bandage around my wrist.
"Or this?"

He nodded.

"Yeah, juvie's no garden party. It got worse than
bad. Anyway, like I was saying, the choking stopped,
and the pot hit my brain. I began to laugh. '*Okay,*'
Gemma said, '*let me try again.*' Then it was back to
me. Gemma was holding the joint the entire time with
the dog still barking when she said, '*Holy shit.*' Her
eyes sailed past my head to Roy's. For a sec, I thought

she was joking around, but when I heard car tires screech behind me, I knew. I just knew. You know how you know? You just do. It's so weird how things crystalize in your mind. Like you don't need see the scene in a horror movie to know a monster is going to jump out with a knife and stab the actor to death.

"The dog's barking went nuclear. I remember weird details. You remember any of it?" she asked.

"Some. After," Pauling said. "The woman with the dog. How she, well, helped me."

"All I remember about the woman is how she held one hand over her mouth. After she helped you. I remember the car sitting weird, like if it could walk off it would but with a limp. And details about Tessa, like I said before. Her bike was under her body. And, blood. She didn't struggle. It was almost like she lay down to take a nap. Like all that bike riding exhausted her or made her dizzy and she ran out of steam, had to stop spinning endless circles. And you know what?"

Pauling shook his head.

"She looked peaceful. Distorted, yes, but peaceful," she added. "But I don't remember some things. There are big gaps. The deputies showed up. You were on the ground. Why were you on the ground?"

Bill Pauling coughed into a fist and spoke. "You dragged me."

"I don't remember. Why don't I remember?" Mac said.

"Shock protects our psyches."

"That's when I hit you?"

"Hit? I wouldn't call it hitting. You were *wailing* on me."

"Didn't you fight back?"

Bill Pauling dropped his gaze and shook his head that he had not.

"Why not? Ohmygod. No one deserves to be hit."

Pauling's mouth bent in a half-smile. "I knew, no matter what happened after, yours was only the first round of the punishment I deserved. And believe me, I deserved worse."

"No one deserves to be beat up." Mac paused, then said, "What exactly did I do? I mean, the whole thing is a fog."

"Honey, when you're ready to remember, your mind will open to that day. Don't rush it. Trust me. You'll be sitting somewhere, like, I don't know, church. Do you go to church?"

"Used to."

"You might want to try it again. Anyway, it doesn't really matter where you are, you'll remember when your mind is ready. But you will. You need time to heal. The memories are part of the healing."

Mac asked, "Is that when the woman helped?"

"Yeah. I think you might have struck her in the jaw. A glancing blow, but yes, that's when she pulled you off me."

The truck rumbling to a stop outside Bill Pauling's house announced her dad's return. Mac spun around on the couch and kneeled to face the window. She glanced back at Mr. Pauling and said, "I guess I better go."

Pauling stood and put his chair back. Mac took her coffee cup into the kitchen and set it inside the sink. "I can wash it?"

"No need," he said.

Mac wrapped her arms around her waist. "Mr. Pauling?"

"I think by now you can call me Bill."

She gave a sad laugh. "Bill?" She had made her way to the door and stepped down onto the porch.

"Yes, what is it, Mac?"

"I'm sorry for hitting you."

"Good God, young lady. I'm the one who's sorry. I can't tell you . . ." His words stopped short and he began to cry.

Mac glanced back to her dad. She whispered, "Please don't cry, Mr. Pauling."

"You'd have to come here every day to remind me that."

He shook out his handkerchief and wiped his eyes.

"Okay, well." she said, thumbing attention to her father. Mac turned to leave and got to the passenger door but stopped and returned. "Okay," she called back.

"Okay? Okay, what?" he said.

"To coming back."

"Hold on," he said. "I have something." Pauling left the door gaping and Mac walked back but waited for him outside as she watched him through the door. He lifted the lid of the silverware box and pulled out a letter-sized manila envelope fat with its contents. When he returned, he said, "These are yours. Well, probably your mom and dad's."

Mac dug inside the envelope and lifted one photo. It was Tessa.

"You and your sister have the same nose, see?" He touched the picture. His fingernail was jagged but short, his knuckles arthritic, his hand shaking.

He was right. She and Tessa had nearly identical features. Her hair was a mousy shade of blonde. Tessa's was dark. But, the eyes. The identical shape.

"How'd…" Mac was saying.

He cut in. "I assume friends, you know, family sent them."

Mac nodded and dropped Tessa's photo back inside, then gazed up at Pauling. "To not let you forget."

He nodded. "That's my assumption." He kept his eyes down but they popped up fast when he said, "Look," he said, "If you don't mind. I mean, well, I don't know but maybe, if you decide it's okay. May I have at least one? But like I said, only if you think it's right. I mean I'm not . . ."

Before he could say anything more, Mac grabbed him by the waist and hugged him. Not for long. She pulled out the first photo for him. And maybe in less than two seconds before tearing off and running to her dad waiting in his truck.

63

Thanks for the Memories, Trés

Pauling was right about memories. Her memory of the day…you know…had altered, shrunk, expanded and came back slowly at first but then suddenly, like *Abracadabra*!

"You know," Mac had said to Gemma that day, "I think I changed my mind." Her head was swimming after only one hit. Her feet had to be seven inches off the ground. "I'm just not the pot-smoking kind."

Gemma blushed and nodded. "Okay," she said.

Mac was trying to return the bag of pot, shoving it back at Gemma, but Gemma screamed, "Holy shit!"

From her peripheral vision, she watched as the scene hung in limbo, when all the activity warped into a fervor, with Gemma stuffing the pot into Mac's backpack when she turned to look. She lifted out a vial of scented oil but froze when she screamed again. Then, they both raced to Tessa, to the car.

A slice in time warped into a vision, a ghost, moth dust on an eyelash. No reaction would have been swift enough.

She had wanted to buy something nice for Tessa, a new dress and shoes for school. She'd been hoarding church and allowance money for months and stuffed it into her backpack that day so they could go to the store after she saw Gemma. She'd saved nearly three hundred and fifty dollars.

Mom had refused to let Mac drive the car. Said gas was expensive, the fuel tank was low, and to ride their bikes instead. Even when Mac promised to fill the tank, Uma refused.

"You don't even trust me!" Mac said to her mom. It had become normal since Dad left, their screaming sessions. Tessa running to her room in tears.

"I'm not fighting with you, young lady," her mom had said.

"Tessa! Let's go!" Mac called. "We're *riding our bikes* to town." She was glaring at her mom while she yelled. "Grab your backpack, twerp."

Mac was angry the entire four point five miles of the ride. Angry with the unnecessary inconvenience. Embarrassed that Gemma could drive and would wonder why Mac wasn't driving. Mac's mom was so lame.

But Gemma was excited about smoking pot together. When Mac took that first hit and coughed, Gemma had laughed. *It's always that way*, she'd said.

Then, "*Holy shit.*" And their family disintegrated into ash.

Pauling's burly Impala wobbled around the corner as if the car needed a walker. Its dingy cream coat covered a monstrous steel chasse. The car had become an island landmark. Most times, it sat askance on the sidewalk down Argyle Street close to Ferry Lane B close to Roy's, and most often at morning. And there it was, the monster with a knife in a horror movie, emerging with Tessa in its sights.

A lapse of five seconds was all it took. When five seconds can mean the difference between living and dying.

64

Baby Steps

How could I not have seen the tall bank of Douglas firs lining the street and running perpendicular to Mr. Pauling's house that first time we talked? I determined it was because of nerves. Nerves prevented me from seeing anything before approaching Mr. Pauling's—*Bill's*— front door.

By the time I reached his car, I noticed how he'd parked the truck a half-inch from the curb.

"Where'd you go?"

Dad opened the front passenger window. "Get in," he said.

Maybe for groceries. But he'd been gone for almost two hours. Dad never spent more than thirty minutes at the store. Hated grocery shopping. He'd been gone as long as Bill and I had been talking.

I rested my elbows inside the window. "Where were you all this time? I started to get a little worried."

"You okay?"

I felt spent, like I had no more words, and gave him a weak grin.

"Get in, babe," he said.

After climbing in, the scent of her cologne hit me like a bat against the back of my skull. I spun around. There she was. Mom. Sitting in back. A cardboard box next to her. She must've hidden on purpose for me not to spot her. The witch.

"What's *she* here for?" I hissed. Then I remembered the tinted glass of the back windows.

They planned this together, the double-teaming band of villains.

"Mac," she said.

I turned away, stared straight. Didn't budge. Wasn't about to listen. Dad didn't do a thing. He didn't start the engine. He did, however, manage to click the locks and roll up my window. For what? To muffle my screams? Possibly. The criminals.

"Mac," Mom said *again*. "I don't know what to do anymore. What to say." She kept her words tight and quiet. For seconds, she said nothing. The silence hung heavily.

Then, a strange noise came from where she was sitting. Was she crying? I glanced to Dad who had a stupid look on his face. How could he smile at a time like this? When Mom was having an emotional breakdown? I lifted my hands like *what the eff, Dad*? He chuckled and faced the street. But again, the sound. Mom's crying? With sound? Proof that everyone *can* change.

"Are you crying or something?" She was so irritating. My voice filled with judgment, but I refused to turn around.

"No. I'm not crying."

Again, the wimpy squeak came. I honestly could not stand it one more second. I spun around. My mouth pursed. My eyes squinting. "What!"

Mom wasn't amused, not like Dad. But she also did not reflect my same mood. She seemed reconciled. Her left hand moved off her lap. She touched the top of the cardboard box and began peeling open the folded slats. Then she reached in.

"They already named him," she said. "Meet Slick." And when she withdrew her hands, in them was this ridiculously tiny black and white tuxedo mix kitten. Both ears bigger than its entire head.

Then Dad broke the silence. "Uma? I've been thinking about something for a while now."

Mom handed the kitten over the seat to me. After that, it was all noise. Sort of.

Mom said, "Yeah?"

"One good thing about Kiki's funeral?" Dad said.

"What's *that*?" Mom said.

He rolled up his window and started the engine. The kitten snuggled into my neck and coiled around my nape then crawled back into my arms.

"At least Kiki had the decency not to fall out of the casket." He shifted the car into gear and set off from Mr. Pauling's.

"Oh, jeez, Ben. That's horrible," Mom said.

And that was Dad. In a nutshell. Making us laugh when we didn't have much to laugh about at all.

Mom repeated, "That's awful, Ben." And it got quiet except for the kitten who mewed between me kissing her.

"Hey, Mac," Mom said, "Will you ever forgive me? I'm so sorry about April, sweetheart. But I do have to tell you, those people absolutely adore her and have promised you visitation rights whenever you want."

Just down the road, a full moon bobbed in the side mirror behind us. It looked as big and golden as the one Tessa and I stared at the night before she died. I wanted to tell them all about that night, about Tessa, how cute she was asking about the moon. But I paused. Some things just aren't meant to be shared.

It was crazy, too, when Dad said, "Wow. Uma," he said, "turn around."

Mom let out a short sniffle. Dad had Mom's face locked in his rearview mirror. "Pretty, huh?" he said.

Nobody spoke the rest of the way back to Mom's house. On the ride home, I decided not to tell them about Tessa's moon. It was my secret. Our secret, Tessa's and mine. How that dang moon follows the sun on its lunar orbit like a fawn after a doe—the fawn's lifeline. That's the pull the moon has on me. The moon is my lifeline to Tessa. Our secret. Forever. Amen.

That night after we returned home, I walked to the road that lines the Strait so I could sit again on Old Man Johnson's fence to stare at the moon. For two hours, I stayed out there in a prayer of sorts. I said to the moon, to God, to Tessa, to anyone listening, that I'd be okay. I'd try to stop being scared.

Finally, I promised I'd watch for her—this time to Tessa only that I would search the moon every time it came out, to catch a glimmer of her face, *our* face, spotting us together bounding around that big old cheese wheel, riding on the back of that white deer—all the remainder of my days.

ONE ENDING

A "SORT OF" EPILOGUE
…Aw, Tessa…

"Mac!" I scream and scream. I laugh, too, at my own joke . . . how Mac looks so, so, *moony*! "Mac," I repeat, "the deer in the moon doesn't eat cheese, it eats stardust and moon beets, solar flowers, and plants. Or are they solar flares and planets? Doesn't matter much; they eat just about whatever the heck they want. And they let me ride them, Mac!

"This one's named Einstein, 'cause he's so blasted smart! He eats stardust straight out of my hand and steals moon beets out of my back pocket when I pretend not to be watching him. He's sneaky, Mac. But so smart.

"Tell Mom and Dad they should stay together, will you? For me? You need them to stay together. For you. And not to split up in spite of me.

"Remember what Gramma Ellie used to say, '*Always try to forget the past and not to dwell on the future. Remember, they call it the present because it's a gift.*' And, yes. She's up here and doing fine. She orders people around. She's no angel, Mac! She and Kiki don't get along. It's a *sort of* competition for my love. It's so silly, 'cause I love them both.

"Also, Mac, try to remember that I love you. It wasn't your fault. It wasn't anyone's fault. I'm happy here. I can see everything, feel everything you feel, Mom and Dad too. It's all about love, Mac. Try to remember that for me, will you? Remember that I love you. Forever, Mac . . . forever."

ANOTHER ENDING

ACKNOWLEDGEMENTS

HOW THE DEER MOON HUNGERS is set on the island where my husband, Bob and I live. We had taken a night walk down False Bay Drive to a spot that looks out at the Olympic Peninsula. The sun had set but the sky still shone the ebbing color of day. That was on the way out. On the way back, the moon had risen over a stand of trees. The moon was fat as a plate, yellow, and soft enough to touch. That's when I started hearing Mac and Tessa's story a story that wouldn't let go of my heart. So, first and foremost, thank you, Bob for taking walks with me. Our walks are high points in my life.

How do I start giving thanks to so many people who touched this story from the idea nucleus to typing "The End" and beyond? Whatever the statements I make here will fall far thinner than my deep appreciation to them. Still, I must try. Other folks were key in my fact-finding mission. People like Sean Thompson of Skagit County Juvenile Detention who helped with information about beds and room conditions at the detention center. People like Teresa Barnett an Assistant Prosecuting Attorney for San Juan County who guided me through legal aspects of prosecuting minors and who helped me tweak the crime so that it fit Washington State laws. I walked away from our meeting feeling as if I'd fallen softly into a catch-net.

To people like Zac Reimer, Undersheriff for San Juan County Sheriff's Office who went through crime scene investigation protocol with me and who gave me a myriad of forms used to book perps, of tests for drunk drivers, and who ultimately organized my next adventure with Sergeant Eric Gardner of San Juan County Sheriff's Office who took me on one helluva eight-hour "ride-along" a memory is etched in my mind for the rest of my life. These people who serve us in law enforcement work every single day to protect and serve us. Their lives are immensely important. Without them? I'm mean, helter-skelter.

I would be remiss if I didn't mention people who were vital in shaping the story, people like Bridgette O'Hare and Billie Hobbs who combed the tangles out of my words. And boy-oh-boy were there tangles! I want also to thank my dear friend and pew partner, Carol for reading the story. Thank you for your bravery. As well, my sister, Elizabeth Ajamie Boyer a fine author in her own right who was my single, first reader and who wrote me after she finishing, "I was terrorized, then I cried." The best review a sister could ever give. I love you but for so much more. For readers like Jo Szczepura, Randall Silvis, Peggy Sue McCrae, Steve Cubine, Vincent Zandri, Pam Stack, Julie Buchanan-Caudill, Kathryn Lane. Thank you also to my AOTSJI pals Jill Urbach, Janet Dann and Sharon Hooper. And to my friend who pushes my books for me, Dorothy Thompson.

And last, but in no way least, a big curtsy to Chip MacGregor who stepped in to help me when I needed him. You amaze me for helping when you are not required to. As a long-ago friend of mine would have described Chip, he's "a true mensch."

Foremost, I thank God who placed all these amazing people in my life. Without them, this story would not have been possible.

FIND SUSAN WINGATE

www.susanwingate.com

www.facebook.com/authorsusanwingate

www.twitter.com/susanwingate

www.pinterest.com/susanwingate/pins

www.instagram.com/susanwingatephxborn

www.blogtalkradio.com/dialogue

Psychological women's suspense at its best!

"I'm still reeling after finishing Susan Wingate's latest, THE DEATH OFVULTURES. Brilliantly written, here is atale that grips you by the throat from the opening prologue to the gut-punch ofan ending. Both tender and brutal,intelligent and visceral, each page carries a reader further down a harrowingpath to a conclusion both inevitable yet also shocking. This novel will leavean indelible mark on your soul. Don'tmiss it." --James Rollins, New York Timesbestseller of The Demon Crown